By Nelson George

WHERE DID OUR LOVE GO?
THE DEATH OF RHYTHM & BLUES
ELEVATING THE GAME: BLACK MEN AND
  BASKETBALL
BUPPIES, B-BOYS, BAPS & BOHOS
URBAN ROMANCE*
BLACKFACE: REFLECTIONS ON AFRICAN
  AMERICANS AT THE MOVIES
SEDUCED*
HIP HOP AMERICA

*Published by Ballantine Books

More praise for
Urban Romance

"Finally a leading man who can hang with my contemporaries—arrogant, brainy, and dogged by juicy class conflicts. George brings us to early-eighties New York, before AIDS and the recession, when buppies thought they had the world tucked away in their briefcases. A page-turner shot with the adrenaline of hip-hop."
                                                    —LISA JONES

"*Urban Romance* is *Waiting to Exhale* meets *Bonfire of the Vanities*—a natural page-turner that chronicles the emotional and political landscape of an era."
            —REGINALD HUDLIN
            Director of *Boomerang* and *House Party*

"In *Urban Romance*, Nelson George lets women in on one of life's great mysteries: how men really feel about love. But this book is not just educational, it's fun reading too!"
                                            —VANESSA WILLIAMS

URBAN ROMANCE

A Novel of New York in the '80s

Nelson George

One World
THE BALLANTINE PUBLISHING GROUP • NEW YORK

Ballantine Books
Published by The Ballantine Publishing Group
Copyright © 1993 by Nelson George

www.randomhouse.com/BB/

Library of Congress Catalog Card Number: 98-96460

ISBN 978-0-345-47273-1

This edition published by arrangement with G. P. Putnam's Sons

Manufactured in the United States of America

146673257

To Blondie
Remember the Times

LONG ASS JOURNEY

Written by Joint-ski, Rahiem, Reggie Olds,
"Mississippi" Rivers

It's been a long ass journey
To where I want to go
But now the hill's not so steep.

It's been a long ass journey
To where I want to go
But now the water's not so deep.

It's been a long ass journey
To where I want to go
But when you hold me now
Baby, I can sleep.

ONE

Dwayne Robinson's raggedy little alarm clock went off at 9 a.m. and its owner, not used to awakening so early in the day, opened his eyes but didn't move. The clock's buzzing seemed an extension of the ringing that remained in his ears from dancing last night at the Roxy. *Maybe I'm still there,* he thought. *Maybe this is just last night extended or something like that. . . .*

Dwayne dearly wanted to avoid the idea that it was morning and he had to wake up. He reached out and slammed the clock down on its back, stifling the ring and knocking off the clock's plastic facing. Then he sat up. *Big day today, my man. Big busy day. Got to be on top of my game. Word.*

Instead of psyching himself up, the prospect of a busy day sent Dwayne falling backwards. His head was back against the mattress and his eyes at half-mast when he heard the sound of the shower through the wall.

Reggie in bed late? Unusual. Whether he'd been up late at a recording session or humping his latest victim, Reggie usually never stayed in bed later than 7:30. By 9 he was either having breakfast, at the Y swimming, or watching his "Putney Swope" tape—the film was a cult item about blacks taking over a Madison Avenue ad agency in the sixties. The strange idea of his roommate running late made Dwayne rise up. *It's a day for the unusual,* he reasoned. Wobbly but now willing, Dwayne ambled out of his wooden captain's bed over to his desk, his white sweat socks sliding across the dusty floor. His date book lay open atop his Brother electric typewriter.

TO DO—APRIL 15, 1982
1-Stop by Post Office for records, press releases, etc.
Look for review in Village Voice.

2-10:30 a.m. Drop off Gap Band review at Musician
office on 23rd Street.

3-11 a.m. Drop off Evelyn King interview at Essence
at 1500 Broadway.

4-11:30 a.m. Drop off Mtume interview at Black
Beat magazine at 55th and Madison.

5 - 12 to 2:30 p.m. FREE LUNCH! Shalamar listening
party at Kee Wah Inn at 57th St., between 5th & 6th.

6-3 p.m. Interview with Kashif in Celestial Studio at
3rd Ave. and 52nd St.

7-Get on E train back to Queens by 4:15 p.m. to beat
rush hour traffic.

*Can't be late with all that copy. Well, actually I'm already
late with all that copy. I can't be any later. I'm already late with
my half of the rent. Late's becoming my middle name.* Dwayne
snatched his white terrycloth robe (borrowed from the Philadelphia Hilton during a press junket for Teddy Pendergrass's
album) and shuffled into the hallway. The shower had been
turned on but Reggie's bedroom door was closed, which struck
Dwayne as strange. Dwayne made the left turn toward the bathroom and was suddenly face-to-face with Latonya Hilltown, a
nineteen-year-old girl Dwayne immediately knew was born to
wear sneakers.

She didn't actually have sneakers on at that moment, but except for her bare feet Latonya's attire—designer jeans, pink
sweat shirt with her name stenciled upon it, and long slender
gold chain with a gold "L" dangling from it—was what Reggie

called "a dirty sock girl" or what Dwayne, with slightly more charity, referred to as a "female b-boy."

"Good morning," Dwayne said.

"What's up?" she replied. Her eyes surveyed Dwayne's skinny bowed legs, then twinkled in amusement. "You got some cute legs."

From behind Dwayne a voice said, "I'd call them undernourished." It was Reggie Olds. His head was stuck out of his bedroom into the hallway. A long, sly smile creased his dark-brown face.

"They're all right, Reggie," she offered. She giggled, said "Excuse me," passed Dwayne, and then entered Reggie's bedroom.

"A touch young, Reg, don't you think?"

Reggie stepped into the hallway and closed the bedroom door behind him. Reggie whispered, "Normally I'd be insulted by that insinuation, but you may be right."

"Do tell. Joint-ski introed you at the Inferno. She wants to rap or sing. Dip, dip, dap. She opened up her ears and you got her to wiggle her behind."

"Shhhh, Mr. Robinson, you have an indiscreet voice."

"Hope you used a rubber."

"Mr. Robinson, I wouldn't worry about my highly successful sexual practices. I'd worry about my half of the rent."

Dwayne saw the turn the conversation was about to take and headed toward the bathroom. "Money coming soon, mon," Dwayne answered with a weak Jamaican accent.

"I'll drink to that," Reggie said and went back into his bedroom.

Since he was already running late, Dwayne passed on a shower and instead slopped soap under his armpits and between his legs. Clean underwear, recently purchased white socks worn only twice before, Sergio Valente jeans, a blue nylon shirt, white shell-toed Adidas with three stripes, and Dwayne was set. He strode out into the hallway past Reggie's bedroom, his bedroom, and into the dining area, where a stack of audio tapes lay on the butcher-block dining table.

Scribbled on the labels in Reggie's chicken scratch was "Joint-ski Demos." *It's about time Reggie manifested his mouth. He's been talking about making rap records before the Sugar Hill Gang and Kurtis Blow. I just hope it's not too late and that this rap thing has legs.*

Dwayne went into the kitchen, his Adidas sticking to the floor in a few spots from too-long-unattended spills, and poured slightly sour milk over Raisin Bran. As he munched on his breakfast cereal, Dwayne walked back through the dining room area and down two steps into a living room containing a Magnavox color tv plopped atop two green plastic milk crates, a dingy dungaree sofa, and Reggie and Dwayne's two thousand or so combined records. On the floor by the Technics turntable and stereo were Lakeside's *Fantastic Voyage*, Stevie Wonder's *Hotter Than July*, Earth, Wind & Fire's *Spirit* and Prince's *Dirty Mind.*

Dwayne opted for the Minneapolis kid. The bright rhythm guitar riff of "When You Were Mine" filled the living room as Dwayne sat on the sofa and scooped raisins, brown flakes, and milk into his spoon. Reggie and Latonya, now fully clothed, entered the dining area. Checking out Latonya in her uptown wear, and Reggie in blue blazer, gabardine pants, and trademark Hush Puppies, Dwayne mused that rap had created some strange bedfellows. Gesturing toward the tapes, Dwayne said, "I see you've been squeezing a little work in."

"Yeah," Reggie said, "we got a song that I feel good about. A real radio record. On occasion he wants to do lyrics about mugging old ladies but I steer him away."

Latonya cut in. "You talking about that song with street rhymes? That was fresh. I mean it was all fresh to me. But that one with the street rhymes, that was da joint."

Reggie said, "Is that so?" with a hint of sarcasm that Dwayne felt was unwarranted but that Latonya didn't notice.

"What's this?" Latonya asked.

"Prince. Do you like him?"

"He made a couple of all-right records, but he's so tiny." Looking toward Reggie, she added, "I like my men chunky."

Reggie cut Dwayne a triumphant leer. Dwayne returned it with a tight jealous smile.

After they were gone Dwayne played "When You Were Mine" again. He should have been out the door too, but he found himself drifting into the record, mesmerized by the interplay of Prince's voice and the music. This had been happening to him all the time since he was about thirteen. Dwayne found himself immobilized by particular songs as if there were some secret inside them that, if he listened long enough, would reveal itself and change his life. This feeling is what led him into rock criticism, a career choice he now often rued. *Did my mother raise me to get paid to bug out to records?* The answer was "No," since (a) she wasn't happy with his career direction and (b) he was making no money. Dwayne played "When You Were Mine" three more times before he finally, reluctantly, put down his Raisin Bran and left the apartment.

Rush hour was almost over, so Dwayne had a little room on the E train to pen his mail. Not a very distinguished crop today: Bob & Doug McKenzie's Great White North comedy LP from Mercury; Bertie Higgins' single "Key Largo" (which Dwayne assumed was some takeoff on the Bogart classic), an advance of the Dazz Band's Motown album and a bunch of press releases and promotion pictures. *Maybe I can write a Dazz Band review if the record's any good.*

Dwayne was about to check out the placement of his *Voice* review when he noticed two sweet young ladies sitting diagonally across from him. They looked like smarter, older versions of Latonya. Homegirls with dreams. One was reading the *Post.* The headline read **KOCH RIPS PETERS** and had an unflattering picture of an otherwise handsome middle-aged black man. The subhead said, "Mayor Chides Renegade Jurist." Dwayne read the headline and then stared at her legs.

Maybe this is a good time to try Reggie's "I'm lost" technique. A favorite trick of his romantic mentor was to feign ignorance of the city's transit system and ask attractive women directions. Reggie assured Dwayne that this ploy had resulted in innumerable phone numbers. Dwayne had tried it only once before, and all he ended up with was inaccurate directions to Madison Square Garden.

Dwayne was about to rap when Teddy Jamerson, known to all as T.J., stepped his way. T.J. was a chunky, oatmeal-colored black man who's white-boyish demeanor irked Dwayne. But whether T.J. was a white negro or a black honky, Dwayne had often suspected him of lying behind his back during their four years at St. John's. The man did a "he said, she said" action that shamed Millie Jackson. In fact the pair shared a long, troubled history. So when T.J. popped up in front of him, in an ugly dark-green suit and a fake smile, Dwayne grimaced.

T.J. said, "Hey man, how ya doin'?" and Dwayne replied, "Hey."

"Haven't seen you in a long time!" T.J.'s enthusiasm really put Dwayne off.

"Yup."

"You won't believe this, but I've been meaning to call you."

"You're right," Dwayne said sharply.

Ignoring Dwayne's scornful tone, T.J. continued, "I gotta ask you a favor."

"Okay, I'll bite."

"There's a friend of mine named Danielle Embry who's going through a career change. She edits books for Doubleday but now she's thinking of moving into tv news and I think she shouldn't."

"Why shouldn't she change her career? And is she fine and do you go with her?"

T.J.'s façade of good humor cracked. "I don't go with her," he said very deliberately. "We're just friends. I've known her since we were kids. She's real cute. Big eyes. Great smile. Smart. Yale with honors."

"She's that bad and you're letting me meet her?" Dwayne said with genuine surprise. "T.J., you have become remarkably generous in your old age."

"Come on, you still blame me for stupid St. John's stuff? We go back too far for that, Dwayne."

Dwayne was getting a little hot. "Look. My stop is next. So tell your story quick." T.J. wanted to walk away from Dwayne's arrogant ass but didn't. Instead he pulled out his wallet and handed Dwayne a card. "Here's her card. Look, Danielle is frustrated. She can't get the books she wants to publish signed. You're a writer. You wanna write books. You hate television. I remember what you used to say in the 'Media and Mendacity' class. I was thinking maybe you could help her change her mind. Of course you could just give me the card back and we could forget the whole conversation."

Dwayne didn't begin to believe T.J.'s story. It didn't make any sense that T.J. would hook him up with the phone number of an interesting woman. *T.J. knows how much I dislike him,* he thought. This was strange. Dwayne did know that T.J. had great taste in women—after all, he'd tried to steal Dwayne's ladies back at St. John's. So Dwayne was going to call her. *If I get over,* Dwayne concluded, *it would just be payback.*

Dwayne got off at 23rd Street and Eighth Avenue. It was already 10:30. Running late again. But instead of hustling over to *Musician* he sat on a bench and flipped to the *Voice*'s Riffs section. His piece was the last of four reviews that week. *Not badly written,* he thought, *but I still need to get better.*

EVERYBODY IS A STAR
BY DWAYNE ROBINSON

Sly and the Family Stone's "A Whole New Thing" album in 1967 changed black popular music, reintroducing the virtues of the self-contained band to an idiom then dominated by solo singers and vocal groups. They were a bridge between the JB's—the black band as backup group—and the everybody-is-a-star aggregations of the current era. The new-breed bands don't swing like Count Basie's boys, nor have most achieved the white-black appeal of Sly and company. But even the mediocrities do manage to utilize the tools of black pop (vocal harmonies, soulful and/or cool lead voices, antiphonal horn charts) with varying degrees of personality, cynicism, and weirdness.

Lakeside's nine members are upwardly mobile craftsmen, whose "Your Wish Is My Command," on Solar, distributed by Elektra (there is an inferior contractual obligation LP distributed by RCA), soothes coolly, boogies intelligently, and slips in social commentary with a technician's skill. Falsetto Otis Smith, in tandem with Thomas Selby's dusky tenor, provides a vocal tension that recalls Earth, Wind & Fire's Philip Bailey and Maurice White. On the ballad version of "I Want to Hold Your Hand" (yes, Lennon & McCartney's) they breathe life into a calculated crossover attempt, their soulful pleading reinforced by the entire band's churchy harmonies.

As last year's "Fantastic Voyage" demonstrated, Lakeside is adept at designing catchy synthesizer-bass grooves and vocal hooks reminiscent of Brass Construction's rough-hewn charts, but performed with a nice refinement, so the title cut and "Something About That Woman" offer both smooth grooves and hummable melody lines. "Urban Man," Lakeside's bow to realism, confirms the values of hard work in terms Solar bossman Dick Griffey (touted as the "new" Berry Gordy) surely approves. Driven by sound commercial instincts and a clean-cut style, Lakeside seems poised to invade suburban living rooms, and happy about the prospect. Some might question that goal, but consider the alternative . . .

Lakeside could turn into the Bar-Kays, a skilled, funky working-class party band without a creative bone in their collective bodies. Sort of Molly Hatchet with a tan. Listening to any recent Bar-Kays album, including the current "Night Cruising," is tantamount to a survey course in black pop, because from cut to cut they can be Earth, Wind & Fire, the Chi-lites, or Prince. Take "Hit and Run," the hit single on "Night Cruising," which cops a keyboard vamp from dance music producers Ray Reid and William Anderson, and sprinkles a Rick James lyric on top for flavoring. It's not unusual for performers to utilize the tricks of others, as we'll see with Kleeer. It's just that the Bar-Kays are so damn clumsy about it. Too bad. In the early 1970s, these Memphis boys were a tough, raunchy funk 'n' roll band as good as any of the new big bands. Check out "Cold-blooded," reissued last year from Fantasy's Stax catalogue, for verification.

At least the Bar-Kays didn't "borrow" much from disco. Like most heartland music fans, they escaped the massive disco hype we were subjected to here. The New Jersey-based players who comprise Kleeer did, and it shows. Their 1977 debut, "Keep Your Body Workin'," was as moronic as any Eurodisco import ever. But Kleeer, like New York's disco scene, has improved by wedding funk, new wave, and even Eurodisco into a weirdly compelling mix. The best tunes on "Taste the Music," an otherwise lackluster follow-up to last summer's "License to Dream," the title cut, and "De Ting Continues," are in this polyglot style. "Taste" is spiced with spacey new wavey keyboard flourishes, thudding drums Cerrone would envy, and the line "Taste the music with your whole body now," sung-rapped in English and then German, a clear tribute to every street kid's favorite import, Kraftwerk. "De Ting Continues" picks up where last album's "De Kleeer Ting" left off, meaning we're treated to a chunky funk-punk beat while Kleeer's members introduce themselves via some witty raps.

Kleeer's multi-format boogie, the Bar-Kays's boorish imitations, and Lakeside's upscale confections are different in texture and intention, yet they are all branches of a tree, continuations of a now-respected tradition.

Danielle Embry put down the *Village Voice* and glanced absently around her small, cramped office. There were the obligatory shelves of books and manuscripts. Copies of *Essence*, *Black Enterprise*, and *Publishers Weekly* were piled in neat little stacks. A Jacob Lawrence print of jazz musicians hung on one wall. Opposite the print were framed portraits of Adam Clayton Powell and newscaster Ed Bradley. Her desk was dominated by a photo of Danielle and her father taken on Easter Sunday 1973.

She'd first read Dwayne Robinson's work in the *Amsterdam News*, violently disagreeing with his review of Diana Ross's performance in *The Wiz*, but finding his writing remarkably sharp in that otherwise desultory journal of the black experience. She still peeked at the *AmNews* only to keep some contact with the local black politics, though she found their coverage as skewered by the interest of its highly connected publishers as the dailies were by racism. Anyway, she saw Dwayne's by-line leap from the *Amsterdam News* to the *Village Voice*, denoting growth in craft and outlook she found fascinating ("fascinating" being a favored word).

For the last year T.J. had been promising to introduce them, but her enthusiasm always made T.J. nervous. Whenever she mentioned Dwayne Robinson he'd immediately start laying on stories about Dwayne's doggish behavior in college and that age had surely made him worse. Danielle had known T.J. through three boyfriends, each time appreciating his loyalty, yet always making romantic decisions based on her instincts.

Despite a suburban Connecticut upbringing, a studied sophistication, and a double major at Yale of English and Political Science, Danielle loved her men like a natural woman, like Aretha Franklin singing "I Never Loved a Man (The Way I Love You)." You know, deep.

Though only twenty-six, Danielle had lived with a couple of her boyfriends, was on the verge of moving in with the current one, and had, she felt in her heart, truly loved them all. (She thought they still loved her too, though Danielle had no hard evidence.) With each something had happened. Despite a deep well of love, Danielle could turn off to a man quickly. A part of her could just brush them off and chalk the whole relationship up to experience. Danielle was with Morris now, though it hadn't been good for a while. Yet Morris needed her and Danielle had never been keen on leaving a man until she had another lined up. She'd just never been good at that.

"Danielle, Jacksina's on the line," her assistant called from the hallway.

"Hey, Jack," Danielle said into the phone.

"Hey, Ms. T-Bag," Jacksina said back.

"T-Bag?" Danielle rolled her eyes. She loved Jacksina as much as her sisters—but the girl could be so damn silly.

"Okay, what does that mean?"

"It means typical black girl. And you are that," Jacksina said and then laughed.

"My, aren't we witty today. Are you up in the Bronx again?"

With mock anger Jacksina said, "Don't try to get in my business, girl," when, of course, the reason she'd called was to talk about her personal life. "You know why I called you a T-Bag?"

"Yes. Yes, I do."

Disappointed that Danielle didn't give her standard rhetorical question the appropriate reply, Jacksina pouted through the phone. "You called me a T-Bag," Danielle said smoothly, "because this guy, excuse me, man, has been telling you how special you are. That you're not a typical black girl, but an African Queen or something like that, and you're reveling in it."

"That's kinda close," Jacksina admitted.

Seizing the conversation from her friend, Danielle wondered sarcastically, "So when are you gonna announce the wedding? I'm sure the *Post* will run the announcement on the front page."

Danielle could hear a man's voice in the background, apparently talking on another phone. Jacksina lowered her voice. "You saw the paper today. These white folks are out to get him. It makes me so angry, but he deals with it so well."

"So how does he plan to explain his relationship with you?" Danielle didn't want to sound so harsh but the *Post*'s headline sounded warning bells in her head. Jacksina's affair with this married man could easily destroy her career. Before Jacksina could answer, Danielle's assistant stuck her head in to say, "Dwayne Robinson is on the other line. Want me to take a message?"

"Oh no, send it through. Listen, Jack, I gotta go. When are you coming home tonight?"

"About ten."

"Don't you have to study or something? I thought you went to school to be an attorney, not to hang out with horny judges."

"I must be confused," Jacksina said facetiously. "I thought it was all the same thing."

" 'Bye, Jack."

"Later, Ms. T-Bag."

Danielle hung up and waited for Dwayne's call to come through. Lunch. *That sounds professional. I'll say, "Let's do lunch."*

Doubleday's editorial director announced an unexpected staff meeting at 2 p.m. on the day Danielle and Dwayne had scheduled lunch. At first she'd wanted to cancel, then realized this was a good out—if they got along, she'd stay in contact. If he was an asshole, as T.J. claimed, she had a legit reason to cut lunch short.

"This place is fast," he assured her as they walked across West 43rd Street toward Broadway. On this mild spring day the two "D"s checked each other out.

Well, she is cute, Dwayne thought. Danielle had a bright smile and shiny ebony dots for eyes. Her auburn hair was blow-dried just right into a flowing set that bounced with every step of the pumps that matched her eyes. Her dress was deep blue, with a swirling beige design. Danielle looked delicious, and Dwayne was grinning like he wanted a taste.

Danielle was a bit disappointed. She didn't like guys with beards. Certainly not scraggly ones. But his round cheeks were cute, his eyelashes long, and his lower lip inviting. With his brown corduroy pants, beige sweater, white open-collar shirt and nondescript black slip-ons, she thought he was dressed more like a writer wannabe than the real deal. Still, he seemed to have brains and an engaging, though rather anxious, personality. A nerd in transition to manhood? Maybe.

They went to a lunch spot called Beggar's Banquet. As they stood in line, Dwayne said, "I suppose I should make your friend T.J. happy and try to convince you to stay at Doubleday so you can continue to advance the course of American letters. You know, that's why T.J. asked me to call."

"Is that what he told you? Well, then, let's hear your argument."

Dwayne began speaking quickly and intensely. "It's not much of an argument, really. In fact I have no argument. Yeah, I think television news stinks—what a brainstorm—and that it would waste your talent. But, speaking with all due honesty, I really wanted to meet you for two other reasons."

Danielle looked at him quizzically.

"You with me?" he inquired.

"Oh, yeah," she replied with a chuckle.

"One," he said, "and this is not in any particular order, I want to write a book in the worst way."

"About what?"

"I don't know. That's my problem. I have visions of myself lying in bed surrounded by books with my name on them. Lots and lots of books. I just don't know what's printed on any of the pages. You see, that's why it's in the worst way."

"Fascinating," she said evenly. *He's kinda crazed—but in a cute way.*

"Reason two is that T.J., though not one of my favorite people, has always had good taste in women. So here I am."

Danielle laughed softly. Then she said, "It's good you're not telling me to leave publishing. I was just accepted into Columbia Journalism School."

Dwayne suddenly turned, then hugged her. She liked it, while thinking, *This is going way too fast.*

"Congratulations. Let's go out tonight and celebrate."

Danielle laughed. "Thanks for your offer, but I've already made plans."

"Too bad—both about tonight and my suddenly poor prospects for a book deal. But then you know what the old bloods at the barbershop say."

"No, I don't."

"Well, they say, 'Never shit where you eat.' "

"Now what does that mean?"

"Well, I figure that if we're going to be friends and—maybe, I hope, if I'm lucky—go out together, we shouldn't do business together."

She laughed again. "So when was it decided that we'd go out?" He was arrogant, she thought, one of her favorite qualities in a man.

"It's not decided. Not at all. I said 'if I'm lucky.' I meant that. You going out with someone?"

She ignored the question. "You know why I wanted to meet you, Dwayne?"

"No."

"I was curious as to what kind of black man wrote for the *Village Voice*."

"Sometimes I wonder about it myself. It *is* a weird place."

"Its political coverage is so slanted—in that paper you're either a saint or a villain," she said. "The idea of compromise, of give and take, isn't in its coverage." *Let's see how he sounds when he's serious.*

I can play that game too, he thought. "I'd say that being so judgmental is the paper's strength. No phony artifical objectivity like the *Times*. Just one-sided—like the real world."

They were so busy trying to impress each other that they missed the signals of the hostess when she tried to seat them. The hostess shrugged and instead seated a single businessman at the only available table for two.

"So why do you want to work in television?" Dwayne asked her.

"I know this may sound arrogant . . ."

He grinned. "Just follow my lead."

"Well . . . I feel like I'd like to make a difference in the world. By covering politics at a local station I think maybe I can."

Damn—she really means it.

"Hard to make a difference in book publishing, huh?"

"It can be done," she said, weighing her words, "but only if they let you sign the right books—and then promote them. They look for blockbusters aimed at a guaranteed mass audience or works by big-name authors. I have no problem with that, but it'll be a long time before I can sign the kind of books I want to work on. In television news you can move up quickly and affect millions."

"Danielle, I like your spirit so much that if we ever get a seat, I'll pay for lunch."

"No, we're going dutch. But probably not here." Looking around, she saw that the restaurant was now jam-packed.

"How about a hot dog at Nathan's?"

"Okay," she said. "I'll just have fries. Maybe we can talk a bit about your book. I'll be gone soon but I can still recommend editors to you."

"Good. Oh—but no."

She looked hard at him. "You okay?"

"I can't show you my birthmark in Nathan's, can I?"

"Your birthmark?"

"Yeah. I feel this is fresh territory for a book." *I'm pushing it,* he thought. *But at least maybe I'll make her forget the fact that I want to write a book—in the abstract—but don't have a concrete idea.*

Smiling politely at what she thought was a silly joke, Danielle said, "Well, then, why don't you send me a proposal for your book."

"No problem."

A week later it arrived in a regular manila envelope. Very businesslike. Even the cover letter didn't give the joke away, though Danielle's assistant, Michele, thought that even if Danielle had signed up *Motherhood & Your Sun Signs*, this proposal was way over the edge. So she wasn't surprised when laughter came bubbling out of Danielle's office.

<u>Birthmarks & The Mind-Body Nexus</u>
A Book Proposal
by
Dwayne Robinson

The birthmark comes in all shapes and sizes. Some are round. Some are square. A rare group are triangular. Yet they are as much a part of what makes each one of us as unique as glorious black eyes. In *Birthmarks & The Mind-Body Nexus*, Dwayne Robinson, free-lance writer with the Village Voice, Essence and Rolling Stone, will go below the surface of birthmarks (so to speak) and look at:

1-Why some are blessed with birthmarks and some aren't.
2-The Birthmark Inferiority-Superiority. Is it better to be marked or "unmarked"?
3-The Birthmark as a Religious Deity
4-The Impact of Birthmark on IQ
5-The Psychological Impact of Birthmark Loss
6-The Birthmark and DNA
7-The Birthmark in Romance (and SEX!)

For further discussion of this project, particularly Chapter Seven, Mr. Robinson would be willing to meet Ms. Danielle Embry anytime, anyplace. He'd *even* return her phone calls.

Yours truly,

Dwayne Robinson

Even return phone calls. Clever Dwayne Robinson. Danielle turned and looked out the window at the East Side of Manhattan. She'd thought about calling Dwayne quite a few times. But there was too much going on in her life already. The Columbia acceptance celebration the other evening with Morris wasn't a disaster. They'd played Trivial Pursuit with Ernest and Von, and later caught Wynton Marsalis at the Vanguard. Things never got really bad with Morris. They just never seemed to get

that good anymore. It was like being married, she assumed, though this marriage seemed to be in its thirtieth year. Morris made Danielle feel so dull and settled. It was comfortable, she admitted. Too comfortable.

Danielle wanted to break loose, roam the streets, be the aggressive, freewheeling woman of her fantasies—and Morris couldn't get to that at all. He was a city planner, a thirtyish career bureaucrat with an eye for real estate—he had already bought a brownstone in Bedford-Stuyvesant through his City Hall contacts and was near closing on another in Fort Greene for almost no money. And, though he'd toasted her acceptance, the sober, pragmatic Morris really couldn't understand this sudden career shift.

"Stability and continuity are the keys to life, Danielle. I really believe that." She sighed. He'd said it more than once. "And you haven't been on your job long enough to be fed up with it," he pointed out.

Danielle felt there was some truth in Morris's words. But another voice told her: *Just because I'm twenty-six, why should I fold up my tent?* She thought of her parents, with their comfortable life and beautiful home in Arthur, Connecticut. She smiled. *That could be me and Morris in some chic brownstone. A real* Essence *couple. I'd just have to say the words. But not yet . . . not yet.* She looked at Dwayne's letter and thought, *This guy is dangerous.* And this letter confirmed what T.J. had said, all right. He *was* full of himself. A cocky nerd. Never been around one of those before. Cocky suited a black man—especially if he could back it up.

Jacksina had already advised her to "Go for it." What else would she say? That girl moved with all deliberate speed when a man made her juices flow. That was her right, but it could be hell on you if you were Jacksina's roommate. Where had she found those niggers? Everywhere—but especially at discos. God, how she loved Justine's and Leviticus and all those other musical pickup joints where they played M.F.S.B.'s "Love Is the Message" like a hymn. Jacksina's lust radar was so accurate that she could pick out bisexual men at gay clubs.

Danielle watched a helicopter fly past the United Nations. She picked up Dwayne's book proposal and noticed the scent of Polo cologne. The paper was scented. . . . Life changes were already under way. *A new man? Morris wants me to move in with him. That's not the answer. That's a bunch of new questions. Morris is so possessive. He wouldn't even leave me alone in the bathroom.* . . .

Alone. A cold and solitary word. She detested the idea. She hated the definition. Danielle sniffed Dwayne's letter again and then pulled out a piece of Doubleday stationery.

"Oh, I do like your spirit. Yes, I do," Dwayne said as he handed her letter to Reggie Olds, who sat across the table finishing a turkey sandwich. Dated three days previously, the letter was on Doubleday stationery. In a mock-formal voice Reggie read it aloud: " 'Your proposal is *most* provocative. It is *truly* the most *unexpected* submission I've received this year. To further discuss this idea please meet me at the China Bowl, on 44th between 6th and 7th Avenues, 7 p.m., May 13, 1982. Signed Danielle Embry. P.S. Please bring your birthmark with you.' "

"Reggie, my man, is that great, or what?"

"This might be too much for you to handle. Let me go and check her out first."

"That's quite all right, Mr. Olds, sir—I think I can handle it." Dwayne snatched back the letter.

"Do you now?"

"Yes, I do."

"She sounds like she might be the woman I've been warning you about."

"Refresh my memory."

Reggie was about to mutate from good friend into father figure. "Dwayne," he began portentously, "you've made a lot of progress. When I first met you, you were a skinny kid who leered at every woman who walked by and had the rap of a one-legged sailor."

"I was weak?"

"Anorexic."

"I had potential, though."

"You had potential. And you have gotten to be a pretty good stickman," Reggie reluctantly admitted.

"Thank you," Dwayne said sincerely. "Thank you very much. I'm glad you noticed the improvement, though my mother feels you've corrupted me."

"Maybe," Reggie admitted. He leaned forward. "But I didn't make you a selfish young man. That happened before me. As of this moment, you haven't really had to look at yourself. The right woman will make you do that."

Now Dwayne was irritated. "You always say that—and it's not true. One, I'm not selfish. Self-absorbed, maybe. Two, why root for me to fall in love and abandon the splendor of the Parson's Penthouse?" Dwayne waved his right arm in a sweeping motion at the stacks of dusty books, scattered pieces of ill-matching furniture, and crates of records that constituted the view.

Trying to sound sage, Reggie replied, "I didn't say you'd fall in love, but you need your heart broken once, maybe twice. You'll be a better writer—and a humbler human being."

"You're almost serious?"

"You know, Dwayne, I've screwed a lot of women, but I feel I loved most of them." No lie ever passed Reggie's lips that wasn't well intentioned, Dwayne thought. His sincerity made Dwayne crack up.

"No," Reggie protested. "I *do* love them. Can you say the same?"

"Hell, no! I'm not a hypocrite. I *can't* say I loved all those ladies—not that it's been that many. Maybe it's because I don't lie to women to get them in bed. You taught me that women like sex as much as I do. You were right. But love? All that concept got you was a wonderful son—one you hadn't been expecting." Reggie's dark complexion reddened at Dwayne's comment but he didn't lose his cool. He just said soberly, "When I first realized I couldn't stop Sweets from having Junior, I was so damn depressed. . . ."

"I know," Dwayne said. He suddenly felt stupid for bringing up the subject.

Then Reggie brightened. "But you know I wouldn't be making records if Junior wasn't on the way. So by loving Sweets I had my son—and it changed me for the better."

"So, you advising me to knock up Danielle for the same reason?"

Reggie patiently explained that "Once you open up your heart, good things can happen. Besides, you might learn about yourself." He stood up. "Okay, that's it for romantic lesson number 143. You coming down the studio later?"

"Yeah. But first I have to finish something for the *Voice.*"

"Do that. Your half of the rent is due next Friday."

Dwayne watched Reggie walk into his bedroom and then reread Danielle's letter. *Sweet thing,* he thought. *But I'm sure she has a man.*

Then he thought about what Reggie had said. *Love. People use that word like a prayer. Like the national anthem, it's been evoked so often it's lost all meaning. Words were invented to be manipulated. Actions show how you feel. Any fool can say "I love you," and every fool does.*

Dwayne wasn't sure he loved himself, so how could he love others? Since moving in with Reggie after college graduation, Dwayne had grown a lot. Reggie had become the older adviser he'd craved since his father split. Then, giving credit where credit was due, Dwayne got extensive hands-on sexual instruction from Mary Johnson and Eloise Peoples, two older women who'd basically turned him out. Mary was a slim, sexy single mother of two who didn't let her maternal duties stifle her ambition. They met at the *Amsterdam News* when she was trying to start a black Staten Island newspaper *and* run for state assembly. Both efforts ended in failure, but the same ambitious energy she expended in business and politics, Mary concentrated on sex too. In an initially humiliating, though ultimately essential experience, Mary taught Dwayne how to kiss. He'd kissed his high school sweetheart, Candi, he'd kissed sundry college girls, but Mary provided his postgraduate education.

"Do to me what I do to you," Mary demanded one night on her living room carpet, using the same scolding tone she reserved for her young sons. It bruised his ego until he noticed "her way" inspired hardened nipples and renewed passion. To Mary, Dwayne was a boy toy whose stamina she adored. It ended because, quite frankly, she never gave his—in her view—immature mind much respect and Dwayne just couldn't stand that.

Eloise was also about ten years older than Dwayne. But, unlike Mary, she really cared about him. Poor Eloise wanted a man so badly it made her cry at night and, even though Dwayne was twenty and she was thirty-one, Eloise viewed him as a potential mate. Dwayne, after the lessons of Mary, found Eloise's attention hard to believe. The first time he ever spent the night at a woman's apartment into daylight was with Eloise. Mary had always thrown him out around 2 a.m., making sure "My kids respect me," though she was so noisy Dwayne figured her kids counted every stroke. Eloise was so sweet, so soulful, that Dwayne felt that if he had been a few years older, they might have stayed together. Sadly, her passion scared him. Instead of simply liberating Dwayne from the solitary joys of masturbation, Eloise's intensity scared him. When they made love he wondered where his sperm was going and what would it do when it got there. About that time he met Reggie at a Graham Central Station concert, and quickly the older music critic, determined playboy, and instant big brother, advised him to cut Eloise loose. Reggie told him the relationship was a dead end.

So for the first time in his life Dwayne said "No" to an affectionate willing woman, a circumstance he assumed was progress. That knowledge made it no less painful. Dwayne didn't return her phone calls. When she did catch him on the phone Dwayne was cold and distant. All of it part of a process Reggie labeled "letting the leash off the dog." It worked. Eloise got the hint and Dwayne moved on to emotionally less demanding adventures.

Mary and Eloise made Dwayne a confident lover, but he knew he'd lost as well as gained. His innocence was gone, and for all his Reggie Olds–inspired glibness, he missed it. During the same time Dwayne's writing grew sharper, and every now and then he wrote phrases that shined. But the words themselves . . . they never seemed any truer or wiser. He knew he spoke louder now, but what was he saying? What was really inside him? Dwayne thought deeply and a childhood memory, as they so often did, slipped to the forefront of his mind.

The sound of running water was all he heard at first. The voices of his parents. They were speaking loudly for so early in the morning. Dwayne lay there, looking at the ceiling to make out the words. At first it was only Ma. Loud. Accusing. She kept asking the same questions, as though she already knew the answers.

Then his father responded with sounds of fury. No substance to them. The smell of overcooked bacon began filling the apartment.

They both were speaking now, yet no one was listening except Dwayne. His eyes grew wet. He wanted to go and tell them to stop it. It had worked before, but on this Sunday morning there was something different in their voices. Whatever it was it made him stay in bed.

Dwayne would have remained there with the covers pulled up to his neck, but when his father shouted, "Put that thing down, girl! You gone crazy?" the boy sat up. There was the smack of flesh against flesh, the bang of metal against wood, and then Ma's sobbing voice.

Dwayne jumped out of bed, ran down the hallway and into the kitchen, where Ma leaned against the edge of the cabinet top. Her left hand was at her mouth. A redness flowed through her fingers. His father stood in the middle of the room, his shoulders slightly slouched, his head cast down, his eyes fixed on his left fist, and the red along his knuckles. Dwayne stood in the doorway, not feeling a thing but still standing. Then his stomach jumped and he vomited last night's dinner square onto the kitchen floor. A moment later he crawled into his closet, shut the door and cried bitterly in the darkness.

When he came out, his father was smoking a cigarette at the kitchen table. He asked about school. The vomit was gone and so was his mother, locked quietly behind their bedroom door. Dwayne asked his father to play catch with him. No one mentioned the morning. Dwayne's mother didn't come out the rest of the day.

A week after they first met, Danielle and Dwayne sat in the China Bowl on 43rd Street, having rice and chow mein and shrimp fried rice. They were giddy, like kids ripping off the wrapping on a new toy.

"So here we are really having dinner," she said smiling.

"Yup, I finally made it. I could use something to make me smile."

"What's wrong? Woman problems?" she wondered with just the right mix of curiosity and ridicule.

Dwayne laughed. "Oh, I wish it was that. That would be easy."

"Really? How fascinating. Why easy?"

"Not *that* easy." Another laugh. Then he added, "At least it would be something I'd done wrong."

"Or done right?"

"Touché. What's bothering me is a piece I want to do for the *Voice*."

"They don't want it?"

"They don't understand it, and until they do I can't write it for them. The thing is that they're the natural home for it."

"What's it on?" she inquired, sensing his desire to unburden himself.

"It's about b-boys! 'What is a b-boy?' you ask?" Dwayne's face brightened. "Well, the best way to describe a b-boy is that he is one of those young people, usually male, usually black or hispanic, with a huge cassette recorder, unlaced sneakers, tons of gold chains around his 'tag' or nickname written across the front, like Rock-ski, D.J. Red Alert, or Joint-ski."

"I've heard that last name before."

"He had a rap hit called the 'Santa Claus Rap' about Santa Claus visiting Harlem."

"That *was* a cute record, especially considering who made it. 'Cause I have a feeling b-boys don't specialize in being cute."

"Well, that record was 'cute' because my roommate, Reggie Olds, helped make it and added his own warped humor to it."

"You have a roommate? So do I."

"I hope your roommate isn't the same sex as mine."

"What sex is Reggie?"

"Dog."

"No problem. Jacksina is an alley cat."

"We should mate them. Create some sort of hybrid. What does she do for a living?"

"Law clerk by day. Law school by night."

"A rapping lawyer. That might work," Dwayne mused.

"Tell me more about the b-boy piece."

"Well . . . I'd go below the surface and see b-boys, not as potential felons but people with their own values. Underneath all their machismo and gear are real live kids and not the stereotypes found on the *Post*'s front page. If I got it right, it would mix LeRoi Jones' *Blues People* with Claude Brown's *Manchild in the Promised Land*." He was embarrassed now by how much he hoped Danielle was impressed.

"Fascinating," she said. "Sounds like it could develop into a book."

"It could be a book if the *Voice* gave it major play and put its credibility behind it."

"That's true, though I know it would be a hard sell at Doubleday even with a *Voice* clipping. Why is the paper so reluctant to run it?"

"It's the editor involved." Dwayne's voice was uncharacteristically bitter. "The music editor understands it. He's the one who encouraged me to pursue the idea. The problem is the feature editor assigned to the piece. It's a black woman who thinks our contemporary culture begins with Toni Morrison and Ntozake Shange and ends with Cecil Taylor and Alvin Ailey. Joint-ski's world bares little resemblance to any of that. It's sad, but I'm getting more support from a hip curious white boy than a highly educated black woman."

"We have a lot in common," she said.

"Tell me about it."

"I've always had a problem with folks like that," she said. "They all have African or Arab names, read poetry, and wear dreads whenever possible."

"Now don't stereotype them, Dwayne," she said. She hesitated. "But you do have a point. They're the self-appointed arbiters of our 'correct' culture. I had some run-ins at Yale with sisters who measured your racial identity by whether you'd read the collected Zora Neale Hurston."

"The talented-tenth syndrome," he said bitterly.

"More like black liberators without portfolio," she said, which made Dwayne laugh.

"That's pretty good. A lot of black politicians fit that description."

"The strongest black leaders are never politicians. They're local people who care. That's the way it was in my town."

"Up in Connecticut, right?"

"Arthur. It's right outside New Haven. When I was a kid the real leaders in the black community were like Ned Davis, who owned the Booker T. Washington Grocery Store."

"Great name."

"And Malik Rasheed, an ex-Panther who ran the basketball league at the Y. He made everyone sing 'Lift Every Voice and Sing' before games and used red, black, and green basketballs with the names of black historical figures on them."

"I love it."

"Mr. Davis and Rasheed, both had more clout in Arthur than the black city councilman. Whenever he wanted the community's support, he went to them before he took a step. There are lots of people like them in Black America, and that's what I want to show people."

Dwayne sat there grinning again—Reggie called it a "greasy leer"—but damned if he could help it. Danielle excited him. Damn. Danielle felt it too. It was that old feeling again. For these two self-consciously smart people, another articulate, quick, ambitious mind was sexy.

"I guarantee you," he said with the confidence of Joe Namath at Super Bowl III, "that if you go out with me, you will have the best time you have ever experienced as a black book editor soon to be entering Columbia Journalism School. Go ask any of the other black book editors in town now at Columbia if I deliver. Go ahead, ask them."

"Well . . ."

"I won't beg you. I'll blackmail you."

"Will you now?"

"Unless you consent to my wishes, every patron in this restaurant will have the pleasure of viewing my birthmark."

"I don't believe you."

"Is that a challenge?"

"I *do not* believe you," she said, hoping he'd do something silly.

Dwayne stood up and, before Danielle could grab his right hand, unzipped his pants. He was working quickly at the belt when she shouted, "Stop!"

"I want to hear 'yes.' "

People turned to look.

"Yes. Fool!" Danielle said, giggling.

Dwayne zipped up his pants and turned to the couple at the next table. "The wedding is April 1983," he said, sitting down. "Bring gifts."

Jacksina stuffed a copy of the *Law Journal* into her duffel bag, hopped up out of her seat and got off the train at Court Street. Out the Montague exit, up one block toward the Brooklyn Promenade, and then right four blocks until she reached the entrance to the St. George Health Club on Clark Street. In less than three minutes she was down the steps, past the front desk, into the locker room and jogging around the rubberized track encircling the basketball court. Almost immediately sweat began pouring from her forehead and from her chest. Judge Peters had often said, with amazement and lust, that Jacksina was the wettest woman he'd ever known—"And I've known a lot of wet women."

It was Jacksina's perspiration that had brought the jurist and the law student together on that same track six months before. As usual, sweat was pouring off Jacksina's forehead. The Judge trotted up beside her and with an elegant gesture slid a towel from around his neck onto hers. The Judge's towel exchange was so well executed that it still thrilled Jacksina just to recall it. Her initial reaction was that Peters looked pretty good for a middle-aged man. But post-towel she realized he just plain looked good: silver hair, bronze skin, firm, athletic-looking ass.

Afterward, at the juice bar overlooking the basketball court, they'd laughed over virgin piña coladas about the irony of their legal connection. At first she peppered the Judge with questions about his notorious decisions and how he parried attacks from the Police Benevolent Association and other conservative organizations against him for what they considered his radical and overly lenient bail policies. Smoothly the Judge shifted the conversation to Jacksina, and soon had her telling funny anecdotes about the antics of men trying to woo her. When Jacksina recalled how one guy accidentally on purpose walked into a stop sign as he waved to her on 27th Street, the Judge roared with laughter. While they chatted she wondered if he was widowed, divorced, what?

Alas, Judge Peters was not divorced. His wife, Harriett, was very much alive. And he claimed their marriage was the key to his stability. Still, Jacksina duly noted, there were no ringing declarations of love for his wife. So when he suggested that they still could be good friends, she cooed "Yes" in agreement. Making her seventh trip around the track, sweat collecting in her headband and rolling down the insides of her arms, Jacksina still found the energy to smirk. . . .

Judge Peters and Jacksina would be friends today, admiring each other from a close distance and still flirting like crazy if Mr. Right On! hadn't gone after her.

Mr. Right On!, so labeled by Jacksina, was a Sugar Ray

Leonard lookalike and NBC cameraman who'd been terrorizing the (white) women at the St. George with his grin and pectorals. One night, apparently for a change of pace, Mr. Right On! decided to put the full-court press on Jacksina. He sat down next to Jacksina at the bar where she always met the Judge for a post-workout fruit drink. The Judge came to the door, saw Mr. Right On! leaning with a smile toward Jacksina and, following a sad little frown, turned away.

Jacksina, who'd been more than slightly impressed by Mr. Right On!'s physical package, who'd decided not to seduce Judge Peters out of respect for his marriage, his beliefs, and his position, made a snap decision. She stood up, almost butting Mr. Right On! in the chin with her forehead, said a quick "Excuse me" and, duffel bag under her arm, ran after the Judge. She grabbed him out on Clark Street and demanded the keys to his Lincoln Continental. Fifteen minutes later they were parked in the shadow of one of the Jehovah's Witnesses buildings by the Brooklyn Bridge. They made love in his spacious leather backseat, with the Judge's robes draped over their heads.

Jacksina sat down on one of the exercise bikes facing the basketball court. Mr. Right On! jogged by. She noticed he now avoided eye contact. *Oh well,* she thought, *another brother lost forever to the evils of white women.* She'd made the right choice. The Judge was a tender lover, a good friend, and the best law professor she'd had. As Jacksina peddled up automated hills she wondered if he would leave his wife. *Do I really want that right now?* She peddled even harder, refusing to answer her own question, and seemed to feel impurities flow out of her skin.

When Dwayne called and told Danielle to bring her sneakers, jeans, and a t-shirt for "later," she wondered if they were going to play basketball after dinner that much anticipated Friday evening. When he said, "Sort of," she savored the mystery. She'd already told Morris she and Jacksina were going to Albany to see an old schoolmate, and that she'd be over Saturday night.

She hated lying, but what's a girl to do? For Dwayne, the week was economically traumatic. *What am I doing?* he wondered after spending two weeks' rent money on a Giorgio Armani suit like the one Richard Gere wore in *American Gigolo.* Danielle found him unbelievablely adorable when he entered her office Friday evening in his olive Armani. He was carrying a scuffy brown duffel bag. She was dressed in a sky-blue silk dress, pumps of the same color, and she wore a delicate gold chain, a present from a man far away but not long ago.

"You're looking good, Ms. Embry."

"*Love* that suit. What's in the bag?"

"You'll see," he teased. "Did you bring the sneakers and stuff?"

"Yes, I did," she said, reaching behind her desk to pick up a Macy's shopping bag.

"Give it here." She did and he stuffed it inside his duffel.

"Where are we going?"

"First, to dinner."

La Scala was a small, dark, family-type restaurant in the theater district. Most of the diners were middle-aged white theatergoers. Many were on a first-name basis with the owner. Dwayne had dined here three days before with *Billboard*'s New York bureau chief. They'd talked of his covering black music for the record industry's leading trade publication. The interview had gone well, he thought. It was for this reason that Dwayne had come back. It had worked once. It could work again.

Over linguini with clam sauce, veal Parmesan, and plenty of good Broglio Chianti, they ping-ponged double entendres between mouthfuls.

"I've never kissed—I mean *really* kissed—a man with a beard before," she said with a giggle.

He volunteered, keeping a straight face, that he believed that the smarter the lady, the better the sex, "and I think you're the *smartest* woman I've had the pleasure of dining with since I met Shirley Chisholm."

It was all garbage and all great fun. In between the compliments and the innuendos came the inevitable personal histories. Danielle told of her life in Arthur, Connecticut. She described her father, a soft-spoken man of considerable intelligence and refinement, a carpenter by trade who had built their home practically by hand, in his spare time, over a five-year period, and her equally hardworking, insecure mother, who coveted grandchildren yet refused to admit her age. Jean Embry couldn't resist forcing herself into her two teenaged daughters' jeans and dresses ("just trying them on for size"), even when the result was bulges and even split seams. From her parents, Danielle explained, she had learned hard, dedicated work, insecurity, and vanity. Love was very important to her, and she insisted with what Dwayne saw as committed naiveté, that she sincerely loved every man she had seriously dated—from the cute young Puerto Rican student who took her virginity at fourteen to the unhappily married, very Republican analyst from Washington, D.C., to good old Morris, with some interesting stops in between.

Dwayne didn't think he'd ever been in love, admitting he hadn't a clue to how it felt, and tried, very discreetly in light of Danielle's comments, to imply that most other people hadn't either. His father had split when he was in high school, which planted an uneasiness in his soul that had chilled into an arrogance even he sometimes found obnoxious. "At night I'd hear them arguing and I'd curl up in my bed," he remembered. "I was always trying to stuff my head into my pillow."

Danielle reached across the table, took his hands in hers, and pulled them to her lips, kissing each finger softly.

"That was nice," he said, turned on and unnerved.

"Poor baby," she said softly. After they had exchanged their fifteenth or sixteenth gooey look, Dwayne stood up and announced loudly, "Time for some music."

"Sure."

The Savoy was a noble experiment in Times Square. Once a respectable Broadway theater, it had fallen dark in the 1970s and been revived in the '80s as an elegant pop-music venue.

The mezzanine and upper level had refurbished concert hall seats, but on the ground floor there were long black tables that gave the Savoy a nightclub ambience. There was a light menu, but the sale of pricy drinks was the house specialty. The aisles were very tight, and you had to turn your chair sideways for a decent sightline. This was the way Dwayne sat, behind Danielle, his notebook clutched in his right hand while his left slowly stroked the back of her neck. He was supposed to be taking notes for a review of Stephanie Mills as a *Billboard* "tryout," but his left hand was having too good a time to be bothered helping his right.

Dwayne knew Mills' show by heart, so instead of getting ready to take notes, just before her cover of Peabo Bryson's soul classic "Feel the Fire" he put down his notebook, leaned forward in his chair, and brought his lips close to the back of Danielle's hair. Midway through, as Mills started building toward the song's melodramatic close, he pulled Danielle slowly backwards and into his arms.

She thought he was going to kiss her—he was at first. Then, no. Just as Mills' soprano added layers to the lyric's secular passion, Dwayne realized what he needed to do. Tension—controlled passion—was the key to great singing, and for this woman, this night, controlled and passionate was what he was going to be.

After Mills finished and the audience stood to applaud, Danielle looked at him for a moment, puzzled. He refused to meet her glance.

"Time to go," he said softly, and snapped his fingers for the check.

"Where to now?" she said as they walked down Broadway.

"We're going to sweat."

"Jogging in Central Park?"

"Boogie with the Bean."

John "Jellybean" Benitez was the deejay at the Funhouse, a grungy ex-factory with a dance floor the size of Herald Square, where Latino and Italian kids, the greasy ethnics of New York's sweltering pot, gathered Friday and Saturday nights in sneakers, sweats, shorts, t-shirts, headbands, and much makeup to update *Saturday Night Fever.* John Travolta's Tony Manero was their older brother. Times had changed. These kids didn't hustle. They bounced and twisted and flipped. Some called it breaking. Dwayne and Danielle paid attention but not a lot. Stripped down to the bare essentials at the center of the floor, cheering and laughing at Jellybean's high-energy edits, the two sweated all over each other anywhere from 90 to 130 beats per minute.

During an unexpected shift from "Love Is the Message" into "Good Times," Danielle turned her back to Dwayne, rubbed her ass against his groin and then reached back and grabbed his ass, running her fingers up and down his buns. He was hard against her body and she decided, right then, as he moved in time with her, that Dwayne was unquestionably a good lover and that night she would have him. Case closed.

In the back of a cab going uptown they slumped over each other, wet and loose. The place she shared with Jacksina was in Lincoln Towers, an immense apartment complex near Lincoln Center. But Dwayne wouldn't have the pleasure of meeting Jacksina that night. Danielle had "suggested" that her room-mate find another place to sleep "just in case." As she unlocked the door, Danielle's mind was flipping through memories of the past, comparing this night with romantic evenings gone by, wondering how to seduce Dwayne with just the right flair. She hadn't had this much fun in months.

While Danielle was feeling happy-go-lucky, Dwayne was tense. *What if she doesn't enjoy sex with me? What if I disappoint her?* He sat on her pull-out sofa as nervous as a clubfooted thirteen-year-old at a hustle contest.

"Dwayne, I had a great time. Jellybean is really good. Fascinating how he arranged those sounds. It was like a sonic collage."

"Fascinating. Sonic collage. You're cute," he said suavely. "I'm gonna steal 'sonic collage.' "

"But I still own the copyright. What do I get for it?"

"What would you like?"

"What you promised me."

Dwayne scratched his head as if he couldn't recall. "You talking about birthmarks?"

"Let me see yours and you can see mine."

"You never mentioned you had a birthmark," he said skeptically.

"Right below my navel."

She rubbed her hands against her thighs, then twisted out of her blue silk dress and stood there in her white cotton panties. No bra. No further prompting needed. Quickly Dwayne was out of his t-shirt. Laughing and tossing their remaining clothes at each other, they stripped down to nothing, and stood facing each other, still laughing, studying each other's contours. She was a little flabbier around the waist than he had imagined, and he was a little skinnier than she preferred.

Still, there they were, standing butt-naked at 3:37 a.m. Danielle bent down and searched for Dwayne's birthmark.

"Where is it, Dwayne?"

"My birthmark?"

"Yes. What did you think?"

"Right there." He pointed to his waist.

"That's not a birthmark. That's a scar from an operation."

"An appendectomy to be precise."

"Dwayne, you're crazy."

"Stand up." Dwayne's voice was husky.

Danielle did, resting her forehead against his chest. "Dwayne," she said softly, "I don't have a birthmark either."

He put his arms around her waist, picked her up and placed her carefully across the sofa. Her eyes were closed now. For a moment he was going to be cute and spout a fake, sexy, porno-movie line. Instead he bent down and tasted her juices, feeling them flow onto his beard. Danielle didn't want to let go so quickly, but then the wave started building and sweeping through her body. His jaw grew tired, but her convulsions brought new inspiration. Just a little longer. Just a little firmer. Then she was over the edge. When she was calm again they kissed. Dwayne's beard dripped moisture onto her chin.

Then she stopped kissing, slipped out of his grasp, and from under the sofa pulled out a long, round toothpaste tube and a plastic injector. She squeezed the contents of the tube into the plastic injector and was about to slip the chemicals into her body when Dwayne took control, gently guiding her back to the couch, and doing it for her. Then he began kissing her again, rubbing his groin against hers. Danielle rolled her thighs in time with his strokes and then they were one, moving with a syncopation as sensual as reggae.

The next morning Dwayne's nostrils filled with Danielle's perfume and the aroma of food wafting in from the kitchen. He stretched his arms and legs and yawned loudly. In the kitchen Danielle scrambled eggs, fried bacon and home fries, rightly guessing that Dwayne wouldn't be into anything too fancy. For a minute she thought about slipping some onion and lox into his eggs, but then decided to play it straight. Which reminded her that it was time to tell Dwayne about Morris. Then she smiled. It might be the correct time, but she wasn't going to be correct. No need for tension this morning. She wanted to make love one more time before she wrote her resignation letter and got ready for Morris. *But what if Morris wants to make love tonight? No, I can't do that.*

"Danielle!"

She stuck her head into the living room.

"Good morning," she said.

"Good morning, Ms. Embry. You look beautiful this morning."

"No thanks to you."

"No?"

"Keeping me up dancing all night when we should have come here right after dinner."

"Damn." Her frankness surprised him. "Why don't you rejoin me then? I've had cold eggs before."

"They say never ride a young horse on an empty stomach," she said.

"I guess I'm not a good jockey." He gestured with his index finger for her to come.

Danielle moved slowly toward the couch, doing a slow striptease.

Later that warm May day, Dwayne sat on his dungaree sofa and watched the Yankees and Red Sox do battle up at Fenway Park. It was an early season game but played with great emotion because of their bitter rivalry. On a take-out at second base, the Yankees' Lou Pinella almost started a fight by rolling hard into the Sox's Jerry Remy. Good, hard, clean baseball. Yet Dwayne's mind was back in Danielle's couch. He rubbed his groin, its soreness testimony to their passion. Staring at the screen as Reggie Jackson struck out with Willie Randolph at third, Dwayne saw Danielle's eyes, black and bright and wide, and felt her warm breath on his neck.

Danielle was with "him" right then. He could feel it. Before they had made love, she was just a cute woman he had decided to chase. Now it might be something more. Dwayne felt inadequate to the feelings exploding inside him. He felt like a badly programmed computer that couldn't cope with a sudden heavy influx of data. There had been a time when he depended on that faulty information-processing to save him from being deceived or trapped by women. Now he wondered for the first time if he'd been fooling himself.

As Pinella doubled-in two runs with a line drive off Fenway Park's "Green Monster" wall in left field, Dwayne downed the rest of his Budweiser and wondered how she was.

The silence in Morris's living room was loud. Behind wire-framed glasses his eyes were bloodshot. His nostrils flared. His mouth bent into an angry snarl, shifted into a sad smile, then curled back into the snarl. His normally beige face was crimson.

"Why are you throwing our plans away?"

"I told you how I feel," she said firmly.

Morris's face grew hard. So did the voice. "How you feel? *How you feel?* That's the stupidest thing I think I've ever heard you say!"

"Morris . . ."

"We were together because I thought that you cared about

everything. Not about this or that. *Everything.* The totality. I thought you were mature. If you wanted a little dick, we could have kept it on that level."

Danielle reached across the coffee table and slapped him. His reflexes told him to strike back, but his head stopped him. Instead he just looked her coldly in the eye. Then his face softened. "I love you, Danielle." He continued to look her in the eye, but now his were wet. "You know I'm here today and I'll be here tomorrow. You know that. You've really hurt me. But I still love you."

"I know that, Morris. I know that. But I don't want to hurt you any more than I have by lying to you. Lying's the worst thing you can do to someone you love."

Morris was shell-shocked into silence. Danielle reached across the table, grabbed his hands in hers, and smiled. "I'm sorry, baby," she said softly, "but I'm doing what's best for both of us. That's all I'm doing. That's all."

"So tell me about him?" Jacksina was jumping rope in the living room of their apartment. Rick James's "Give It to Me Baby" was pumping from her stereo. But Danielle, editing a manuscript, ignored her. "Too busy to talk about your latest love? That doesn't sound like you. Plus it violates the rules of the house. You told me all about good old Morris. Tell me about this writer—I'll tell you about my Bronx judge."

Danielle looked up wide-eyed through her glasses. "There's no comparison. That man is twenty years older than you."

"I think he looks at it differently," Jacksina said in her usual confident manner.

"Do tell."

"He looks at me as if I'm twenty years his junior," Jacksina said, wiping sweat off her dark chocolate forehead. Jacksina was big-boned, with a large dramatic head and a taut, athletic body that Danielle had often gazed upon with envy. She was a striking sight whether in her current blue Spandex workout suit or in the pants-suit combinations she adored. Danielle glanced up at Jacksina doing stomach crunches and sighed. *I should be tightening up myself,* she mused. Then, as always, she decided she had too much work to do and looked back down at the manuscript.

"Dear, this flat stomach means much more to him than it would to someone our age," Jacksina said. "You and I both know how young guys are. Once you start dating them, they just wanna hang around your apartment and raid your refrigerator. They're users. They give a little in bed—maybe—and they are nice to look at. But I'm nobody's mother." She thumped her stomach with her left hand. "And don't come at me with that 'I'm looking for a father' mess. I'm not the one who sleeps in her father's pajamas."

"But *I* don't bed my father figures," Danielle said with mock meanness.

"Metaphorically you do," Jacksina shot back playfully.

"Who's the book editor here?"

Jacksina came over and flopped on one of Danielle's paper piles on the sofa.

"Hey!" Danielle said, pushing her aside and yanking her papers from under Jacksina's butt. "Why don't you go study?"

Ignoring Danielle, Jacksina said quietly, "He was in the *Post* again today. They called him 'Put-'em-on-the-street Pete.' They said, 'The Bronx is a zoo and he's left the cages open.' Just because he wants to give young brothers a chance, they attack him."

"I'm sorry, Jack," Danielle said, "but how much integrity can he have if he's married and sleeping with a law student?"

Jacksina took no offense at Danielle's harsh judgment—this was an old argument.

"The law and sex are two different things, dear. The Judge believes in keeping the judiciary out of the bedroom."

"So you don't do it with his robes on?"

"Now I didn't say that!" They both laughed.

"Honestly, the Judge is the best man I've met in—"

"Weeks!" Danielle interjected.

"No, not weeks or months. Stop that. He's the best in a long time."

"But he's married and famous and if it gets out—"

Jacksina cut her off. "You're my roommate, but this is my life. Okay?"

There was a long pause as Danielle wondered if this was worth fighting seriously over again.

"Okay," she said finally, "it's your life. Just do like you promised and invite him over for dinner."

"I'd like to, but he might be scared you'd recognize him."

"Tell him if he wants the brief back he lent you, I want him to tell some stories about Adam Powell," Danielle said. "From what I've read they had some sort of relationship."

"Your Powell fixation is getting worse," Jacksina replied.

"You know that when I get in J school I'm gonna make my first-year project a comparison of Powell and Congressman Rangel. It's just research, Jack. That's all."

"Have you been doing dirty things with that old picture of the Congressman you used to have?"

"Why?"

"Because I don't see it around anymore."

"Mind your business. Anyway, it's hanging up in my office."

"Dear," Jacksina said sweetly, "I'm gonna miss you. Where will I find another roommate like you?"

"The Judge perhaps?"

"You know, honestly, I really just want his robes."

Jacksina entered the courtroom, walked up the center aisle, and slid onto a bench, pushing past two smug-looking white legal-aid lawyers and a lovely young Puerto Rican woman wearing a blue New York Yankees jacket and a teary expression. The room was filled with the low mutterings of deals being done, families faced with disaster, and men with shattered dreams of freedom. In her gray pants suit and well-manicured nails, Jacksina looked decidedly out of place in a roomful of people who dressed for function, not style. There she sat, a slick buppie, surrounded by harried attorneys, distraught mothers, and yawning, bored-to-the-bone cops waiting to testify.

But in Jacksina's case looks were deceiving. She was a

regular in this courtroom. The black bailiff who stood near the door to the Judge's chamber winked at her. The stenographer, a fortyish white woman who wore thick blue glasses, noticed Jacksina and rolled her eyes. *Same to you, fishface,* Jacksina thought. The assistant D.A., a reed-thin white woman in an ugly, mismatched blue jacket and skirt and a ridiculously frilly pink blouse, glanced Jacksina's way as she drummed her fingers on the mahogany prosecutor's desk.

"All rise!" the bailiff announced, and Judge Alvin Peters strode in from his chambers with a file in his hand and his robes dangling off his wide shoulders like a coatrack. The first case was announced. Two black men in their twenties were shuffled before him. The Puerto Rican woman stared anxiously at the shorter of the two men. Jacksina caught the woman's look, then turned her attention toward the Judge.

He didn't look as youthful up on the bench, with his reading glasses perched on the bridge of his nose and the weight of his job creating creases in his brow. Yet, to Jacksina, he seemed sexier up there on his throne than he ever had at the gym.

"He's so damn cocky," the gaunt-looking legal-aid attorney whispered to his chubby partner, who replied, "Who cares? He's on our side, isn't he?" The thin attorney was not mollified. "The *schvartze* just wants to make trouble, that's all."

Jacksina had been with men who weren't willing to risk anything—cute buppies who challenged neither her nor themselves. They'd left school determined to fit in. Cool and handsome her men had been—but she also knew that most of them were as shallow as babies' bathwater. Maybe it was just because they were young—they hadn't yet acquired anything worth risking. She had no problem with black folks getting paid. Hardly. Yet when she met the Judge, Jacksina was struck by the contrast between the young men she knew and the grown man he was. She'd been consistent in her men until the Judge: Ivy League types in Brooks Brothers suits and wing-tips, who were happily building investment portfolios. Men who were happy to define themselves at Harvard Club lunches by their paychecks.

The Judge was middle-aged, yet committed to life in a thrillingly youthful outlook. He was a connection to a past era of black masculinity and class. The men her age had profited from the work of the Judge's generation. They'd taken those public triumphs and then turned inward, selfish, satisfied. She didn't want to be around that. By loving the Judge, she felt tapped into a noble legacy, a more noble part of herself. Maybe the Judge had once been a callow young man too. But the man she loved was, in her mind, defined by his integrity.

Well, even she had to admit that "integrity" was a relative term in the Judge's case. After all, he was letting off accused felons on such a regular basis that the entire city establishment was after his hide. And he'd refused to explain his motivations to anyone—even refusing interviews with the sympathetic black media like the *Amsterdam News* and Gil Noble's "Like It Is" tv show. And she couldn't ignore the fact that Mr. Integrity was carrying on a lusty affair with a law student, namely herself. All of which was politically, racially, or morally questionable.

"Tamak Leland Jones and Elijah Anderson, you are alleged to have struck a police officer, John Neal Ireland, just a few blocks from here, the corner of 164th Street and Grand Concourse," the Judge said. "You young men were, according to all involved in this unfortunate incident, carrying a turntable out of the D train exit. There is, I've heard in testimony from all parties, a dispute over what was said when officer Ireland intercepted Jones and Anderson. Even the two gentlemen in possession of the turntables differ in their recollections of the conversation." Then, with a sardonic smile, the Judge added, "What is clear is that the turntables landed on officer Ireland's right foot. According to the medical report he sustained ligament damage. Whether that was a malicious act or not is the root of this dispute."

The chubby legal-aid lawyer whispered to his comrade, " 'See-'em, free-'em' is starting to feel it." The thin one snarled, "Yeah. Time for your regularly scheduled outrage." The Puerto Rican woman heard this, and for the first time since Jacksina had sat down, her face brightened. Jacksina noticed a stillness in the courtroom, a sort of collective breath-holding.

"The Bronx D.A.'s office," he resumed, "apparently at the urging of the Police Benevolent Association, is pursuing felony assault along with what Howard Cosell would describe as a veritable plethora of charges. As I look over the testimony of Messrs Jones and Anderson, several facts leap out at me. Both these young men are products of the usual urban ills—wayward fathers, welfare mothers, bouts with drug abuse, larceny, and—looking at these reports from their schoolteachers—some bad grammar."

Jacksina couldn't help laughing at his awful joke. The Judge peered over his glasses and smiled at her, then returned to his performance.

"But these young men, despite their disadvantaged environment, are filled with ambition, good old-fashioned American ambition, and apparently an abiding love for something they call 'b-beats.' Mr. Jones carries the records, which is understandable since someone must. Mr. Anderson takes these records, and according to his statement, 'cuts' them, and young people dance to these cut records. Mr. Anderson, does this damage the records?"

The assistant D.A. rose on cue to raise an objection. She was on automatic pilot, knowing that objecting to Peters' courtroom procedure was futile. She didn't even bother to open her mouth. The Judge raised his left hand to signify "Stop," and as mechanically as she had stood up, the assistant D.A. sat back down. "Please, Mr. Anderson," Peters insisted, "answer the question."

Nervous, but anxious to have a last crack at pleading his case, Elijah said, "Well, Judge, you know, it's like this. The way we cut records is, like, playing the turntable, you know, like a guitar or something like that." Then Elijah got what he thought was a bright idea. "It's like jazz, Judge. Turntable jazz. T-jazz."

"Jazz, huh?" the Judge said skeptically. "So you stole your cousin's turntable to play jazz?"

"Well, Judge, you know, I was gonna bring it back, you know, after we'd gigged at the Dance Inferno."

"The idea of turntable jazz disturbs me." His voice was deeper and now grave. "The phrase suggests your profound misunderstanding of this music and the complexity it represents." Jacksina glanced at the assistant D.A., who had been sitting slumped in her chair. Now her back stiffened, her head shifted forward, and her hand now lay flat on the table. "My contempt for this turntable jazz concept is profound. But"—he paused for fake dramatic effect—"it is outweighed by the frivolous concept that dropping turntables on the foot of police officers constitutes some form of assault."

The assistant D.A. resumed her slumped posture, and the two legal-aid attorneys looked on disdainfully. The Puerto Rican woman, still riding her emotional roller coaster, appeared optimistic.

"The proper punishment for Mr. Anderson's 'borrowing' his cousin's stereo equipment—and the Bronx D.A.'s presentation of the case—is that next Friday during lunch at the Bronx D.A.'s office Mr. Anderson and Mr. Jones will perform for the entire staff. Afterwards the defendants will do charity performances at local precincts over the next month. I expect the PBA to help select which precincts will benefit from this enriching entertainment."

Jacksina looked over at the assistant D.A. to check out her reaction. The woman was staring at the ceiling with a blank look. No angry objections. No spiteful remarks. As usual, the assistant D.A. was resigned to Judge Peters' outrages and only wanted to move on to the next case, which might offer some hope for a conviction of some sort.

As Mr. Anderson and Mr. Jones were led away, the Puerto Rican woman blew a triumphant kiss at Mr. Anderson.

After this comic interlude, the Judge looked increasingly blasé as the daily parade of South Bronx horrors came before him. Whenever he could, he discreetly made eyes at Jacksina.

As usual they ate lunch in Judge Peters' chambers—take-out food from a bodega on the Grand Concourse. The Judge scooped up a forkful of rice and beans across the desk from

Jacksina who, savoring her sweet plantains, noticed that the picture of the Judge and his wife that used to sit on the desk had been replaced by a photo of a much younger Judge Peters standing with ex-Mayor John Lindsay and the late Governor Nelson Rockefeller.

He looked at her dreamily and said, "I love your hair."

"Tell me why."

He stood up, reached over, and gently placed his right hand on the side of her head. "Because it's all yours. It's thick and kinky and short—and it's yours."

"You saying you wouldn't love me if I had extensions or a wig?"

"No, I can't imagine not loving you under any circumstances." He spoke with his heart but Jacksina wanted something more.

"Your wife wears wigs, doesn't she?" A mischievous look passed across her face. She could feel the Judge's hand tense. His first reaction was to take his hand from her head, but he resisted the impulse.

"You," he said in his grave judge's voice, "believe in your own beauty. You don't worry whether your hair is long or wavy or big and bouncy. You don't spend hours at the hairdresser and God knows how much money. You love yourself, which makes it easy for me to love you."

Peters never mentioned his wife by name around Jacksina. Whether he was being cowardly or astute, Jacksina gave it little thought. Nevertheless, he sometimes obliquely communicated his dislike of his wife of twenty-some years, and as a result, Jacksina knew about Harriett's fancy for gaudy wigs of auburn hue. Just last week, in the *Amsterdam News*, Jacksina had seen a photo of Harriett Peters, overweight and huge, sporting an unnatural-looking hairpiece, at the 100 Black Men Dinner. Jacksina had cut out the picture and intended to enlarge it and use it as a dart board.

The Judge was, in her estimation, too classy to dog his wife in front of his mistress. But, for now, these verbal love strokes were enough for Jacksina. He leaned over the desk, wrapped his

hands around her head, and kissed her with a college boy's enthusiasm and a mature man's skill.

The phone rang. The Judge picked it up, listened, and the
smile vanished. "Listen," he shouted. "Listen, you silly white
son of a bitch. I have power. That's right, I said *power*. And
that's why you're afraid of me, 'cause I'm the *only black man*
you motherfuckers have ever seen who isn't afraid to exercise
power once he's got it. And furthermore—"

But the caller had hung up.

"What was that about?" Jacksina asked.

"The usual," he replied, much too offhandedly. "The swine
are afraid of me. That's all, baby. Just afraid."

"Daniel, I don't know if your daughter is growing up or getting
sillier," said Jean Embry, Danielle's mother, hands on hips in
her bedroom as Danielle unpacked on the other side of the wall.

"Now, Jean, that isn't necessary," said Dan Embry, Danielle's
father.

"I don't know that, Dan. She *is* twenty-seven."

"Twenty-six," he corrected.

"All right, twenty-six. It's still old enough," Jean replied
irritably.

Danielle tried to ignore them, continuing to hang her vast
clothing collection in her closet. The first time she'd moved into
this bedroom, Danielle was eight and awed by how much closet
space she had. So much room, she remembered, compared to
the bedroom she and her sisters had shared in New Haven.

"Morris was perfect for her," her mother claimed.

"Maybe, Jean. I liked him too. But *she* didn't think so."

Closet space meant "middle class" to Danielle. It meant
"things." Extra dress shoes. Dance shoes for her classes. The
pretty pink outfit she wore at her first piano recital. The rabbit
coat back when a rabbit coat was *the* important fashion statement of 1973. That prom outfit she and her mother had argued
about her entire senior year. Now it meant a place to come to in
the summer before attending graduate school, a place happily
where "rent" means cleaning the bathroom on Saturdays.

"This is an important transition for her, Jean. Remember how you worried when she was living with those guys? Remember? She's just trying to continue that process of growth, I think."

Danielle laughed lightly at that. *Daddy always looks for the best side of me. Even when I make awful mistakes he just hugs me and says nothing. His brown eyes are so warm when he's extra-nice. . . . That's why I'm so understanding—too understanding.—I got that from him. . . .*

"Dan, I have nothing against Danielle quitting Morris, quitting her job, moving back home, or going to graduate school," said her mother. "But why do them all at the same time?"

Mother's right again. Always is. The voice of pragmatism and common sense. They'll close Connecticut Bell when she retires. They'll have to. People on the job say Jean Embry is the most stable, diligent person on the entire plant. And, at work and at home, she expects everyone else to be the same. That's probably why Jack, Danny Jr., and Jeannette are all so crazy.

Jack was a fire-and-brimstone Pentecostal preacher in New Haven; Danny Jr., a rarely employed bisexual actor in San Francisco; and Jeannette, an old-fashioned bohemian living on Great Jones Street in the Village with a struggling white painter; all these choices made, at least partially, in reaction to their mother's straitlaced way of life. Only Danielle, the baby, was taking a straight career path, though her intense tossing and turning with men—living with them and leaving after a spell—drove her mother crazy.

"I think it's great she could come home. Feel comfortable enough to come home. I don't think the other kids would."

"That's true, Dan. That's so true. She's the youngest, but she's the sweetest. We have some crazy kids, Dan."

"*We* did it. But in this world what else can you be? It's good for them," he said laughing.

"You are so easygoing—you get along with everybody."

Danielle closed the closet and sat down on her bed, then got up and reopened the closet door. *I shouldn't be spying on them,* she thought. But the back wall was a wall to their bedroom. She had discovered her secret listening spot in junior high school and, with a sly grin and some guilt, had savored her gateway into her parents' private world ever since. She'd heard much: tension over the flirtatious Mrs. Williams from down the block, the shock of Jack's receiving the call to preach, and the many nights they'd made love, just as they were doing now. It wasn't as action-packed anymore. *Mother rarely screams now; she sighs. Sex for them now isn't so much an act of passion as one of sweetness.* Lying back on her bed, Danielle imagined her parents in each others' arms, moving slowly together as if they were dancing to those Nat King Cole records Daddy so adored. Danielle picked the Columbia J. School material off the floor, leafing through it quickly and wondering if Dwayne was writing on this clear spring evening.

Why am I doing this? Dwayne thought to himself. He sat on his sofa with Sandifred Spencer, a nineteen-year-old Hunter College premed student and part-time employee at a McDonald's in Queens, where he first laid his leer on her. Tall, light-skinned, with light-brown eyes and full breasts, Dwayne saw that with time Sandifred could be a quality woman. But she wasn't there yet, though Dwayne thought an older man could get her there. So did Sandifred. Dwayne, however, had decided rather quickly that he was not going to be that man. He just wanted to do her.

How Dwayne got to the point he was now—sucking on the brown breasts he had fantasized about while downing two cheeseburgers (no onions or mayo), an order of fries, and a medium Coke at McDonald's—said much about his pre-Danielle love life. He'd flirted with Sandifred for a couple of months. A little joke. A compliment about her hair. Occasionally he'd sit in McDonald's and scribble in his notebook, trying successfully to stimulate her curiosity. When he had a piece in *Musician* or the *Voice*, Dwayne made sure he told Sandifred about it or dropped her a copy. He knew she wondered why he hadn't asked for her phone number.

Reggie Olds had schooled him well. "Patience is a weapon

that not enough niggers know how to use," Reggie said one night while they sat up watching the Phillies' Steve Carlton shut out the Mets. "That is particularly true when you are scoping on a beautiful woman. She is used to the full-court press. What you have to do is use a zone defense. Draw her into the corner and then drop the ball. Just take your time. Get her confidence. Know this: anybody can pull a beautiful woman but not everyone does."

It worked. Dwayne was actually just a few years older than Sandifred, but he had succeeded in giving off that "older man" vibe. Sandifred was now seriously interested and, man, was Dwayne glad, because he was almost out of patience. Since he'd left home three years before to room with Reggie, Dwayne's only major preoccupations were writing or thinking about women. So when Sandifred accepted his offer to stop by his apartment after work, Dwayne's experience told him he had a seventy-five percent chance of getting over. For things to work, however, Dwayne knew he had to depend on several variables: that she liked the way he kissed, that Reggie wasn't screwing someone, loudly, in his room; that the apartment and Dwayne's room weren't *too* funky; if she really *did* want to do more than talk; and *so* crucial, that Sandifred wasn't on her period.

These conditions of the heart were all "go" as Dwayne, still licking and biting her breast, slid his right hand into her jeans, then her pantyhose and panties. Dwayne was engaged yet detached. Excited yet mechanical. Lustful yet way too cold. Maze's "Golden Time of Day" played on the stereo, sounding all warm and sensitive. But Dwayne knew, for this moment, the song was a lie. This was a raw hip-hop movement. Stripped of romantic emotion and the aura that surrounded loving Danielle, Dwayne knew this was going through the motions, sexy motions, yes, but motion without emotion.

Later, as Sandifred, with more enthusiasm than skill, placed her mouth against his chest and then below, Dwayne sat back and knew something had changed. When Dwayne closed his eyes and moaned, it was Danielle's face he saw.

* * *

"This is my last day of work," Danielle said proudly into the phone.

"That's absolutely correct," Dwayne agreed in a preoccupied voice.

"So what are we going to do?"

"I thought your parents wanted you to do something with them?"

"They do, but," she said sweetly, "I want to do something with you."

"Why can't you hang out with them tonight?"

"Why?" she questioned, quite surprised at his attitude.

"Two reasons. One, I have a piece I have to finish. Two, I won't have time to finish it the rest of the weekend."

"Let me come over tonight," she pleaded. "I won't disturb you."

"Yeah, right." He laughed. "Baby, your not disturbing me would disturb me. Just meet me at our spot at Grand Central tomorrow at high noon. And remember, bring a couple of changes of clothes."

She hung up reluctantly and then called up T.J., who was more than happy to go out with her, though he didn't tell her he'd be canceling a date to do so.

While taking a break from his work, Dwayne called his mother and tried to impress her with the latest lady of his life.

"She's cute. Big eyes. Real bright. Went to Yale. Worked at a publishing company for a while and is now getting ready to attend Columbia Journalism School for graduate work. Nice family. Great personality."

"Uh huh," was Miriam Robinson's response.

"Ma, are you listening to me?"

"Yes, Dee, I am."

"What do you think?"

"I think what I always think. You met a nice young lady. You are excited. You're *not* ready to settle down, so I don't have to worry about being a grandma."

"I see where I get my tact from."

"I'm not going to get excited every time some girl gives you some."

"Ma!"

She laughed.

"All right, Ma. Next time you call trying to get into my business, I'm just going to say none of your business. Now, one, you'll be hurt, and, two, when I do that your nosy little old heart is going to die of curiosity. I'd hate to be responsible for your death."

"Is that right?" she said with a smile.

"Yes, it is. One of your friends is going to ask how Dwayne is doing right after I hang up and you won't know and you will be mad you passed up this opportunity to find out."

"Uh huh," Miriam said in the professionally noncommittal voice she'd developed for listening to students' problems. Dwayne hated when it was directed his way.

"Ma!"

"Does this lady have a name?"

"Danielle Embry of Arthur, Connecticut. I think she's the best woman I've dated since Phyllis."

"What about Ellen?"

"Well, yeah. Ellen was real sweet."

"And the one attending medical school in Chicago?"

"Donna Stewart? She was crazy, Ma. She was smart, but she was crazy. She would call at two in the morning, and every other word she used was out of a medical dictionary."

"So why should I get excited about this particular young lady when you're always moving from one to another?" A quite logical question. She continued, "Ever since you hooked up with that Olds character you've been a wanna-be gigolo. He brings out the worst in you, you know. Until you get away from him you'll never settle on a steady girlfriend. I know you don't like hearing that, but that's how I feel."

"I just think Danielle's special. I really do." He was trying to sound resolute. "And besides, Reggie's got nothing to do with what I do or how I feel about women."

"And if you are still seeing her in six months, I'll believe you."

"You'll see." *Who am I trying to convince here?* he wondered.

"How's your writing coming?"

"Got an article coming out in *Essence* about jazz reissues next month."

"I'll tell my friends at school." She loved showing his work at school.

"How are they treating you at 396?" he wondered.

"All right. The principal is a black woman, Mrs. Holmes, and she seems to care a little more about the children than most. The assistant principal is this simple white man, Mr. Kaplan, who just sits on his butt and doesn't read our lesson plans. There are some good teachers. But it's still the same as P.S. 189. Always—loud black kids, silly white teachers, and lazy black teachers. I'm glad this year is almost over."

"Your class is cool?"

"I have a couple of dummies. Had to grab one by the ear today. But we are moving along at a steady pace. Got some parents who don't like black teachers, and of course their kids are the worst."

"It's like you say, Ma. They don't know how to deal with their own people in positions of authority. It's a slave mentality. A lazy white teacher is better than a strong black one in their eyes."

"All I know is that I'm knocking one down the next time a parent jumps in my face." They both laughed.

"I know because you're little, you have a special license to pick on people. But please remember what happened the last time you straightened out a parent."

"It's babies making babies," she retorted, ignoring her son. "Half these mothers never grew up themselves and here they are trying to raise a child when they are still children themselves, living off their parents or welfare or both. A baby doesn't make a girl a mother or a woman."

"These 'ladies' have really got you mad, huh? Well, you don't have to worry about me, Ma. I won't make you a grandma until I'm really ready, which should be a good ten years from now."

"At least," she agreed.

"That's right. At least ten years."

"That is why I don't get excited when you keep telling me about these girls."

"Young women."

"These young women. It'll be a minute before you find your way to love. You have too much on your mind and, I have to admit it, I spoiled you. It'll take a very together young woman to put up with you and keep you in check."

"Maybe." Dwayne wasn't sure if he should agree or not.

"Has your father called you?"

"No . . . he called you?" Dwayne was surprised at his own curiosity.

"He's back in town. Says he wants to see you."

"No. Thank you for telling me, but no. I'm pretty mellow right now. Seeing him would depress me."

"You should see him." It was more a plea than an order.

Trying to escape her words, he responded, "I'm eating better. Made some pork chops the other night and they were passable. Not great, but genuinely passable."

"Dwayne, don't be smart with me," she said with some heat.

"Ma, I'm not being smart, I'm being honest. It just upsets me to see him. Even when I have a good time, later on I feel so damn melancholy. It's like I'm supposed to feel good about being with him. I can make myself smile. But Ma, I feel angry inside. Usually I hold it in when I'm around him. Then I feel bad later. Why should I feel bad? I'm not the one who stepped off from his responsibilities. So why do I have to be the one who's uncomfortable?"

"I understand how you feel," she said in her best sympathetic Mom voice. "But he is your father. Whatever happened between us was between us. He loves you and you know that."

Dwayne sighed into the phone. "Okay. I know he loves me. . . . Look, I better get back to work. I'll call you next week."

"Be sure to send me some extra copies of *Essence* so I can take some to school."

"You got it, Ma."

" 'Bye, 'bye."

"Later."

Dwayne looked straight up. To his left was the Knicks' 1970 championship banner. Turning his head right, Dwayne peered at the 1973 championship banner. The banners, orange and blue lettering on a white background, hung from Madison Square Garden's ceiling straight and limp, more like useless appendages than a reminder of glory past.

The last Knick championship was less than ten years ago, but in basketball terms that's a century. Down on the court a mediocre Knick team was down by ten to Julius "Dr. J." Erving, Moses Malone, and the Philadelphia 76ers after only three minutes gone in the first quarter. Boos were cascading down from the half-full arena. So far the only Knick to score was forward Bernard King. Everyone else looked outclassed.

From their spot in the green seats halfway up from the court, Dwayne could see the listless look in the eyes of several Knicks. White-haired coach Hubie Brown is red-faced and screaming, but his players either won't or can't respond. *When I was a kid this building was a magical place,* Dwayne recalled, as he surveyed the empty seats. *Now it's just another gym haunted by its championship seasons.*

"How could any real brother say that?" Joint-ski asked Reggie.

"I'm black and I said it," Reggie replied, "but I am also a true b-ball fan."

Joint-ski, with real outrage, shot back, "Naugh, man, you couldn't be nothing but an oreo sayin' that. Am I right, Ra?" Rahiem, sitting to Joint-ski's right and munching on a hot dog, mumbled, "Word." Dwayne was going to jump into the debate but instead focused on watching Dr. J's modest Afro and lean body glide upcourt with the Knicks' Bernard King in close pursuit.

"You guys can say I'm not black, not African-American, street, whatever," Reggie said with mock defiance. "Anybody who would take Bernard King over Dave DeBusschere doesn't really know ball." Joint-ski couldn't believe it. "Come on, man, I know ball. If it wasn't for this rap game I'd be serving niggas right now at some big college. I had scholarship offers. Right, Ra?"

On this point Rahiem wasn't as anxious to cosign his partner's pronouncement. "That's what you told me, bro," Rahiem said in a tone that suggested he didn't necessarily believe his boss. Joint-ski cut Rahiem a mean look, which Reggie took as an opening.

"Hey," he said, "Your pedigree doesn't matter. The question is would DeBusschere do Bernard, and any real student of the game would know that DeBusschere just had way too many tools." Joint-ski wanted to cut in but Reggie was rolling. "King's a very passionate player. Has a great turn-around jumper. Goes to the hole with authority."

"Now you're talkin'," Joint-ski cut in.

"But DeBusschere could outrebound, outpass, and outdefend Bernard on his best day. And he had a lot more range on his J. It's not a race thing; it's a game thing. DeBusschere was more versatile."

An irritated Joint-ski shook his head at Reggie and said, "That's all fine, Reg, if you're into that team-ball concept shit. That pick 'n' roll, give 'n' go mess. But I ain't checking for all that. A real ballplayer's got to have attitude; gotta be able to take a nigga off the dribble. 'Nard does that and that beer drinkin' DeBusschere couldn't beat Rahiem off the dribble. Right, Ra?"

"And you know that."

Bernard King got a pass at midcourt from guard Rory Sparrow. The 76ers' Lloyd Free had missed a long jumper, creating an equally long rebound. There were two 76ers back on defense, so King probably should have held the ball and set up the Knicks' half-court offense. But number 30 saw an opening. He split the two 76er defenders and drove toward the hoop. Seventy-sixer guard Doug Collins tried to grab his arm, but

King just shrugged it off and dunked powerfully. The referee indicated a foul. The crowd jumped to its feet.

"See, motherfucker!" Joint-ski shouted. "See! DeBusschere never did no fly shit like that!"

Dwayne stood and clapped along with his three friends. Then a man carrying a tray of Cokes, popcorn, and hot dogs strolled past them on the crosswalk below. Dwayne stared at the man's profile. There was a sprinkling of gray near his temples. Big cheeks. Brown Kangol cap. Brown overcoat. Short man with round, sloped shoulders. "Sit down!"someone shouted from behind and Dwayne complied.

"Yo, D, the play wasn't that good." Joint-ski was commenting on Dwayne's delayed reaction, but the writer was somewhere else. His eyes followed the man four sections over, where he then went up the steps. Now the man was parallel to Dwayne. He sat down next to two people, one of whom was a woman. Dwayne said, "I'll be right back."

Joint-ski asked him to bring back a Coke and Dwayne nodded. With fear and anticipation Dwayne moved down the aisle, across the crosswalk, and followed the path the man had taken. He went past one, two, three sections. Then he slowed down. His eyes narrowed.

Yes, it was him. Dwayne's father was sipping on a soda and smiling. Next to him was a comely woman with pretty eyes and too much rouge on her cheeks. Looked about forty. Next to her was a boy—seven or eight—wearing a brand-new Knick cap and leafing through a Knick yearbook. The crowd leaped to its feet. Dwayne turned to see Dr. J landing gracefully behind the Knick basket. The rim swayed, people were giving each other the celebratory new slap called the high-five. Dwayne had clearly missed something special.

In that moment time melted away for Dwayne and he was transferred back over ten years. He was in the same physical space but he was a foot shorter and a lot less hairy. That evening the Garden was full and the hated Baltimore Bullets were being slain by the Knicks. Frazier outplayed Monroe. DeBusschere, Bradley, and Barnett rained in jumpers from the outside. Reed dominated Unself off the boards. The Knicks were up by 20 in the fourth quarter and Dwayne, holding his father's hand, left their seats early and walked—Dwayne now could feel—past this very spot. Dwayne smiled. Holding hands with his father at a Knick game. Dwayne smiled wider. "Excuse me, mister." The memory was gone. Back to the realities of '82. The kid he'd seen sitting with his father had bumped into Dwayne. The kid had a fresh twenty squeezed into his hand and moved down a corridor where the concession stands and restrooms were located. And Dwayne followed him. The kid headed straight to a souvenir stand. Dwayne watched him purchase a blue t-shirt with an orange Knick logo in front. Anxious and envious, Dwayne stared at the kid, feeling the past weighing down this moment.

The first-quarter buzzer sounded. Fans started to fill the hallway. The kid took the t-shirt and pulled it on over his head. Dwayne wasn't sure what to do now. Following the kid was a little psych, he thought. But he felt compelled to. Suddenly he noticed a look of distress on the kid's face. Dwayne walked over.

"Yo, you look lost."

"Naugh, I ain't lost." The kid was suspicious.

"Your mom told you not to talk to strangers, right?"

The kid just eyed him suspiciously and looked anxious to walk away. "Listen," Dwayne said, "you go down to the next hallway and it'll take you back to your section."

"How do you know where I'm sittin'?"

"I know that section. That's all. Enjoy the game."

Dwayne walked away from the kid and attempted to look back. Maybe if I hadn't talked to him I might have gone. Now it would seem so spooky. He knew that wasn't a very good explanation. *But what could I say? It blows me away just to see him,* Dwayne thought. *Just to see him with another woman and another little boy.* Dwayne knew he was adept enough at polite conversation for that. Besides this was not the place to say what he wanted to say or ask all the questions that troubled him.

Dwayne moved into the soda line. *Reggie's right. DeBusschere is probably a better all-around player than Bernard. But we have Bernard now and we should be happy about that because there's no way to go back. No damn way. So why am I angry? Why am I so damn angry?*

TWO

T.J. *was* jealous, yet they'd been friends so long that Danielle didn't think he'd lie. He started by saying, "I thought you wanted a professional consultation, not a new boyfriend."

"Dwayne is not my boyfriend," she said defensively into the phone. "He's a new friend who's an attractive male. He's fun."

"We both know how you can't have a relationship with a man and not get superserious with them. With a guy like Dwayne—not a bad guy but one with zero self-control—you'll get burned. You shouldn't have quit Morris."

Danielle was pissed. "You act like I can't change. Well, I can. I *can* have a good time, enjoy a man's company, and not immediately want to move in with him."

T.J. was trying to be wise but instead sounded condescending. "I know you and I *know* Dwayne very well. Dwayne is too ghetto for you. Yeah, he's a writer, but his mentality is still Brownsville. When it comes down to it, he's still got that hit-it-and-quit-it ghetto attitude."

Danielle quickly got tired of T.J.'s nasty view of Dwayne. More disturbing, though, was the sense that T.J.'s hostility was deep and not just a friend trying to properly advise a friend. "How well do you know Dwayne? Is there some problem between you and him?"

Sounding very defensive, T.J. shot back, "Look—you and Dwayne won't work. Simple as that."

"I am so disappointed in your lack of confidence in me. I really am, T.J. Talk to you later."

After she hung up T.J. justified his comments to himself. It

57

was for her own good—that sort of thing. Inside he knew it was just jealousy.

Neither Dwayne nor T.J. admitted it to Danielle, but there was a time when they were tight. Back at Brooklyn's Meyer Levin Junior High School, Dwayne, the bookworm from the Brownsville ghetto, and T.J., the glory of black middle-class parents who'd never let concrete chip under their feet, shared a love of blaxploitation and kung fu movies, and spent many Saturdays on the subway to Times Square seeking bloodthirsty double features. T.J. had been attracted by Dwayne's mind and wit. Dwayne was impressed with T.J.'s real-life nuclear family, where he lived, and T.J.'s remarkable ease with whites.

But before it blossomed into one of those lifelong, through-thick-and-thin friendships, T.J.'s parents saw that East Flatbush was changing. His insurance-selling father and his cosmetics-pushing mother owned a house three blocks from the school in East Flatbush, which was then an overwhelmingly Jewish and Italian area. But the old ethnics were fleeing, and other American blacks and, in large numbers, Caribbean immigrants were buying up the newly available homes. Delis were giving way to beef patty emporiums; yiddish to patois. Not that T.J.'s folks were prejudiced. "Hell, no!" they'd reply if challenged. They were just pragmatic. The equation "Blacks in = Whites out!" meant this to T.J.'s folks: negligent teachers, callous cops, lazy garbagemen. They reasoned that's what happened in Crown Heights and Brownsville, and the Jamersons weren't going to wait to be proven wrong. Like many black middle-class families, they joined the white ethnics in their escape. Again they took pains to emphasize that this move reflected no silly self-hatred or any particular love of whitey. You work hard, you want the best, and Brooklyn couldn't provide it.

In the summer of 1973 they moved from East Flatbush to a house in Rego Park, Queens, where T.J. enrolled in Christ the King High School. His folks made it clear he shouldn't venture back to Brooklyn. What about Dwayne? Yeah, he was well-mannered, especially for a child of those terrible Tilden Projects. But don't lock yourself in to the past. His mother told him,

"At Christ the King you'll meet Italians and Irish and black kids too." His father told him, "If you're gonna make it in this world, you got to get along with everybody." Always a follower, T.J. listened and never thought of rebelling. By his sophomore year in high school T.J.'s world was Rego Park, Christ the King High, and a slew of interracial friendships (Italian, Asian, Dominican) that left no place for Dwayne.

Dwayne's family would move to the Fairfield Towers development in Spring Creek, Brooklyn, where Dwayne made his own white friends. But Fairfield, just three blocks from poor-ass East New York, was already tipping black when the Robinsons arrived. Within three years of their arrival all the whites were gone. Watching them run, as well as his father's exit, made Dwayne's world view profoundly different from T.J.'s. It wasn't until T.J.'s junior year when, after drinking his way out of Syracuse and transferring to St. John's that the two met again.

Dwayne had entered college in 1976, seeking a world that didn't exist in a world he needed to know. He had a romantic notion that college would be intellectually stimulating, politically broadening, and sexually fulfilling. Maybe if he'd been accepted by Columbia or by his first choice, New York University, college might have been all that. Commuting every day into the Village or living on the Upper West Side would have been fun. He also had the option of accepting a scholarship to Ohio's Oberlin College sponsored by his Congresswoman, Shirley Chisholm, but spending four years on a campus where Cleveland was the closest big city was no way to live. New York City is where he wanted to be (a) because he loved it and (b) because leaving his mother for four years would have seemed like desertion and he already knew what that was about.

So he ended up in a place he needed to know—St. John's University. Instead of the Manhattan urbanity of Columbia or NYU, Dwayne found himself at a Catholic school in Jamaica Estates, Queens, surrounded by the sons and daughters of the Irish and Italians who'd been exiting Brooklyn as his family was arriving in the '50s. It was the first school he'd ever attended without Jews—none as students, none as teachers, and precious few in the curriculum. With a crucifix over the blackboard in every classroom, Catholic theology was a required course and many classes were taught by red-faced priests he'd see later suds-guzzling at the Rathskeller. St. John's was so removed from East Flatbush as to constitute another frontier of urban ethnics. It was there he learned to like the Eagles, tolerate country rock (Poco, Dan Fogelberg), and accept Billy Joel's "The Stranger" album as the prophetic work of the age (at least on Long Island).

For Dwayne, his Irish and Italian schoolmates were simple to understand or, at least, accept, since Dwayne didn't view them as people, but as beer-drinking, rock-loving, no-dressing, hair-flinging, pasta-eating, confession-taking, Long Island-and Queens-living, hockey-loving types. On anything but a superficial level he didn't connect with them nor they with him. Still, learning to get along with the student body, to come to terms with their existence, to acknowledge that along with Jews, the Irish and Italians were running New York—well, it was good for Dwayne to absorb all that before trying to make a living in Manhattan.

It was the black students of St. John's who really caused Dwayne grief because they were, in so many damn ways, similar to the white kids. Unlike the brothers and sisters he knew in Brownsville, the majority of his black St. John's peers had never been poor. Even those getting financial assistance had some item of middle-class value—a car, a home with a basement and driveway, a working parent, a lawn or, to Dwayne's amazement, they lived on Long Island. To Dwayne's narrow, ghetto-based view, to be "black" was to be from the projects. The students at St. John's forced him to take a broader view.

At St. John's, his fellow black students huddled in a corner of Marillac Hall (aka "the black corner"), where they congregated to play spades, plan parties, and practice, always practice, the art of the hustle. To the strains of Silver Convention's abominable "Fly, Robin, Fly" or the Ritchie Family's "Brazil," they twirled and untwirled themselves in front of vending machines, showing off their graceful superiority to their white, Fogelberg-listening schoolmates, while simultaneously confirming every nigger-hating stereotype the Fogelberg listeners learned over the dining room table. *No, they are not living stereotypes,* Dwayne told himself, *they are just enjoying themselves, carrying on in the same lunchroom style as they did in high school. But that's the problem. High school. This isn't high school, it's college, a white college.* And in this context, watching them do the hustle and play spades and plan parties made him self-conscious, even when he knew he shouldn't be. Growing up, he'd been ridiculed by some brothers for being a "four-eyed, white-acting, bookworm" just because he read books. Even as a child Dwayne was savvy enough not to buy that ignorant crap.

Then one morning, while buying a cup of bad coffee from a vending machine near the dancers, Dwayne spotted T.J., eating a bacon and egg sandwich. T.J. circa 1978 was still oatmeal-colored. However, his hair was short, black, and clumpy, matching his short, stumpy, well-muscled torso—the kind of body made by deadweights. To Dwayne, T.J.'s musclebound build was as corny as his clothes—the same rugby-shirted attire the white boys favored—and his voice had acquired the nasality of that all-purpose New York accent all local civil servants possessed. Culturally, T.J. was now white or at least very vanilla. He knew enough to own the Ohio Players' *Honey* and that black girls were endowed with adorable rear ends.

But he was so comfortable around white kids and so versed in their culture (T.J. could tell you which was Loggins and which Messina with no problem) that Dwayne found his old/new friend a puzzle. They shared Science 102 notes and, on occasion, talked music in the Marillac lunchroom. T.J. and Dwayne would never be as close as they were as kids, but they communicated regularly. Dwayne studied him like a specimen, and unknown to Dwayne, in the tunnel vision of his own perceptions T.J. was studying him too. To T.J. it was amazing after all these years in the projects that Dwayne's interests had remained broad. Most of the ghetto kids he knew seemed to value the use of "motherfucker" as much as his mom did "Hail Mary."

Given time, and continued mutual curiosity, Dwayne and T.J. might have enjoyed a real friendship again. But all that was derailed when Evette Murray transferred from Hunter College to St. John's.

The first thing Dwayne noticed about Evette was her hair—burnt auburn just like Clairol intended. Then the large mounds of flesh she wore covered by a jacket, no matter the time or weather. When she arrived on campus in September of Dwayne's senior year, many pursued her, but by Thanksgiving Dwayne and Rod Crawford, a backup point guard on the basketball team, seemed most likely to succeed. Rod was given the edge by the brothers simply because, well, he was a ballplayer and Dwayne read books.

But despite the conclusion St. John's brothers drew from Evette's body, this pharmacy major was no bimbo. This was a lady who actually enjoyed *Beowulf* in the English literature class, something even Dwayne found unbelievable. Because of her body Evette had gravitated toward poetry as a way to express the part of herself that young men didn't care enough to discover. In reality it was Dwayne who had the inside track on Evette.

The wild card that ultimately decided this romantic duel was T.J. who, to the chagrin of Dwayne and Rod, knew Evette through his parents. T.J.'s dad sold the Murrays life insurance after Mr. Murray was stabbed by a thief in his Jamaica, Queens, muffler shop and their families had grown friendly. Like Danielle would later, Evette perceived T.J. like a big brother or cousin, not a potential mate. T.J.'s dad worked hard to hook up his only son with well-bred bourgie girls. Time after time, however, T.J. turned romantic opportunity into frustratingly platonic friendships. With the right words T.J. could have laid the groundwork for his ex-childhood chum. Instead, a bout of jealousy led him to poison Evette against Dwayne.

"Dwayne is always talking about you," T.J. said innocently one day in Marillac Hall's black corner.

"Like what?" Evette inquired.

"You know," he teased.

"Come on, T.J., you know I like him. I really want to know what he's saying."

"Damn," he said regretfully. "I hate to do things like this."

In her mind, Evette, used to being talked about because she was so busty, was already concocting tawdry scenarios.

"Like what, T.J.? Tell me what he said. I won't tell him you told me."

"No. I hate to have to hurt your feelings."

"Did he say something nasty?"

T.J. leaned forward as if about to reveal an ugly secret. "He talked about your breasts and how he was going to find out if there were water balloons underneath your bra."

Yes, Dwayne had remarked about her breasts—so did every other brother in the corner and several white guys too. It was rather juvenile and Dwayne should have shown a lot more class. However, T.J., under the guise of alerting Evette, had violated one of the key tenets of male bonding: never tell a woman how she's really thought about, especially sexually. Evette's breasts were a sensitive issue for a young woman desperate not to be stereotyped by her body. T.J.'s comment wasn't the death blow to Dwayne and Evette. It did, however, plant a seed of distrust that made Dwayne's endearments and jokes suspect.

Then one afternoon Dwayne went to play ball in the gym and noticed Evette hanging with the "jock sniffers"—the nickname for the school's basketball groupies. He went over and she played him cold as ice.

"Hey, lady," he said.

"Hey." Not a note of enthusiasm in her voice.

"I tried to reach you last night."

"I was in Philadelphia. Went to the Villanova game."

One of the girls, garbed in a crimson St. John's sweat shirt, said to Evette, "We're going downstairs. You coming?"

"Oh, yeah. Got to go, Dwayne."

"When can I call you?"

"You can try anytime," she said. Then she was off with the posse of well-developed, well-groomed girlies who ran with the ballplayers. Evette had made her choice and Dwayne had no clue why. It took a while to find out—she didn't return his calls and was elusive in the hallways. Finally Dwayne cornered her at the St. John's—Georgetown game at Madison Square Garden.

He damn near pleaded before she said, "I didn't appreciate you bragging all around campus about what you did and were going to do. I thought you were different, but I was set straight. You really disappointed me."

"Where did you hear these lies?"

"From your best friend."

"Best friend?"

"T.J."

From that night at the Garden and until that fateful E train ride four years later, Dwayne had spoken to T.J. four times, and each time Dwayne had worked hard to control his desire to churn T.J.'s oatmeal head into flakes.

Dwayne leaned against the wall under the huge clock that dominated Grand Central Station. He was eating a brownie and reading the *Voice*. There was a Cheshire Cat grin on his face.

Danielle frowned slightly. "You certainly enjoy reading yourself."

"As a matter of fact, I don't. I rarely read my stuff once it's in print. I was reading my man Robert Christagu's 'Consumer Guide.' It's like studying Egyptian tablets. You have to learn the code, but once you do he's very funny."

"Well, I don't want to hear that," she said.

"No?"

"No." *Today's going to be about us.*

"Well, frankly, Scarlett, I don't want to tell you anything else about it either." He dumped the *Voice* into a nearby garbage can. "I just want you to know that if we hurry we can catch a double feature of *Vertigo* and *Rear Window* at the Thalia."

I knew that's where we were going.
"Disappointed?"
"Only if I was wrong."

Danielle was a passionate Hitchcock fan, something Dwayne discovered one night on the phone when a conversation on the worst thing that could happen to each of them—for Dwayne, being drafted into the Army, for Danielle, to awaken one morning as a bag lady—flowed into a dissertation on Alfred Hitchcock's films. Danielle chided him for daring to compare *American Gigolo* to *Marnie*, citing the superior "psychological depth" of Hitchcock compared to Paul Schrader's work. She called it "ersatz Hitchcock." As she talked, Dwayne chuckled, amazed that she reminded him so much of how he and his high school friends used to rap about movies. Just another reason to fall for Danielle.

Throughout Hitchcock's two masterpieces they sat whispering to each other about camera angles and zooms, dissolves and psychology, like the Thalia was film school. Dwayne, to use Danielle's word, found this fascinating. But for her it was nothing new. Her interest in Hitchcock had led all her previous men, even dry old Morris, to pick up a film history book and study the playbills of Manhattan revival houses. As Jimmy Stewart dangled out of his window near *Rear Window*'s conclusion, a nickname for Danielle came to Dwayne.

"Ersatz," he said, as they exited the Thalia.
"What in the world does *that* have to do with me?"
"You kept talking about 'ersatz Hitchcock' the other night."
"Okay, keep going."
"Few people use the term in general conversation—so few that you may be the first person I have *ever* heard use it. But you use it, and use it correctly too. I know it means 'second-rate' or something like that. But it's not the word's meaning that gets me—it's that you would use it."
"I'm not convinced," she said dryly. "Try it on me later and I'll see how it feels."

They were walking east toward Central Park on West 95th Street. "I really love that about you," Dwayne said, adding,

"The problem, Ersatz, is when you finally work in television, you'll see words like 'ersatz' won't work."

"I already don't like being called Ersatz," she said sharply. "And I certainly don't think I have to change how I speak to work in television."

"You don't?"

"Not much."

"Okay. You think Hitchcock is a deep, strong artist. I do too. But if he hadn't made thrillers, he'd just be some artsy director shown only in the Village."

"What's your point?" *Why is he picking a fight?*

"That to be a mass communicator you have to simplify complicated ideas. And you know, words like 'Ersatz' get in the way."

They sat down in Central Park. A Puerto Rican kid in shorts, red Adidas shell toes, a bare chest, and a ghetto blaster playing "Bounce, Rock, Roll" walked by. Dwayne bought two red Italian ices from a vendor pushing a metal cart. Danielle was silent for an unusually long moment. Then, looking Dwayne straight in the eye: "People always tried to hold me back. No, change that. *Men* have always tried to stifle me, accusing me of being too smart for my own good."

"I'd never say that. I love your mind." Now he was on the defensive. He wished the kid with the blaster were back to drown out this conversation and the tension in his forehead.

"What about the rest of me?" They were now walking sensitive ground.

"I like that too." Dwayne was being way too glib to suit Danielle. Which is why she said, "You are not going to make me happy today, are you?"

He came back with, "Why so grouchy?" and realized that was the totally wrong tone.

"Because *we* like each other but have some things to work out."

Dwayne wasn't sure where this was going, but now *he* wasn't happy. He pointed downtown. "Let's walk this way."

As they walked she decided it was time to set Dwayne

straight on who Danielle Embry was. "You need to be sensitive
to the fact that my intelligence has always caused problems
with men. I'm proud to have graduated Yale. I'm proud to have
landed an editing position at a major publisher. I'm proud I'll be
attending Columbia Journalism school in September." Dwayne
was going to cut in but wisely held back. "You say you like me,
you say you like my thinking. But brothers have this strange
way of liking my intelligence but resenting it too. I'm not an ersatz anything. Men use words like those to belittle and box in
women."

"I totally understand your point, but I am not all men," he
said slowly and deliberately. "Judge me as Dwayne Robinson,
not as all black men. Too many sisters do it. That whole 'black-
men-aren't-shit' deal. Don't fall into that. I am me. I want my
individuality as much as you do. Sometimes I'm simply too
slick with my words. I just got caught out there. Runs in the
family, I guess."

They strolled past the doormen, awnings, and joggers of
Central Park West on this glorious spring day. Danielle wondered whether she'd been too open. Dwayne, who too often de-
valued the spoken word by speaking before thinking, was
equally uncomfortable. These conversations never happened
with the Sandifreds of the world—but then the Sandifreds
never enjoyed Hitchcock double features.

"I know that even with the best writers," Danielle said,
"talking about feelings can be uncomfortable."

"I always talk. But," he admitted, "too much of me bores
even me."

"I like hearing what you have to say." Danielle now realized
she'd somehow pushed through Dwayne's glib defenses. Here
was a chance to dig deeper. Switching gears, she asked, "What
are you going to be when you grow up?"

"I just want to be great." He looked around, his eyes shifting
comically. "Please don't tell anybody. Please don't. I don't usually admit that. It sounds arrogant and corny, but that's what I
want." Now Dwayne searched for the right words. "In my heart
I don't think I have the discipline it takes to be great. But if I just

end up good, I'll have done something. I mean, I just want to write a book but I'm blocked. I can't come up with a topic. I have all this ambition but no direction. I envy your sense of direction. I really do."

"Fascinating," she said reflexively as they walked through the park behind the Museum of Natural History and past the Hayden Planetarium.

"Danielle!" A good-looking black couple came striding toward them. "Hi, Von!" Danielle leaned over to kiss the woman. And then she said, "Ciao, Ernest" and pecked him on the cheeks. Both wore Gloria Vanderbilt jeans—it was back when wearing designer jeans still meant something—soft brown suede jackets, and Etonic running shoes. Ernest, thirty-four, had a receding hairline, gray strands in his close-trimmed beard, and long legs. Von, twenty-seven, was a cute buxom brunette, whose hair was as bouncy and carefully cut as Danielle's.

"Why don't you introduce me?" Von said.

"Dwayne Robinson. This is Von Palmer and Ernest Douglas."

"How are you?" Dwayne said, trying not to be too self-conscious as they surveyed him. Immediately he sensed they had been around Danielle and her previous (still current?) boyfriend and, judging by the intensity of their inspection, probably liked him. They also seemed quite bourgie, a quality that always set Dwayne's teeth on edge, though he wasn't sure why. Maybe it was all that self-conscious sophistication? He was hoping that Danielle wouldn't want to hang; Danielle was wondering about the chemistry between Dwayne and her favorite couple: both wondered how the other would respond.

And, as if on cue, Von suggested, "Why don't you stop by? You're not in a hurry, are you?"

"We were just going to hang out on Columbus Avenue," Danielle said. "But I'd love to stop by." No way out for Dwayne, he forced a smile and went along.

Von and Ernest's apartment was like an *Essence* magazine photospread—the kind in which some oh-so-happy black couple sprawled laughing in bed or soaking in the bathtub of an apartment/condo/home with exquisitely arranged furniture. There was the required African art, including a multicolored kenté wall hanging picked up last summer in Ghana. The state-of-the-art component set was surrounded with Bob Marley's "Kaya," a couple of Grover Washington, Jr., albums, some Herbie Hancock, Děniece Williams' "My Melody," Joni Mitchell's "The Hissing of Summer Lawns," and Ernest's comprehensive collection of Miles Davis' pre-fusion recordings. There was a framed reproduction of Ernie Barnes' cover of Marvin Gaye's "I Want You" right over the leather sofa. In front of the sofa was a glass coffee table holding a small African statue, a marble ashtray, the current issues of *Black Enterprise, Essence, New York, Cosmopolitan*, and a hardcover edition of Toni Morrison's *The Song of Solomon*.

"Danielle says you're a music critic." It was Ernest.

"I started out just writing about everything but found music the route of least resistance."

"You did a piece on Rick James in the *Voice* I liked. You almost made him sound intelligent," Von said.

"A difficult job, I assure you," Dwayne said, producing chuckles in his listeners.

"Would you like something to drink?" Von asked, then added, "I must warn you all we have is juice—apple, orange, or carrot. We don't drink alcohol or soda." Apple juice for Dwayne.

Danielle sat back observing. Von and Ernest were Danielle's friends when she lived with the lawyer, Ronald LaCross, up on West End and 103rd Street. LaCross had been their friend first, but they so enjoyed her that when Danielle moved out they retained their ties. The energy between Ernest, an investment broker, and Von, a remedial reading teacher at City College who was to start law school in September, made Danielle envious. Though committed to professional excellence, Ernest and Von refused to lead dull lives: opening nights at the Negro Ensemble Company, evenings at City Center watching the Dance Theatre of Harlem, fund-raisers for the Studio Museum of Harlem and the Urban League and lectures at the Schomburg Library were essential to and, in fact, inspired their careerism.

Listening to Miles or reading Langston Hughes made them feel connected to a rich tradition of achievement they definitely planned to contribute to.

"So, Dwayne, what is the next big thing coming in music?" Von asked as she handed him the apple juice.

"Something called rap music."

"Rap music? What's that?" Von wondered.

"Did you ever hear a song called 'Rapper's Delight' or 'Christmas Rappin'?"

"No."

Then Ernest got into it. "Wait, Dwayne, are you talking about that stuff where these young boys are going 'hippity hop' on those ghetto blasters?"

"That is it."

"Oh man, that stuff is horrible."

Von, attempting unsuccessfully to be diplomatic, observed, "That music is negative."

"Why is it negative?" Danielle asked.

Von, abandoning diplomacy, replied, "Because it is loud, obnoxious, and has nothing to do with anything but drugs and getting our young girls pregnant. Some of the young men at City College spend all day in the student lounge blasting it, talking it, and not coming to class."

Genuinely disturbed, Ernest looked at Dwayne and added, "If this is the direction black music is taking, then I feel sorry for you having to listen to it for a living."

Dwayne said, "I like it."

"You do?" Ernest or Von said, but Dwayne was so embarrassed and mad he couldn't discern who. Before they could ask "Why?" Dwayne went into his defense of rap. "I like it for several reasons. One, it's a reflection of the life and attitudes of young blacks in this time, like the blues in the twenties, bebop in the forties, or soul in the sixties. It's called 'ghetto music,' but 'urban music' is a better term. If you listen to rap records you'll hear the subjects talked about are wider than just drugs or sex, though let's be clear: almost every great black artist has dealt with them in his or her experience." He slipped in the zinger. "Not everyone goes to Sag Harbor on weekends."

Danielle hastily cut in. "One of the things I like about Dwayne," she said, smiling as warmly as she could, "is that he really appreciates the wide range of black experience and sees the connections between them."

"That is important," said Von, nodding and smiling back at her friend. Ernest said nothing as he struggled with his temper. Sensing an opening, Dwayne said to Von, "As a reading teacher, I think rap music could be helpful in reaching your slow learners."

"How?"

"You could have some of the kids write raps. It'll show them rhyme, alliteration, metaphor, all that good stuff."

"I guess I'd have to listen to some myself."

"Why don't you make her a tape of the best rap records?" Danielle asked.

"Sure."

"Rap music in this apartment?" said Ernest with mock indignation that wasn't mock enough to suit Dwayne. Still, everybody laughed, though the words "elitist pig" ran through Dwayne's brain.

"I think they liked you," Danielle said as they rode the R train downtown.

"I don't think so."

"Why not?"

"I just didn't." The little boy in him was spilling out, she thought.

"You are a little too articulate for that answer."

"I'm sure they thought I was a little too 'street' for you."

"Because you like rap records? That's paranoid."

"If you look at rap music, it's just a metaphor for a way of looking at the world."

"What about Ernest and Von's way of looking at the world?" she countered.

"It's been successful for them. I can't criticize it."

"You sure it wasn't *you* that didn't like *them?*" Danielle was picking up where she left off earlier.

"What makes you say that?"

"As relaxed as you were in the theater, that's how tense you were in the apartment."

They got off the R train at Prince Street, walked over to Greene Street, and stood in front of a beat-up black metal door next to an art gallery. As Dwayne pushed the button on the intercom next to the door, he said, "We'll talk about this later, okay?"

"Okay. What are we doing here?"

Dwayne smiled for the first time in hours. "You'll see."

A buzzer sounded, the door opened, and they descended some squeaky steps into a comfortably appointed basement that was the foyer for the Greene Street recording studio. Sitting on chairs, smoking cigarettes, sipping on beers, and eating junk food from a buffet table in the center room were several b-boys and b-girls.

"It looks like a sepia Funhouse," Danielle said.

"Tonight it is. You see you, I and all these lovely people are about to become recording artists."

"What?"

"My roommate, Reggie, is recording a record on D.J. Jointski tonight. He's the guy who did 'Christmas Uptown.' In the background we're gonna have party sounds, and you are part of the party."

Surveying the crowd, Danielle joked, "I must be the oldest woman here."

"Not true, my dear. Some of these folks are older than you and me."

Danielle peered at the people around her. They had on sweat suits, sneakers, and baseball caps worn backwards, sideways, and at a variety of extreme angles. "That may be true, but they still look like high school kids to me," she said.

"I'm going to go into the studio to see what's going on. Since they might still be recording, you'll have to wait out here."

"Okay."

Danielle sat down in a chair by the studio door, feeling distinctly out of place. It wasn't that she feared them. That was crazy: something her mother would feel. But it struck Danielle that she'd rarely spent any time in New York around people like this. *I'm not stuck-up,* she told herself. *The opportunities just haven't presented themselves. If I'm going to be a reporter in New York, one who really reports on New York, this is really what I should be doing. So relax. Relax and smile.*

"Yo, homegirl, what's up?" A muscular young man wearing a red knit sweater featuring a black and white design, a big gold chain with the word JOINT written in block letters hanging from it, tight-fitting Jordache jeans, and Nike sneakers with fat laces approached her. His arms were folded. His hair was short, with a sharp, razor-cut part on the left side and slick waves, which Danielle hadn't seen since her daddy wore a stocking cap around the house.

"I'm fine. How are you?"

"I'm fine myself meeting a young lady such as yourself. You know you're gonna be on *my* record don't you?"

"Are you Joint-ski?"

"And you know that." He had a pretty smile.

"My name is Danielle," she added politely.

"Danielle, Danielle/ look so sweet/ can't be beat/Danielle, Danielle/ look so sweet/ won't you ring my bell?"

"That was nice."

"So are you, baby doll."

Danielle was getting nervous again. Not because of Joint-ski. Actually he was kind of cute—reminded her of Ricardo Ponce, the too-cool Puerto Rican boy whom she'd lost her virginity to in Newark. She was tense because Joint-ski's overtures suddenly made her the center of attention, and several tough-looking "ladies" didn't like it.

"You know my boyfriend, Dwayne Robinson?" she asked loudly.

"You! Home piss Robbie D."

"Home piss?"

"Yeah. Here my man is."

Dwayne came out of the control room.

"Hey, man," he said and slapped his hands with Joint-ski.

"Hey, home-ski, is this yours?" Joint-ski gestured with his right hand at Danielle. Dwayne winked at her and said, "Yo, homie, yeah. It's mine." Joint-ski looked at Danielle appraisingly and then said, "Just checking, baby doll. Well, I better get over to the other side and see what I can bust out."

"Dwayne, what was *that* about?"

"Just how he talks."

"It's mine?"

"I can't apologize for him, but I'm sorry you're offended."

Joint-ski walked by with two teenaged girls. The trio entered the studio's one restroom and closed the door. Danielle looked at Dwayne. He smiled weakly.

"Black culture?" she said.

"Enlightenment comes from many sources."

"Are these the people you spend your time with when you are not with me?"

"Just some of the time."

Reggie came out of the studio. "All right, ladies, gentlemen, and others. Welcome to the D.J. Joint-ski recording session for 'Break It Down.' You have been invited to add your wonderful singing, shouting, whispers, and any other guttural expressions at your disposal."

"That's my roommate," Dwayne said, trying to switch the subject.

"He's funny."

"Please don't tell him that."

Danielle smiled. "Lacks confidence?"

"You got it. Reggie! Joint-ski is in the bathroom. He is not alone."

Reggie strode over to the closed door and hit it with the evil authority of a prison warden. "It is time." No answer. *"It is time!"*

There was much stirring. The toilet seat could be heard flapping up and down. There was a sound of flushing. One of the girls giggled. The door opened and a cloud of smoke floated out of the door, hovering over the heads of two sheepish-looking young girls as they exited. As Joint-ski walked out, Reggie put his hand on the rapper's chest and pushed him back in the restroom. The door slammed behind him. Dwayne smiled at Danielle and was about to say something when Reggie walked back out.

"It's party time, team! Party time!" he said, leading the collected partygoers into the studio. Amid microphone stands, a covered piano, and sundry stools were pictures of Joint-ski on the walls, and one large microphone set in the center of the studio.

"All you have to do is make noise and shout out one phrase, 'Break It Down! /Just Break It Down!' whenever I raise my hands and we'll be straight."

Everybody put on earphones. Joint-ski stood on one side of the microphone with half the group and Reggie faced him with the other half.

From the 'phones came the sound of funky music: a stuttering bass line, clicking guitar, cowbells counterpointing the beat, and Joint-ski's boisterous rapping flooded their senses.

"I can't understand what you're trying to say," declaimed Joint-ski's voice. Then Reggie raised his arms.

"Break it down/Just break it down," Dwayne and Danielle shouted facing each other.

"Politicans talk in a maze/Feel like your life is clouded with haze?/Well, children let's break it on down/Good God yes!"

And the music fell away, leaving only the sound of the bass and drum. Danielle felt like she was back in the Funhouse again. She and Dwayne bumped bodies and yelled so loud that Reggie gestured for them to cool out.

Dwayne waited at J.R.'s, a dark, wood-paneled restaurant-bar on 46th Street near Eighth Avenue he'd been introduced to by two dancers in *Dreamgirls*, which was playing down the block. But this early evening Dwayne wasn't thinking about any dancers or singers or any other women but Danielle Embry. He sipped on a Heineken and watched the door. He'd planned the weekend out. What they'd do, when they'd do it, etc. Still, there was the unexpected element of romance that worried him. He'd planned to do no writing this weekend. *Can I do that,* he wondered, *and not turn neurotic?*

Reggie was on the road with Joint-ski, so the apartment was his. No pressure from Mr. Sarcastic. No last-minute love tips dipped in put-downs. Just me and her. Danielle walked in and stood by the door, seeking him out with bright eyes. When she saw Dwayne her smiled sparkled. And when she kissed him he noticed her lipstick was cherry flavored and sweet. "I already got the tickets," she said when he'd finally loosened his grip.

"You work fast."

"Enjoy it now. Once I start school I'll just be another poor college student."

"You better pay for dinner, then."

"Popcorn, Dwayne. I'll get the popcorn."

They wolfed down dinner—he had an extra-thick hamburger and she shrimp scampi—and then walked over to Broadway, where they melted into the thousands of tourists, residents, and couples walking under the neon lights in Times Square. The line for *E.T.* was long and sprinkled with couples and kids and their parents. "My family used to come into the city to go to movies and plays all the time," Dwayne said nostalgically. "I remember we all went to see *Mary Poppins* at Radio City."

"So did my family."

"Really? I don't believe you. Spell 'Supercalifragilisticexpealadotious.' Anybody who saw *Mary Poppins* at Radio City must be able to spell that word."

"Fascinating," she said. Then, deciding to be cagey, she added, "I admit I can't spell it. Why don't you go spell it for me."

"C'mon, you know writers can't spell. But look, I'll do something better." At the top of his lungs Dwayne began singing Dick Van Dyke's show-stopping song for all those waiting in line. Dwayne's voice, far from beautiful, wandered up into the Times Square night like a sick puppy. A little white kid with his mother began singing along. Dwayne had a giddy look on his face, while Danielle laughed, both embarrassed and amused. Thankfully for all involved, the line began to move forward.

"Great voice, huh?"

"After a performance like that," she said, "*E.T.* can only be a letdown."

But it wasn't. Dwayne tried to stay above Spielberg's fanciful pyrotechnics, but Danielle let the film's sci-fi sentimentality fill her up. *E.T.*'s death scene found them holding hands and, like the throng around them, they exited as happy as Hollywood can make you. Later that night, at the Parson's Penthouse, they discovered that *Cooley High* was playing on Channel 7's late movie at 1 a.m. She wanted to stay up to see it. He had other ideas.

First he told her to take all her clothes off and lie spread-eagle on his bed. "Not very romantic, are we?" she said. "You won't regret this," he replied. Danielle did as requested. From out of the living room came the sound of a muted trumpet and castanets. As Miles Davis' "Sketches of Spain" filled the apartment, Dwayne entered the bedroom with a newly purchased bottle of massage oil and slowly, yet firmly, just as he'd read in *The Art of Sensual Massage*, rubbed Danielle down from her tense little shoulders to the very tips of her toes. *Now for the loving*, he thought. "Danielle, Danielle." Her reply was silence. The lady had fallen asleep back when Dwayne was still fondling her legs. Apparently she didn't have sensitive feet.

But Dwayne did. Later that morning he woke up startled. There was Danielle's tongue, licking his big right toe. He apologized for almost kicking her, but she didn't speak. She just continued about her business, licking and sucking her way up his body until her face was at his chin.

It was two hours later and the Saturday-morning sun shone on their naked bodies. "I'm gonna cook you dinner tonight," she said.

"You don't have to do that," he insisted. "I have money for us to go out with."

"I want to. And I'm going to. End of discussion."

That afternoon they wandered up to the 165th Street Mall,

where at Key Food they bought steak, broccoli, and baking potatoes. Dwayne picked up a bag of records at the post office. That afternoon she chopped onions and seasoned the meat, while he played records and took notes. As the meat simmered, Danielle called Jacksina (for a change she was home studying), her parents (mother was at the local mall, father was repairing a broken kitchen chair), and T.J. (on his way to a Mets game with someone from St. John's).

Dwayne started playing selections from a three-record boxed set of Delux Records, the defunct r&b label. Pammi Lewis and the Vibes were Danielle's mother's favorite group and she began dancing around the living room using Pammi's trademark hip-sway shimmy. Dwayne joined in and did his best to keep up, but his hip sway was no match for Danielle's. "Just sit down!" she ordered. "You're throwing me off." Dutifully he sat back on the sofa, kept the Delux records coming on the turntable, and watched his lady hip sway the afternoon away.

Dinner was at about 6:30. Dwayne was pleased but Danielle spent much of the meal complaining about the quality of meat in Queens. On the E train Danielle reread Toni Morrison's *Sula* and Dwayne perused the *Voice*, carefully working his way through Stanley Crouch's review of Elvin Jones at the Vanguard. In the encroaching darkness they walked through Washington Square Park past the trey bag sellers, roller skaters, homeless men, potbellied police, NYU students, and hordes just hanging. At West Fourth and Mercer they entered the Bottom Line. At this showcase cabaret journalists usually sat in the back. This, however, was to be a traditional date, so he didn't want to be surrounded by industry types.

Instead they were seated front and center. They were, in fact, so close to the elevated stage that both had to stretch slightly to see over the edge. Ashford & Simpson, the ultimate in bourgie r&b, presented an ultraslick soul set that featured the great songs they'd written at Motown ("Ain't No Mountain High Enough," "For Your Precious Love"). During a spirited rendition of their hit, "Tried, Tested & Found True," Valerie Simpson's right earring popped off and bounced into Danielle's lap. She laughed to herself as she squeezed the earring, thinking that it would make a great toy.

Later, back in his bed, Danielle massaged Dwayne's back and then asked him, "Do you trust me?" He turned and looked at her curiously.

"Sure, Danielle. You know that." Adding, "What's up?"

"I want to find out how much."

"Okay," he said nervously. "What's up?"

She reached down to the floor where her pantyhose lay. She pulled the hose taunt in her hands and held it before her. She said, "Give me your hands." He did. The surge of pleasure on Danielle's face shocked him. She locked his hands firmly before him, then reached down and pulled out Valerie Simpson's earring, which she began rubbing across his body. "Don't move, okay?"

"I'll try not to."

"It'll be fine."

"I'm sure."

"Fascinating, right?"

"Ohh, that tickles."

"Good. But try not to move too much."

Sunday afternoon they sprawled out on the living room sofa. He was looking at the *Daily News* sports section. She was leafing through the *New York Times* "Week in Review." Later he scrambled eggs and made toast while she looked through a book collection heavy on novels from the '20s (Hemingway, Fitzgerald, Dos Passos, Anderson) before turning her attention to Gil Noble's "Like It Is," the top black public affairs tv show in town. Noble, a lanky, graceful man with a deep voice aired an old documentary on Adam Powell that had Danielle transfixed.

"Your eggs are getting cold."

"You should watch this," she said.

"I saw it before," he said. "I'm just gonna go in Reggie's room and check out the ballgame."

"The Yankees?"

"Yup."

With a take-charge tone Danielle said, "Soon as 'Like It Is' is over we're going out."

"Why so aggressive?"

"I know from my father. Let a man watch sports on a Sunday and the day is lost."

Ninety minutes later they were back in the Village. It was one of those spring days on which summer feels a heartbeat away, on which those with great bodies put themselves on premature display, and the air fills with the aroma of rotting garbage, sidewalk hot dogs, and spilled beer fermenting on the concrete. On Bleecker Street the smell shifted to that of coffee, espresso, and fresh baked goods mixed in with car exhaust. Dwayne glanced up at the marquee of the Bleecker Street Cinema and stopped dead. The marquee read, **HITCHCOCK ON PARADE: 24 HOURS OF TERROR**.

"You knew this, didn't you?"

Being coy, Danielle replied, "I knew if we came down here, we'd run into something interesting."

"Okay. How many do we see on this beautiful day?"

She reached into her pocket and pulled out a Bleecker Street Cinema program. After scanning it she said, "*Vertigo* is on in an hour. Then *North by Northwest*. You like that, don't you?"

"I think you know that."

She hooked her arm around his and walked him toward the box office.

"You know," he said with amused resignation, "at one point I thought *I'd* planned this weekend."

She kissed him lightly. "It was teamwork," she said. "You start things. I enhance them. I think that's something to build on."

"You know what?" Reggie asked as he walked into the dining area. Dwayne sat leafing through *Essence*, the black woman's magazine, at the table. He looked up and said, "What?"

"I've just made a list. It's called 'A List of All Those Women I'll Never Get Around to Screwing.' "

"Run that by me again."

"It is a list of women I could have and should have screwed but for whatever reason did not."

"Okay, Reg," Dwayne said with a chuckle.

"My reason is very simple. There comes a time in every man's life when he realizes he's just not going to sample all life has to offer. Circumstances are against you. Opportunity slips away. And who has the time? If it was just meeting them, undressing them, and laying pipe, it would be one thing. But it's not."

"Unfortunately you got to get to know them, huh?"

"Nope. The problem is they have to get to know *you*. All the talking, the storytelling, the seducing. It takes its toll." And, no, Reggie wasn't being facetious.

"I can't believe *you* said that. You're the most talkative person I've ever known."

"I'll be thirty-four next month, Mr. Robinson. Thirty-four. I was sitting at the bar at Possible 20 after a session the other night, engaged in deeply frivolous conversation with a dark lady of ample proportions. 'Flying Burrito Brother's' on her chest. Big legs and lips. She was E.P.—the entire package. I might have gotten it that night. I would have gotten it soon," he said with professional pride, "but for the first time that I can remember, I didn't care enough to even play her. The sport of the chase wasn't there."

"Doesn't sound like you, Reg."

"Which is why I wrote this list."

"Sounds like a good way to frustrate yourself."

"It may have begun that way, but it has taken an unexpected twist. I'm thinking of instead of this being a wish list, maybe it could become a hit list." He flashed it in front of Dwayne's face, but when Dwayne tried to read it Reggie snatched it back.

"How many names are on it?"

"About fifty," Reggie said as he surveyed it. "I'm going to attempt to screw twenty-five of the women here, with hopes of realistically compiling a free-goal percentage of about thirty-five by the time I hit thirty-five."

"*You* have definitely been listening to too many rap records.

You sound as pussy crazy as Joint-ski or, for that matter, me. Look, Reg, if you want a thrill, I have a better idea."

"All right, Mr. Robinson, what's that?"

Dwayne handed Reggie his copy of *Essence*.

"Looking for clothes," Reggie cracked.

"This magazine helps me to pay the rent."

"Which is late, Mr. Robinson."

"Hey, man, I'm trying to help you. Look at this."

The page was turned to a new *Essence* feature called "Say Brother," in which men were invited to write a one-page essay about life on their side of the bed. In this particular "Say Brother" a young man discussed his homosexuality. Dwayne cautioned Reggie to "Ignore the subject and study format."

"I was about to say."

"The editors there are looking for guys to write these things, and given your good humor, know-it-all attitude, and gift for bullshit, you are uniquely qualified."

"I see. This does look like a fine vehicle for getting into the pants of the fair sex." Then Reggie smiled lecherously and said, "I have just the topic. Fatherhood and the single life. The balancing act of your personal life and child-rearing. A couple of jokes. Some heartwarming anecdotes."

"You already sound better."

"Almost as good as I will when you come up with your half of the rent."

"Yo man, I just gave you a great idea. I'm gonna hook you up with *Essence*, get you paid and probably pussy on a national basis. Then you harass me for rent?"

"Friday. I expect a check on Friday. I've already put out your half and I need the money to take my kid shopping for shoes." Then his voice softened. "And, yeah, thanks for the idea. You're a good friend." Of course Reggie's cynical side, integral to his nature, couldn't accept this charity without suspicion. "So how come you're not doing one of those 'Say Brother' pieces? Don't tell me you've done one already and I'm just getting sloppy seconds."

"No, man," Dwayne replied. "I haven't written one. They

approached me. But what I wanna write about I have to wait on. Have to see how things turn out."

"What's the topic?"

Dwayne's face got red with embarrassment. "It's about whether I can fall in love," he said sheepishly.

"Giving your expert opinion, huh?" Well, let me explain love to you."

"Not another damn lesson, Reg."

Undeterred by his roommate's reluctance to listen, Reggie began, "This is love. The first night she ate me to ecstasy. The second night I screwed her to utopia. The third night we made love to Shang-ri-la. The fourth night I fell asleep in the saddle. The fifth night I was alone."

Dwayne said, "You are in rare motherfucking form today, Reg. Rare, rare form. I hope you're saving all this creativity for the studio. What's up with Joint-ski and 'Break It Down'?"

"Still shopping it. Got interest at CBS, B.C. and PolyGram, but they don't understand what it is or aren't sure a market exists for it. That reminds me. I have a suggestion for you that'll help us both."

"Preach."

"Wednesday night at the Dance Inferno, Joint-ski's appearing. You haven't been up there have you?"

"No. The way you and Joint-ski describe it, the Inferno doesn't sound all that inviting."

"Your bourgie soul is showing, Mr. Robinson."

"I didn't survive Brownsville by walking into danger. I did it by avoiding obvious danger. But if you're saying it's important for me to go up there, you're right. That's where the action is."

"So sell a piece to the *Voice* on a night at the Inferno. Joint-ski *might* be featured, of course."

"I'm a little slow, but I get it now."

"You'll get a paycheck—those hip folks will probably play it on the front page—and maybe you'll meet the dirty-sock girl of your dreams." That's what Reggie called the young girls who hung there getting high, causing fights, and wearing sneakers and dirty socks.

"You got sex on the brain tonight, Reg."

"Come, come, Mr. Robinson," Reggie said as he got up from the kitchen table. "This is Reggie you're talking to. You may tell your new girl you're a saint, but I know you're a bow-wow."

"I've reformed. That's why I'm trying to help you in a time of need."

"Mr. Robinson, you may have slowed down, but every time you sit in McDonald's I fear for the well-being of the freshman class of Jamaica High School."

THREE

As the red Electra 225 went up the Grand Concourse in the Bronx, Joint-ski began looping extra gold chains around his neck.

"Don't have enough, huh?" Dwayne wondered.

Joint-ski ignored him and just continued to adjust the gold chains that encircled his bare chest. "You all right for someone who ain't run this track before. Can't lose with Lee's and a t-shirt, money. Could use some gold, though."

"Maybe one chain?" Dwayne asked.

"One chain?" Joint-ski said as the car turned left on 167th Street. "One chain will make you totally whack. I'd have to loan you two or three if you want to get in this game even at a low level."

"No. I'll probably feel more comfortable without it."

"No prob. Hey, Robin, drive by first."

Robin's real name was Rahiem, but whenever he drove Joint-ski's "Batmobile" (also known as The-Deuce-and-a-Quarter) he automatically became Robin in Joint-ski's eyes. Joint-ski, however, never allowed himself to be called Batman, though throughout the Bronx and Harlem his apartment on 149th Street and Lenox was known as the Bat Cave.

Dwayne immediately knew why when he'd entered it two hours earlier. The four rooms were dark and jammed with cheap furniture, the walls were papered with graffiti, and the floors were weighed down with plastic milk crates packed with records from the front door to beneath the kitchen sink. The windows were painted black, and the only bright objects in the place were Joint-ski's crimson waterbed and the red light on the turntable in the living room.

"You like it dark?" Dwayne asked.

"Yo, money, that's the way the world looks to me. That's what the places I go to look like."

"The Dance Inferno looks like this?"

Joint-ski didn't answer because Rahiem entered the bedroom with a bag of records bearing the legend "Downstairs Records." Among rap fans Downstairs was known for its extensive collection of obscure old records from which creative deejays found fresh old beats to confound their rivals.

"You find it?" Joint-ski asked.

"Word 'em up," Rahiem said and pulled out two 45s with identical logos.

As the Batmobile cruised past the Dance Inferno, and Joint-ski peered intently at the flow of the teenagers going through its doors, Dwayne instead looked down at the two records leaning against Joint-ski's white-leather pant leg. Now they were in different sleeves; one said Atlantic Records, the other was plain black. The original labels had been peeled off by Rahiem after he soaked them in hot water while Joint-ski dressed. They were Joint-ski's secret weapon for tonight and he wouldn't tell Dwayne what they were.

"Okay, go back now," Joint-ski said.

"Waiting for the crowd to build up?" Dwayne asked.

"You know it, money. Wednesday night the Inferno is where you build a rep. With the holidays coming up there's extra flavor in the mix. Fresh girlies, you know. With that record coming out, I'm about to blow up."

Dwayne detected some insecurity. "Sounds like you still feel you have something to prove."

"Nah, it's not like that. The Dance Inferno is *my* house. Ain't that right, Robin."

The normally silent Rahiem said, "Word up." Then Joint-ski said, "Yo, Robin, pass me the piece." Rahiem reached into the glove compartment, pulled out a gun, and handed it back to Joint-ski. Dwayne's eyes got wide. "This is a Glock," the rapper explained. "It's a plastic gun." He tucked it into his pants. "Lets you go through metal detectors and never have to feel naked."

Rahiem pulled the Batmobile over next to two stretch limos double parked in front of the Inferno. Rahiem got out of the driver's seat and came around to open the door on the right side where Dwayne sat. The faces of those collected turned to them, registering "Who's that?" when Dwayne appeared and then knowing smiles when Joint-ski emerged, resplendent in white leather boots, pants and jacket, and a dozen gold chains dangling from his slim neck. As Joint-ski moved forward, black teenagers reached out to slap his palm, kiss his cheek, and just touch him. It reminded Dwayne of that Ben E. King song, "A Star in the Ghetto."

After successfully fooling the metal detectors set up at the club's entrance, Joint-ski turned left, Dwayne and Rahiem at his heels, and climbed a narrow iron stairway. There had been some smoke downstairs, but now the air was thick and blue-gray, and everything was blurry and indistinct through the haze. Even before Dwayne's foot touched the top step he was coughing and, his eyes were red and streaming with tears. Now Joint-ski stood at the threshold of a large room, smiling, waiting to be recognized. Rahiem moved around them, carrying a carton of records, crossed the room, and entered a tiny glass deejay booth. Dwayne could now see that the room was filled with girls, some barely thirteen, none older than twenty, drinking, waving cigarettes in the air, and giving off a don't-fuck-with-me aura. Dwayne, more a shadow than a companion, followed Joint-ski across the dance floor and into a smaller room, one that was even darker and smokier than the one before.

In it, faintly illuminated by their cigarettes and tiny candles on the tables, were some of Manhattan's best-known rappers and deejays. Grandmaster Flash. Cowboy. Kurtis Blow. Love Bug Star-ski. There were others, too, but Dwayne couldn't make them out as anything more than dim figures in Kangol caps, jeans, sneakers, and lots and lots of gold.

Joint-ski announced: "Yo, yo, check this out! I brought two surprises."

"How old are they?" a voice snapped through the haze.

"Same age as when I had your mother. Same number of strokes I needed 'fore she screamed."

Dwayne was getting nervous. Not because these dudes sounded angry—he knew Joint-ski and the crew were just playing the dozens. He worried how Joint-ski was going to introduce him, or even if he was going to. And if he did, how would they react? Joint-ski turned and faced Dwayne. "Here he is. Dwayne Robinson, of the *Village Voice*. He's chill." The half-visible rappers murmured greetings. Dwayne offered a self-conscious "What's happening?" and hoped he hadn't sounded too upscale. Joint-ski continued. "And my other surprise is that Rahiem found the joint break records that's gonna rock all comers tonight."

"Nigger, you got more mouth than a little bit," someone in the back said. Through the haze Dwayne made out a kid in a velour sweat suit with "Sugar Dice" written across the chest. Everybody laughed except Joint-ski. Judging by the intensity of the laughter and Joint-ski's obvious discomfort, Dwayne realized that his host wasn't the total uptown hero Reggie had advertised. That idea was confirmed when, after a solid hour of drug ingestion, the rappers and deejays collected in the main room and Joint-ski was the next-to-last man allowed on the mike.

Dwayne almost didn't care. After Blow's boasting, Cowboy's resonant bass, Love Bug's humor, and Melle Mel's politics—Dwayne's jaw dropped when he invoked Malcolm X, Marcus Garvey, and Patrice Lumumba in one line—Joint-ski seemed a minor attraction. But that changed when Joint-ski took the stage. Compared to the street-hardened looks of the others, Joint-ski's face was open, and, in the words of a dirty-sock girl standing next to the stage smoking Kools, "He's fly and fine." Dwayne remembered that even Danielle thought Joint-ski was cute.

Then Joint-ski rapped, "Here comes my secret/It's not no cute trick/It's old and it's cold and it breaks the mold/Rahiem show them that I'm in control." Rahiem began mixing MFSB's "Sexy" with a bright-sounding record with tinny guitars. Dwayne and everyone else were shocked as Joint-ski rapped over the opening section of the Jackson Five's "Stop! The Love You Save." Michael Jackson's first line was counterpointed with Joint-ski's catchy but corny rap. Dwayne had heard better, but it was working for the young ladies, and that was the point. Most of the star-rappers had returned to the back room. Those that remained seemed contemptuous of Joint-ski's teeny-bopper attack. *This fool is some kind of new-style teenage love man,* Dwayne thought. *Maybe Reggie will get paid after all.*

Jacksina hadn't been so nervous since she took the LSAT. The food was ready—fettucini alfredo with a big tossed salad—and the apartment was unusually clean because Danielle had arrived early to help. Danielle sipped red wine and talked about running into Von and Ernest and then performing on Joint-ski's record. Jacksina, who actually liked rap, wasn't listening too hard. This would be the Judge's first time around any of her friends, and she still wasn't sure it was a good idea. When she suggested it, the Judge agreed right away—he wanted to meet Danielle. Jacksina wanted them to meet as well, but it seemed unusual for a man having an affair—a sitting judge—to have an elegant dinner with his mistress' friend. Mistress! What a word. So old-fashioned. It didn't mean anything to Jacksina. Not a damn thing. To this determined woman, "mistress" was a meaningless word on a piece of paper, like so many of the opinions about crime and pain and property she had studied in law school. The Judge was her man, and no matter what the legal papers between him and his wife said, Jacksina knew she was his woman. After years of romantic wanderlust, Jacksina found loving a married man neither ironic nor frustrating. It was just love.

The doorbell rang. The Judge had a key, but for this evening, he elected to play the guest. Jacksina thought this was unnecessary— Danielle knew the deal. But that's what he wanted and that's what he did. In his arms was a bottle of red wine and a dozen white roses, six for Danielle and six for Jacksina. Danielle thought he looked like a beardless Ed Bradley, but better because he was giving her roses, which Ed Bradley never had. After he kissed her cheek, Danielle looked at Jacksina and winked. If you were going to screw a daddy figure, the Judge would certainly do.

"The range of human emotion is wider than the range of our expression," he said during dinner. "As a result many people die of constipation of the heart. I mean, how much love have we missed out on because we couldn't express our love when we should have?"

"I'd never thought of it in those terms, but it certainly sounds right," Danielle responded carefully, her mind wandering back through his words, deciphering his reasoning. "Are you saying simply that actions speak louder than words?"

"To some degree yes," he said calmly, "but it comes down to the quality of the actions. People, particularly men, too often rely on grand gesture to make up for their overwhelming verbal constipation when it comes to emotion. Over the long journey the minute details of love opportunities missed overwhelm the grand gestures like water seeping through rock. Sooner or later, to paraphrase the play, the rainbow isn't enough if the foundations are eroded. That's why I try to display my love whenever possible."

Jacksina had been quiet, watching the Judge and Danielle interact, noting with amusement her friend's surprise at the Judge's philosophical pronouncements of love. She'd heard most of it before, but his manner still enthralled her. As he talked, the Judge flowed from topic to topic like a comedian going from joke to joke.

Danielle couldn't figure out if he was wise or just trying hard to sound like it. She was glad Dwayne wasn't there, because he'd have thought the Judge full of shit. Though slightly skeptical, Danielle had to admit he was an engrossing talker. Must drive attorneys crazy with speeches from the bench.

"That's my personal philosophy, and if I could let you in on a secret?" he said to Danielle, leaning forward conspiratorially.

"Please go on."

"Lots of blacks, blacks who have made it, give lip service to the idea of helping their less-fortunate brothers and sisters. Talk. Talk. Talk. When I go to some of these Urban League dinners and listen to the platitudes that emanate from the dais, I want to put on a gas mask to protect my lungs from the stench."

The conversation was degenerating into a monologue, but the Judge seemed happy to be talking. Danielle figured she'd eventually get him around to talking about Adam Powell, and Jacksina was content to adore him—so everybody was getting something out of it.

"You think the Urban League is hypocritical?"

"My dear, throw in the NAACP, Jesse's organization out in Chicago, and the Black Caucus as well. They all say the right words, but if they had to deal with the people I do every day, they would not survive with their empathy or dignity intact." Jacksina got up and began brewing some coffee. Danielle couldn't believe how quiet Jacksina was, but the Judge wasn't missing a beat.

"What I do is give what society views as the unredeemable one last shot at earthly redemption. I give lighter sentences, affordable bail, and a chance—their last chance—because after being in my court, every other judge in the city will try to bury them."

"According to what I've read, many of the men you've granted light sentences have long, violent records of criminal activity."

The Judge took a sip of wine after Jacksina refilled his glass, turned to her sweetly to say "thank you," and then rolled back into his conversation with Danielle. "You cannot be redeemed, in the Biblical sense of the word, unless you have first admitted sin or failure. The fall must precede the rise, though it would be useful if one didn't fall at all. It would be highly unlikely, however, that any of my 'clients' would be in front of my bench if they hadn't fallen a bit."

"And many of them are pushed?" Danielle offered.

"How's that, dear?"

"By the police, social conditions, racism, a poor education—" He cut her off. "Good points. Good points. But"—he paused to finish off his coffee and then continued—"that is too easy an excuse for many. Newspapers complain about my actions. Yet they don't report on the many stiff sentences I've imposed or how I refuse to allow the D.A.'s office to plea-bargain my court into a charade. My point is that ultimately people have to bear responsibility, if not for what they are—poor, uneducated, whatever—then for what they do. Not every poor girl gets pregnant at fourteen. Not every boy steals. At some point individual decisions are made, and I have to make judgments based on that knowledge."

"If they—the papers—only made judgments about you as fairly as that," Jacksina said, her first comment in an hour.

"You certainly don't sound like a subversive," Danielle added.

" 'Mau-Mau Judge.' That's what the *Daily News* called me." Jacksina was rubbing his neck. "Well, Danielle, he said, "you want to be in the media. What do you think of that?"

"That's *why* I want in," she said with characteristic earnestness. "There must be a better way than what's being done on the news now. I'd like to be part of the change."

The Judge heard her but didn't appear to be listening too hard. While Jacksina still continued to massage his neck, the Judge looked hard at Danielle and said, "Every Sunday edition of the *Daily News* they used to print a mug shot of a black man arrested on Saturday night on page three or five. Some black man from Brooklyn or Harlem looking into the camera, into the kitchens of Irishmen and Italians and Jews for digestion over coffee, toast, and lox. And," he paused dreamily, "I'm the Mau-Mau Judge."

Jacksina and Danielle exchanged glances. Jacksina wanted her to leave, and normally Danielle would have taken the hint. But he hadn't yet talked about Adam Powell, and Danielle really wanted to hear his comments.

"You knew Congressman Powell, didn't you?"

"Adam? Certainly. I knew the man very well."

Jacksina looked at Danielle again. She was annoyed but not at all surprised. *Keep going,* she thought, *but you may not like what you're going to hear.* She started clearing the table.

"Jacksina told me you were researching him," Peters said.

"That's right."

"Could you give me your impression of Powell as a man and as a politician?"

The Judge leaned forward confidentially and said, "I'm not the sort of human being who looks forward to his memories. I'm still living." Danielle immediately thought that it was fortunate Dwayne wasn't there to comment on that pompous revelation.

The Judge sensed her skepticism and quickly changed his tone. "Well . . . Adam was a sharp dresser." He chuckled. "And a fantastic talker. He could hold up his end of any bar in town when he decided to."

"What about his politics?"

"Adam Powell was one of the cagiest motherfuckers in politics. Are you surprised by my language?" Yes, Danielle was. "Well, that's exactly how I feel about him. He wasn't what you'd call charitable toward me when I was just another hungry young lawyer out in the world for the first time. Adam Powell wanted my total commitment, and he promised me no guarantee of return on the investment. At least he was honest about that. He informed me one late evening at the Red Rooster that I lacked *rage.* I just didn't have enough *rage.* I had asked him in all sincerity for his blessing, and that's the baloney he gave me. He was in his turtleneck-and-medallion phase—he'd given up the sharkskin suits. What did my dreams of reforming the world mean to him? The answer was, nothing! I didn't have enough *rage.* So today I'm Judge Mau-Mau Peters. How time does pass." He finished his coffee.

"Don't you think he did a better job for Harlem than Congressman Rangel does now?" Danielle asked.

"Powell was Harlem's representative in Congress from the 1940s into the 1970s," the Judge replied. "During that time Harlem, once a grand community, went to hell. But of course it wasn't his fault. When the black middle class took advantage of integration and moved to Queens, Long Island, or Jersey, Harlem was doomed. It turned into a wasteland for the weakest, least educated, least motivated of our people. So today I do the best I can for these losers. Powell, when he wasn't busy with the ladies or on the sauce, did what he could. One man can't defeat the forces of history. It would be nice to think so, but only young people believe that."

"I respect your opinion."

"You know, Danielle, if I were you I'd stop studying Powell and focus on that neo-con prophet Dan Winfrey."

"I hate him," Jacksina interjected. "He's just a slick mouth-piece for your enemies."

"But he's shrewd. I hate his politics, but I always give my respect to a shrewd young man. He's charismatic, ambitious, and cynical. In essence he's not that different from Powell. He's just a product of a more vicious, self-serving age." On that note the evening ended.

The next day the two friends hashed over the evening on the phone. Danielle opened with: "Your judge sounded pretty sour last night—like he'd been betrayed by somebody."

"Maybe he wasn't expecting a third degree from you, Danielle."

"Third degree? I was a pussycat! They'd toss me out of school for interviewing that gently. Please, Jack, don't ever let a man turn you out like that."

"Okay, I won't blame you for interrogating him."

"So what are you blaming me for, then, Jack?"

"You really want to know? If you hadn't been there, we would have made love before he had to go. That's what I'm blaming you for."

Danielle said nothing, then: "Jack . . . are you always so tame around him?"

"I like to hear him talk, Danielle. Don't you?"

*　*　*

Walter Gibbs stood in back of the lightman, occasionally reaching over and moving the switch when he thought a change in mood was in order. The lightman cut him a couple of dirty looks, but Gibbs was the club's manager and he took the title seriously. After the show, Gibbs took every "celebrity" (examples: a Knick bench warmer and the daughter of a black city councilman) he could find backstage for promotional shots with the band. Click. Click. Snap. Snap. Smile. "You think *Billboard* will take these?" he asked Dwayne. "I'd love to get something about the club in the trades, man. You know that." Dwayne knew. It was part of the Process. The Process was the world of hype, glad-handing, and payoffs that made careers in the recording industry, a world that both fascinated and repelled Dwayne. It thrilled him to be a part of exposing well-made, pleasing songs; it disillusioned him that more of the business was about hustling than music. He was at this dingy Brooklyn club precisely because Gibbs had had his big chance stolen and Dwayne felt sorry for him.

Gibbs, a twenty-seven-year-old songwriter-singer-manager-music publisher and all-around mediocrity, was part of the legion of New Yorkers who search for that "big score" like safecrackers near retirement. He had enjoyed some success, written a couple of post-disco crossover hits and just gotten a nice writeup for a solo twelve-inch in the *Village Voice* from Dwayne Robinson. But, to Gibbs, the money and power were in management. Building careers. Making stars. No more song hustling. No more ass-kissing at those Sixth Avenue record companies. That was his dream. He might have already pulled it off.

"I heard about Marcus Silver from some friends in Newark about three years ago," the round-faced Gibbs recalled after the photos had been taken, the band had been paid, and the few patrons lingered at the bar. Gibbs wanted to tell Dwayne his story, not for publication, but because he just needed to talk about it. "One night at their club in Englewood I saw this tall, lanky boy on stage. He had this lavender jumpsuit and a straw hat on. White platform shoes. Tall guy, you know. The band

sucked. But he had that 'thing.' Wasn't really the voice—it was
okay. He had energy, personality, all the stuff I never had as a
performer." A smile. A long sip of Harvey's Bristol Cream.
"And the girls were there already. About five of them. Despite
those tacky clothes and that lousy band, he had what it takes."
"Did you smell money?"
"I was tasting it, Dwayne. Twenties and fifties in big fat rolls.
It was sweet."

Two weeks later, in a room filled with people drinking for
free, a slender, bowlegged twenty-two-year-old singer named
Marcus Silver did a split, his sheer lavender shirt ruffling
through cigarette smoke. The wide, white cowboy hat cocked
sideways on his head didn't budge. He sang "Oh baa-baa-by,"
milking the syllables and savoring the shouts of his frantic female followers. His narrow, breathy tenor, which on occasion
rose into falsetto range, was engaging, and the brother man had
a sweet, quite tender, way with a ballad.

The band was a crew of top New York session cats: tight,
professional, and amused by Marcus Silver's gymnastics. The
crowd was dotted with the usual mix of parasites, groupies, barristers, and actual music lovers that populate record biz. Among
the invited guests were Dwayne and Danielle. They sat in the
back, sampling the free butterfly shrimp and rare roast beef
when not holding hands.

All were gathered at B.C. Records' 40th Street studio to celebrate Marcus Silver's signing to the Multinational label. A slim,
pretty boy deejay from the city's leading "sophistic-soul" station and a short, business-suited black record executive traded
patter about how "dynamic," "commercial," and "crossover"
Marcus Silver could be, and what a "fine addition to the star-
studded B.C. roster." Various record company functionaries
were mentioned, and then Mayo, hot producer ex-band leader,
and self-described "musical conceptualist," stepped into the
spotlight.

"Thank you," he said, one hand holding the microphone, the
other fingering the zipper in his green army jacket. The badges
of a general were on the breast pocket. On the other side were a

couple of five-cornered stars and a "Jimi Hendrix Lives" button.

"Tonight we have seen the first stage of the Marcus Silver experience: a deep and profound emotional rendering of song. Starting soon we move to phase two: the capturing of this unique talent on record and cassette, bringing this man's gift to the world through the auspices of B.C. Records." *Ye olde record company ego massage,* Dwayne thought. "This is a challenge to me and my organization. One I look forward to! We have been challenged before and . . ." He paused meaningfully, waiting for the applause to come, then bowed. He continued. "In this age of space and man's search for the sustaining energy of life, music can be a vital force of spiritual and psychic communication. Through Marcus Silver this strength can be channeled to the masses, warming their lives in the winter of the everyday world. This is our gift and our destiny. So be it!"

With Mayo's words ringing in their ears and images of Thor in their brains, Dwayne and Danielle went backstage to meet the singer. Surrounded by comely young ladies with "Marcus Silver Is Serious" buttons on their bosoms, the center of attention sipped on apple juice and wiped sweat from his bare chest with a towel bearing his likeness. It was hardly an unusual scene. Every night, somewhere in America or the world there were girls and there were singers. Dwayne whispered these things to Danielle, who found it amusing. Dwayne was there to meet Silver, under the impression he might do a piece on the vocalist for a couple of magazines. "I know you'll have a lot to ask him after the show," the perpetually upbeat B.C. public relations lady assured him.

There was really only one thing Dwayne was really curious about, and he couldn't wait to hear Silver's answer. Following some typically hearty introductions by the p.r. lady ("Ooh, Marcus, this is someone you *must* meet. He's a *very* influential writer . . ."), Dwayne and Danielle sat next to him, Silver's body funk mixing with the perfumes of his female followers to produce a most unappealing aroma.

"How did you like the show?" Silver inquired. Danielle smiled affirmatively. Dwayne answered, "I thought it was really good. Have you always worked so hard on stage?"

"Oh, yes, I love that feeling of being up there and having the people looking at me. Ever since I used to go to church with my mama, and I would sing solos in the choir, performing made me feel good. It's the best thing I knew about—the very best." Dwayne mused to himself all r&b singers must buy the same interview instructional tape because they all have the same answers.

"Must be looking forward to working with Mayo."

He did a Little Richard-like roll of his eyes and said softly, "Mayo is a genius. He takes those knobs and those musicians and those keyboards and creates beautiful music. The thought of it makes me warm, you know. There is strength in his music—and that's what I need behind me, something strong."

"You know we have a mutual friend."

"Who's that?"

"Walter Gibbs."

"Walter? Oh, that's nice. He helped me a lot at a certain point in my career." Realizing that sounded harsh, Silver caught himself. "Walter was an important person. He helped get me here. Next time you see him tell him to call me, all right?"

"Sure," Dwayne said.

The dressing room was now full of the previously mentioned parasites and barristers, etc. Dwayne eased Danielle toward the door, stopping only to ask the p.r. lady if he could interview Mayo. She was quite accommodating.

Manhattan is full of unknown rooms like this: long control boards, wood paneling, dimmed lights, windows that look out upon other rooms where pianos and drums lie in wait. Behind the board, emperor of this domain was Mayo. His New York Yankee jacket was zipped up and his brown eyes darted about as if his brain were on fire. Dwayne had on a tape recorder because Mayo spoke too fast for notes.

"Yes, that is just my point, sir. Music is both art and commerce. But one can't leave the spiritual out of it too. Here, in this piece of ever-expanding technology, spiritual energy is harnessed and refined. We are past the period of raw emotion. For example, the days of Delux Records, of Hudlin-Harrell-Hudlin, of 'Mississippi' Rivers and that marvelous rhythm section are for scholars. People like us love those sounds, but they are the past. My mission is to crystalize feeling through the power of digital recording. This is my music. An anthem for our age."

"What do you think of rap?"

He laughed. "What is there to think about?"

Dwayne didn't need the argument right now. "How is the Marcus Silver project progressing?"

"Wonderfully. Wonderfully. This youngster will be the ultimate—at least to this point—expression of what I and my organization can do. His voice is fertile soil from which will grow fruit for the soul and the feet." Then a bit of his business acumen came through. "Off the record, I think he'll go double platinum if B.C. handles it correctly. But that is always a question."

"What's your reaction to Walter Gibbs' suit against you?"

"My lawyer says I shouldn't discuss it."

"Okay."

"I'll speak on it, but only if you promise not to quote me directly or attribute these thoughts to me in any way."

The "musical conceptualist" was trying to use the journalist, but Dwayne was down for the game.

"Okay, what do 'undisclosed sources' say?"

"I say that this is a most reprehensible action on Walter Gibbs' part. Something one friend shouldn't do to another."

"So, then, he is both morally and contractually wrong?"

"Marcus Silver was under contract to Paul Michael, owner of Michael's Cabaret, when Walter began working with him. During that period, Walter was unable to sign him officially due to this contractual relationship. A shame really since Walter really acted as manager, while Paul Michael was wasting Marcus' time sipping brandy. This is why I was needed."

"Really?"

"Yes. Paul Michael provided nothing. Walter provided too

little. He gave Marcus a 'cute' image," Mayo said condescendingly. "But I provide an overall musical concept. When Michael's contract ended, Marcus Silver came to me because I had the vision."

"And the connections," Dwayne added.

Mayo laughed again. He may have been pretentious, but he was also jolly. "Mr. Robinson, in this time of depleted resources, isn't that what it's all about?"

The day after the Mayo interview Dwayne and Gibbs sat in McDonald's with a Coke, a strawberry shake, and two large french fries. Gibbs' treat.

"I introduced the motherfucker to Mayo," Walter recalled bitterly. "Then he had the nerve to ask me to work for him."

"You?"

"Yeah. Still, it's not all his fault. Marcus didn't have to do it."

"He sees stardom in Mayo's mind."

"I did too. Mayo only sees money. He's producing him, got his publishing, and manages him. He's got that boy's shit locked up tight. Mayo advances him money. I know I used to give him money before I had stuff. Paid his light bill when he didn't have any bank."

"Forget all that. At least until your suit against him goes to trial. What else is happening?" Dwayne asked.

"That band that played the other night is gonna give me their publishing," Gibbs said proudly.

"Got it on paper?" Dwayne sounded skeptical.

"Soon, man, soon. Don't worry. I got it."

"They had some strong songs."

"Soon, man." Gibbs started into his strawberry shake. "This was just a lesson to me. A serious lesson. Ain't nothing around the record business but the greedy, the star-struck, and the smart. I've been the first two."

"Took you long enough to get there," Dwayne scolded.

"Now I'm just gonna run over kids, abuse women, and get them to sign outrageous contracts with lots of options."

"Sounds promising."

"Might even make somebody a slave for life, you know, Dwayne."

"I see potential in you, Walter Gibbs. I'll keep an eye out for the *Billboard* profile."

"C'mon, that won't happen until you get in there. You know this ain't just about music; it's about life. You go out there unprotected and you will get hurt."

Dwayne enjoyed Gibbs' cynicism. It made him feel comfortable, even though he knew there was something inherently stupid about embracing negativity this way. Yet he found himself raising his Coke in toast. "Isn't it good to be in the record business?" Dwayne said. Walter grunted and finished his shake.

"Wake up."

Dwayne slowly opened his eyes and quickly closed them again. The curtains were open and the bright morning sun attacked his pupils.

"Ugh!"

"Dwayne, come on." Danielle, dressed in her cute white-with-blue-trim tennis outfit, sat on the edge of the bed, tying the laces on her white sneakers.

"What time is it?"

"Seven-fifty."

"What?" He moaned again, lifted his head, and looked at Danielle's back. "Why are you up?"

"Because we are in the tennis tournament and everyone is going to jog together this morning. Sounds like fun, right?"

Dwayne's head made a "puff" sound as it landed against his pillow.

"Dwayne."

No answer.

"Dwayne!"

"Baby," he said finally, "I thought the point of these weekends on Gilligan's Island was relaxation. The crack of dawn is not relaxing."

"It is seven fifty-three. That is not dawn, and relaxation is not lying in bed all day."

Without getting up from his prone position, Dwayne continued the conversation. "Now you know you like doing the all-day bed thing."

"Not every weekend, sir. We came out here to break up our routine. To be more active and to hang with our friends."

"That last part was Ernest's idea. Not ours or, at least, not mine."

Danielle stood up and looked down at him. "You can be stupid some mornings."

"At the crack of dawn? Yeah."

He reached out and tried to pull her into the bed but she anticipated him and stepped away.

"See you outside." The door closed loudly. Then it opened again. "Dwayne, if you're not downstairs in twenty minutes I'm getting another partner for tennis."

Dwayne wanted to say, I don't give a fuck, but thought better of it. Instead he said, "I hear you, *dear.*"

Downstairs in the kitchen Ernest, Von, a few people she'd met at the party the night before, and a bunch more she hadn't, were talking and sampling from a fruit platter. All together there were about twenty of them, most dressed in tennis whites or trendy sweat suits. The brothers were a rainbow of brown and yellow hues, but the women, including Danielle, were no darker than honey brown.

They were investment bankers and lawyers and accountants and engineers and midlevel bureaucrats who wore suspenders or pearls during the week. Every last one of them was, at least in material terms, living better than his or her parents had at the same age. *These people contradict all stereotypes about us,* Danielle thought. *Talented, smart, well-trained, and ambitious.* There was something wonderful about being in their presence. *Harness this talent,* she mused, *and we'd run this country.*

"Danielle, almost ready?" Von was in white shorts, prissy white blouse, white sneakers, and socks with little white balls at the heels.

"I haven't had breakfast yet," Danielle protested.

"Sleeping late is not allowed here, at least not on Saturdays."
Von turned to the counter and came back with a piece of toast
and orange juice.

"We're all going to go jogging on the beach."

"Really? I should get Dwayne."

"He's still asleep?"

"He shouldn't be. I already told him to get up."

"If he doesn't want to, you shouldn't force him. It's a
weekend." Then, smiling mischievously, Von added, "Knowing
Dwayne's taste, he'd probably find our jogging music a little
unfunky."

Ernest entered the kitchen, dressed in a blue Fila sweat suit
and white sweatband. He was carrying a long JVC portable cassette player.

Danielle asked, "What are you doing with *that*?"

Ernest smiled. "This, dear lady, is my suburban blaster. I use
it on weekends as an anecdote to the mugging music back in the
city. Speaking of mugging music, is your friend up yet?"

"Don't start that, Ernest!" Von said, cutting a sharp look at
him. Danielle laughed and replied, "He's upstairs relaxing."

"Is that right? I just hope your friend brought a tennis
racquet."

"He'll probably borrow mine."

Ernest said "Good" to Danielle and then shouted, "Okay,
everybody, it's time to share the wealth."

Dwayne had on a Knicks t-shirt and his blue Tilden High
gym shorts when he finally arrived in the kitchen. There were
dishes in the sink, a couple of half-empty juice glasses on the
table, and a copy of the *Times* in a chair. Dwayne grabbed a can-
taloupe out of the refrigerator, sliced it in his usually sloppy
fashion, and quickly ate his quarter. He considered reading the
paper and then decided not to. *I did come out here to get away
from the city, didn't I? Lighten up a bit. Should have gotten out
of bed and gone with the rest of them. These are my peers,
right? My attitude toward bourgies is silly. They are just trying
to make it. So am I. Maybe one day Danielle and I will be like
Von and Ernest.* Then he decided they'd be a lot better than Von

and Ernest. There *was* a lot to like about their lifestyle. Sag Harbor did beat the hell out of Prospect Park. Still, somehow, it struck him as pretentious and vaguely whitewashed.

Just then Dwayne heard classical music coming from outside: it was light and filled with the trebly charm of bright, shining trumpets. Dwayne walked to the back door and peered out. His eyes opened wide.

White clothes, brilliant in the morning sun, even more intense because of the brown faces, arms, and legs they hung on, moved toward the house. The JVC player, its metal parts reflecting light, bounced on Derek's right shoulder, pouring music into the air. It was Handel's "Water Music Suite," which Ernest had fallen in love with while a sophomore at Yale. Flanking Ernest on his right side was Von and on his left was Danielle. They were sweating, happy, beautiful, and, to Dwayne, looked unbelievably content.

That evening a chill wind blew in from the Atlantic, dropping the temperature into the low sixties. None of the guests ventured out onto the balcony except Dwayne, in his slightly faded Tilden High sweat shirt. He looked out at the ocean, trying hard to ignore the people in the room behind his back.

Danielle, Ernest, and Von sat at a card table with several others, playing spades for pennies and sipping the mixed drinks Von concocted in the blender. Chuck Mangione's "Children of Sanchez" provided the sonic backdrop. Danielle looked up from her cards and stared at Dwayne's back. Von noticed, looked at her cards, and announced, "I'm out this hand."

Ernest, who had a strong hand, said, "Well, come on—somebody take her place. I could use some more pennies." Von went into the kitchen to freshen her drink. She then strolled by the table, sipping her piña colada, while peeking at the cards of the players. As she passed Ernest she made a big deal of staring at his hand. He looked up at her, rolled his eyes, and pulled his cards against his chest.

"May I help you?"

"Just trying to see how you're cheating this evening."

"In the usual manner. I'm good."

Von smiled and joined Dwayne on the balcony.

"Hi," she said. "You're not having a good time, are you?"

"No, that's not true. I'm just a little moody, that's all."

"Why is it that you always get moody around Ernest and me? Danielle says you can be very funny."

"She says that because she's sweet. I'm really a dick."

Dwayne's response shocked Von into a loud laugh. "Is that right?" She sipped at her drink. "Yeah," Dwayne said, "it's hereditary."

"Oh."

"We've had three generations of boring dicks in the Robinson family. I'm just trying to build a better life for myself so maybe my son won't be as trapped as I am."

"Does Danielle know this? I hope you're not keeping this important information from her."

Dwayne turned and looked at Danielle through the window, then he said, more seriously than he had intended, "I find it hard to keep any secrets from her. Sometimes it seems that love requires more honesty than I can stand. You're lucky to be so comfortable with Ernest."

"It's not luck," she said firmly, "it's work. And time, too. Ernest and I put work into it. We've taken the time to get to know each other."

"How long does it take?" Dwayne was half serious, half facetious.

"It's never over."

"Damn."

"Could I make a suggestion? It might be nice if you made more of an effort to fulfill Danielle's desires."

Dwayne's mouth fell open. "Did Danielle say something?"

"Nothing direct. But I know her well—and I feel it."

"You said 'desires'?" He wanted to ask what kind of desires, but couldn't force himself to do it.

"Let me give you an example." Von glanced over her shoulder suspiciously to see if anyone was watching or listening, then whispered, "You need to learn how to play tennis."

Dwayne's tense breathing lightened. He chuckled. "Tennis? If our relationship depends on that, we must have broken up today."

"I'm not saying you have to be Arthur Ashe. But by participating, you'd show you cared about something she liked, that it mattered to you what she enjoyed. See my point?"

Dwayne did, but decided not to cooperate. "No," he said, "no, I don't."

"Relationships—real relationships—are about partners being sensitive to each other and doing the little things to make each other happy."

"I know that, Von, and I do things for Danielle. I just don't like tennis." He tried to smile and make a joke of it. Von frowned and said, "Too bad," sucked up the last of her piña colada, and went back inside, where she took a position behind Ernest, tickling his ribs with her left hand while trying to expose his cards to the other players with her right. Dwayne looked at the scene. *You are a dick, you know. And not a big one.*

The sweating, helmeted policemen on big brown horses were not smiling, and all the cologne in the world—and it seemed like all the cologne in the world, or at least in Manhattan, had been poured over the people in line—couldn't overcome the smell of the horse manure that had been deposited onto 52nd Street. Inside Roseland a party was being sponsored by WKTU radio station, aka "Disco '92." Outside, swarms of young black and Latino teens were pushed, shoved, and crushed as they squeezed erratically through Roseland's glass door. The bulls (aka the New York City Police) were out in force. To Dwayne the warm, early summer evening possessed an intoxicating blend of excitement and tension, as if the kids' desire to party and the threatening presence of the police had blended to create some exotic, hyped-up form of oxygen.

Danielle merely imagined myriad opportunities for violence. "I don't want to stay, Dwayne."

"It's not that bad. Just a lot of random energy."

"Random energy is not what I want tonight."

An argument erupted between a big-gutted, thick-necked Italian security guard in a rumpled gray nylon suit and a wiry, feisty, Puerto Rican teen in a tight, elegant black suit and unbuttoned red silk shirt. The Puerto Rican youth suggested that the guard get his "fuckin' greasy hands off me, fatso!" To which the guard countered, "Step back from that door, sonny, and there'll be no trouble."

"No, man! Trouble is already here."

A nervous murmur rippled through the crowd. The horses edged forward. Dwayne felt the tremor.

"You're right," Dwayne agreed. "It's way too tense out here. Let's go."

"Where to?"

"Let's walk east."

Hand in hand they went past the parking lot on the corner of 52nd Street and Broadway, past the Americana Hotel on Seventh Avenue and over to Sixth, best known to tourist and brochure writers as the Avenue of the Americas. From where they stood on the corner of Sixth Avenue and 52nd Street in front of CBS's "Black Rock" corporate headquarters, they looked downtown and saw the neon red Radio City Music Hall sign and, facing north, the treeline of Central Park.

The enormous glass office buildings on the Avenue of the Americas make for treacherous winter strolling. But on this summer night they created a delicious cool breeze that blew past the lines of yellow taxis, hotels, and the two lovers who kissed softly and moved on toward Fifth, where there were no hot dog vendors, no b-boys, no "random energy." Just arrogant stores and echoes, sad echoes, of a fading sophistication.

They moved leisurely eastward through the narrow alley that is Madison Avenue and the deep canyon that is Park Avenue. Lexington was nothing special. Neither was Third. But Second and First were filled with sex and money and the desire for desperate adventure. Each bar and restaurant was a mini-series, and every wayward glance an installment.

And then they were on Sutton Place.

"I've never been over here before," Danielle said.

"Neither have I, at least not in person. There's something I want to find. I'm pretty sure it's around here but I'm not completely sure where."

"I hope it has seats."

"This is an adventure, baby. I mean, how often do you get to enjoy all of New York?"

"Walking all the way from Broadway at night is a lot more adventure than I expected. My feet hurt."

"Have faith."

They walked up the east side of Sutton Place, past castle-like apartments with little booths for security guards. It was calm, and so unnaturally quiet that it was hard to believe Sutton Place and bustling Seventh Avenue shared the same rock. At 55th Street they turned into a tree-lined street with elegant, country-style homes all snug together.

"Each one of these must be worth millions," Danielle observed as they tried to peek in illuminated windows, feeling self-conscious and guilty.

"I think it's up ahead," Dwayne said.

At the end of the street and down a staircase was a pocket park with thick green bushes, three benches, and a black iron fence that overlooked the immense, glistening, swirling East River. Across the river was wealthy Roosevelt Island, with its recently opened apartments. To the north, dominating the sky with its strings of lights, was the 59th Street Bridge. Danielle patted Dwayne's ass. "This was definitely worth the walk, Dwayne. It's beautiful here. And familiar somehow."

"I don't think this is the same spot," he said, "but it was somewhere near here that Woody Allen shot a scene in *Manhattan* of himself and Diane Keaton sitting watching the bridge at dawn. When I was at the *Amsterdam News*, I got a copy of the press kit for *Manhattan* and had that picture taped over my desk. One day someone in the office ripped it off the wall. Trying to create a more stable work environment or something silly is what they told me. But I always remembered that shot."

Dwayne leaned back against the black railing that separated the park from the river below and looked up into the dark sky.

The night was moonless, but a few stars peered through the summer haze. "There are," he started, "let's say two million stars in the sky. Can I get away with using that number?"

"Go ahead."

"Okay. We agree on the million figure. Now that two million really only applies if you're on some mountaintop or in the desert or the ocean. In other words one of those spots where pollution isn't so bad. Still with me?"

"Sure," she said, "but you haven't gone anywhere."

"Okay. Of those two million stars most are weak. Between the clouds and the haze and space rocks their light never reaches earth. Then there are the mediocre stars that have enough juice to cut through mere clouds but lack the intensity to penetrate pollution. Know what that means?"

"I have no idea."

"It means that between the distance to the earth, the natural cloud cover, and the unnatural pollution, only the strongest stars reach earth. Now, since the United States is so polluted and New York is the dirtiest place in the United States, that means that the stars we are looking at right now are the brightest in the universe."

"Fascinating. Now sit down and don't say anything else."

"Why?"

"Just sit down."

"Sit down."

He obeyed. She was in the middle of the bench and he sat to the right of her. She wrapped her arm around his neck and pulled him close, kissing him and rubbing the back of his neck. Then she slid her hand inside his shirt to caress his chest. This went on for a minute or two. Then Danielle twisted her body so that her legs lay atop his. She kicked off her loafers. "Rub my feet, Dwayne." Again he obeyed.

"How are you feeling now?" he asked.

"Weird," she answered dreamily.

"What? Are your feet cold?"

"No. I just feel anxious about really starting my life. I want to be into what it's going to be. I wish I was married, successful, had a child, and one of these mansions overlooking the East River. We'd be having cocktails with Ernest and Von. We'd be talking by the windows, savoring the view."

"Sounds nice."

"I want it all now!" She said it with a ferocity that made Dwayne stop massaging her feet.

"You sure?"

"Don't say anything. Just let me listen to the cars."

It was quiet for a minute. Then Danielle slid her feet back into her shoes and stood over Dwayne. She put her hands on his shoulders, pushing him back against the bench, and studied him like a painting.

Danielle took her hands off Dwayne's shoulders and stepped back, never taking her eyes off him. A gust of wind rolled across her.

"I'm acting crazy?" she inquired.

"Maybe a little. I don't know. Maybe that long walk was too much for you."

"You know how hot it is at Roseland right now? Dancing. Fighting. People all melting in the heat like grilled toast."

"I thought you didn't like all that action."

A shadow in the curtained picture window of one of the houses caught Danielle's eye. A woman. Danielle wondered how many times she'd stood there and spied on lovers. *Is her husband home? Is she lonely? Divorced? Got the house as a settlement maybe? Maybe as she watches others, she touches herself. Maybe she's as jealous of our lust as we are of her money. Night after night this lady watches lovers by the river's edge. . . . So it's time to make everybody happy.*

"Dwayne. Do what I say."

"I haven't exactly *been* resisting you, have I?"

"Shut up and don't move. Don't move no matter what I do."

And he didn't . . . at least until he couldn't help it.

The Pink Tea Cup, situated on the south side of Bleecker Street just before you hit Seventh Avenue, was an anomaly in Greenwich Village. Painted pale pink, decorated with framed photos of celebrities and furniture from the owner's old kitchen set, the Pink Tea Cup was a traditional soul-food restaurant nestled in the bosom of the West Village, an area known for handsome, expensive brownstones, quaint little bistros, and smoky gay bars down by the piers. By contrast, the Pink Tea Cup could have been in Brooklyn or Harlem or Newark. With its tacky interior and its heavy scent of grease and vinegar, it was a small, pungent outpost of black reality in bohemia.

Whenever the Judge swung down to the Village to hear jazz he stopped at the Pink Tea Cup for dinner. He knew the ham hocks, greens, and handy little bottles of Red Devil hot sauce were bad for him, but so was a lot of what he did. Life is to be lived, he reasoned, not fretted about. So he indulged his palate, just as he was now savoring the presence of Jacksina.

She sat across from him, eating potato salad and making fun of him for eating pork, and he absolutely loved it. He looked down at her long, athletic legs and suspected these would give him a heart attack long before eating the flesh of swine would. He smiled at that idea and reached down to touch her knee.

"Get those greasy paws off me," she commanded playfully. So he just squeezed harder before he let go.

The Judge turned to look behind him. The cook, Thomas, and the head waitress, Vanessa, stood by the kitchen door checking him out. Thomas, a man the Judge's age, known to have pinched a customer's butt as women made their way to the rest room, was amused to see the Judge being so flirtatious with a fine young lady in public. *More power to him* Thomas's eyes said. Vanessa reacted differently. Through round, rose-framed glasses that complemented her pink uniform, Vanessa viewed the couple with a cold contempt she felt no desire to hide. Years ago, before the Judge became notorious and his hair silver, he and his wife would eat at the Pink Tea Cup before hitting the Vanguard or the Gate. Vanessa had served them often and wasn't thrilled by the Judge's current company.

The Judge motioned for her to come over to the table, and reluctantly, she did so. "How's the sweet-potato pie tonight, Vanessa?" he asked.

"You been here enough to know, Judge." She looked down at Jacksina and rolled her eyes so hard it felt like a slap.

"No need for you to be rude, Vanessa. I've been coming here too long for that kind of treatment," he said.

Vanessa wanted to smack him—feeling that woman's knee right in front of *her*. Yet business wasn't good enough for her to justify reading a regular customer the way she wanted to. So, biting her tongue, she asked, "You want it or not?"

"No, thanks."

Vanessa ripped their bill off her pad, plopped it onto the table, and stalked back toward the kitchen.

Why did he bring me someplace he'd been with his wife? Jacksina waited until they were outside, walking up Seventh Avenue a bit, before popping the question.

"It's no big deal," he answered testily. "I always eat there before I go to gigs down here. I've eaten there with other women aside from my wife. And with male friends as well. Vanessa's just one of those evil sisters who's been working in the same place so long she hates it."

"No. Even before you grabbed my leg—which you shouldn't have done—she knew. Women can tell."

"So you women say."

"Your wife will know—if she doesn't already."

"Fools worry about consequences. I do what I do because it's the right thing."

"The right thing?" Even Jacksina thought that interpretation of their relationship was farfetched. But the Judge was resolute.

"We have a special chemistry. Don't you agree?"

"Yes."

"Then we need to be with each other. That's what's crucial for us." Now they stood outside the narrow doorway of the Village Vanguard, where a vertical sign by the door read, **ELVIN JONES QUARTET**. The Judge faced Jacksina and stared into her eyes. "You came into my life for a reason, Jack. What that reason is, time will reveal. But I'll be damned if I'll be timid about the fact that your fine self is with me."

Then he kissed her, on Seventh Avenue, in front of a famous

jazz club, in front of passing cars, pedestrians, and customers stepping into the club. Jacksina felt her knees grow weak. *Maybe he loves me,* she thought. *Or maybe he's just crazy.* Then she decided he was both, and kissed him back.

It was a rainy Friday evening in late autumn. The after-work crowd at Sweetwaters on 67th and Amsterdam jammed the bar. They were almost all black. The men were in business suits. Some wore their ties loose or had opened a button or two on their shirts, but most still looked as crisp as Grant's profile on a fifty-dollar bill. There were women in pearls, wearing dresses with sexless shapes and white sneakers. Underneath the corporate garb, when the boss was bugging them and white junior executives were letting their contempt show, these brothers and sisters perspired in little puddles of sweat. Men and women, soul children and corporate clones, these buppies walked hand in hand through minefields of ambition and racism, wanting the best, mindful of the worse. At Sweetwaters they drank and forgot their jobs or at least tried to.

T.J. and Danielle sat at a table near the front window, he with a Harvey's Bristol Cream on the rocks, she with a piña colada, talking animatedly about a camping trip that never happened.

"No, no, no! It was *not* my fault the canoe came off the car," she said.

"Yes, yes, yes!" he countered. "Nobody told you to make that turn so fast. That thing flew off like a rocket. Just missed that old lady's rose garden."

Danielle laughed giddily.

"No, it's *your* fault!"

"How's that?"

"You shouldn't have brought that stupid old canoe in the first place. We could have rented one up there. We'd have drowned in that old thing. Probably full of holes."

"That was a precious family heirloom," he said with mock defensiveness.

"Junk!"

"Heirloom. Handed down from my daddy to me. My son was gonna use it."

"Your yet-to-be-born son would have been better off using it as tree-house material."

T.J. swallowed the last of his Harvey's and chuckled.

"You know, despite the dead canoe, the blown tires—two damn flat tires in three blocks, oh God!—we still should have gone upstate. It might have changed our lives." T.J. reached across the table and touched her hand. His touch wasn't innocent. It was a caress that flushed his yellowish face.

"T.J., you know we weren't supposed to make that trip. We never even got out of Arthur."

As Danielle spoke she eased her hand out of his grasp. T.J. laughed weakly. "Guess you're right."

"So who are you dating these days?" she asked.

"No one I really care about."

"Playing the field?"

"Maybe."

"Or is the field playing you?"

"What?"

"T.J., you are not cut out to be a playboy. You need a girlfriend. Want to meet Jacksina?"

"I've met Jacksina a couple of times and I'd much rather take my chances at the bar here. That girl's insane."

"No, she's not."

"A flake. A head case. Plain old crazy."

"So she made an impression."

"Danny, you love these off-the-wall characters. I mean, Dwayne Robinson . . ."

"You introduced us, remember?"

"You're gonna make me order another drink."

"My mother asks about you. She asks if you still drink too much."

"Does she now?"

"She still remembers Christmas 1978."

T.J.'s face turned beet-red. "That was just one of those things. It happens."

"She still misses the curtains you threw up on."
As if on cue the waitress asked if they wanted another round.
"No," Danielle said. "We'll take the check now."
"What's the big rush?" T.J. asked.
"Got to finish an article for school tonight so the weekend will be free."
"Got plans?"
"Don't you?"
"Yeah. I got plans," he said in a monotone. Then, with a sudden surge of energy, he said, "Hey, Danny, we need to get together more often. We don't talk enough anymore."
"Soon as I'm more in the groove at Columbia, I'll be able to make more time."
T.J. wanted to complain that she seemed able to make time for Dwayne, but he figured she'd probably say something he didn't want to hear, like she loved Dwayne Robinson or something stupid like that. Still, he was too weak to let the evening pass with no comment on Danielle's love life. "Has Morris called you?" This question stopped Danielle. Her eyes narrowed.
"Why do you ask? Did he call *you*?"
"Yeah . . . he did. We always got along. In fact I kinda like him."
"So what did he say?"
T.J. couldn't resist twisting the knife. He pretended that he was having trouble recalling the conversation. "I believe he was real excited by how much Bernard King has improved the Knicks."
"Stop that. You're not very funny."
"He asked how you were. What did you think? Whether you were happy. Whether you were being treated well. And"—T.J. dropped his carefree tone and spoke slowly—"he said he'd take you back in a second."
Danielle didn't reply.
"Well, what do you think about *that*?" T.J. insisted, gathering courage.
"I'm happy with Dwayne, T.J."

"You sure?"

"Yes." She slid into her coat and stood. "I'm going now, T.J."

"I love you, Danny."

She looked down at him and said, "I love you too, T.J." She touched her lips to his forehead and then, as if in one of his tortured dreams, she was gone, walking up Amsterdam Avenue in the rain.

The waitress arrived with the check.

"One more for the A train," he ordered. Two attractive sisters sat down across the aisle from him, and he assured himself, as he had for years, that Danielle was just a terrific friend and big waste of heartbeats, forgetting that he had just said he loved her.

Standing at the bar was a tall, willowy lady in a sky-blue silk dress and thick strands of pearls. She cut a look his way. *Promise yourself,* T.J. told himself, *that tonight you won't be stupid and you won't throw up and you'll sleep alone.* He looked down at his latest Harvey's on the rocks and realized that none of those promises would be easy to keep.

There was hysteria, conniving, and displays of ego backstage at Madison Square Garden. Since none of this was unusual before a big concert, no one seemed too concerned—certainly not the stars, who still hadn't arrived yet from their hotels. Or the fans, who were filling the seats in anticipation of ballads and funk by two popular black bands. Or the roadies of the two bands, who throughout the thirty-city tour had been sabotaging each other's activities with a fervor their employers rarely matched onstage.

The only person in all of Madison Square Garden who seemed to survey this professional madness with undue concern was the unannounced warm-up act. "Break It Down" was a big local hit, and Reggie, through his contacts with the promoters (plus cutting Joint-ski's fee) had got his young charge on as the show opener.

As the crowd trickled in, Joint-ski walked around his dressing room in blue jockey briefs, constantly poked his head out the door and talked at a rapid pace.

"Homies from the Inferno be in the house. Girlies, all my

girlies from uptown, be in the house. Uncle Cecil. Aunt Bee Bee. My whack cousins from Yonkers. Billie Bill. Bobby Bee. Youngblood. Tyrone. Hey, Rahiem! Everybody be in here, right?" Rahiem, earphones on, his face impassive, hovered over two spinning records, oblivious to Joint-ski's ramble. Rahiem had just eaten three big apples from the promoter's complimentary fruit basket and was now intently practicing his mixing.

Joint-ski stuck his head outside again, but this time pulled it back with a smile. "Yo, here comes Reggie Reg, Billie Bill and Bobby Bee. Even Dwayne Robinson's in the house." When they entered he turned cool. "Yo, homies. Check it out. My own dressing room in the Garden."

"These are your roadies," Reggie announced.

"My roadies?"

"That's correct."

"Yo, that's the joint."

"Okay, guys," Reggie ordered, "let's move the equipment."

Billie Bill and Bobby Bee, two young b-boys dressed in matching red Kangol caps and Adidas sweat suits, began moving the turntables and record crates.

"No soundcheck?" Dwayne asked.

Reggie cut him a "Don't ask" look. Dwayne nodded, then asked, "Can I help move the stuff?"

"Go 'head," Reggie said. "It'll be more fun than cleaning up our apartment."

Dwayne picked up Rahiem's cross-fader and followed Billie Bill and Bobby Bee into the hallway. Reggie was holding the door open. As he walked by, Dwayne whispered to him, "Your boy needs a pep talk."

"Don't worry. Insecurity brings out his best."

Down a long corridor usually frequented by the Knicks and the Rangers, Dwayne walked with the cross-fader in his hands. There were fine young ladies, dressed tightly and brightly, standing in clusters along the white walls. Beefy security men and roadies with walkie-talkies strutted about. Slick men in expensive suits talked shop. Dwayne and company then moved through a big empty space filled with burly roadies stuffed into t-shirts bearing the headliner's logos. Past a tall curtain, up some steel steps, and there was Dwayne Robinson, standing center stage at Madison Square Garden.

You couldn't see any fans out past the first three or four rows, just as all the singers he'd interviewed had said. Standing with the cross-fader in his hands, looking out at Madison Square Garden, it was easy now for Dwayne to understand megalomania. Dwayne felt like a world-famous pop star. He felt like a dictator . . .

. . . and then he felt like a roadie. Billie Bill took the cross-fader out of his hands. Dwayne stared out into the crowd one more time and then walked off stage. Joint-ski, resplendent in white leather, gold chains, and fresh jheri-curl, waited at the bottom of the steps.

"Good luck," Dwayne told him.

"No prob, money. I'm gonna cold-rock niggers."

Joint-ski did. So did Rahiem. Reggie wasn't bad either. Between Joint-ski's juvenile charisma, Rahiem's ability to "cut" records—a skill most of the audience had never seen before—and Reggie's "Break It Down" production, the Garden clapped like thunder when they left. Backstage, Joint-ski's once empty dressing room was now a party. The Inferno rappers had, some grudgingly, come to pay their respects. A couple of the hallway girls were sipping on Cokes. Reggie was explaining Joint-ski and rap to two fat, perspiring white men in slick suits. Rahiem had slipped out to watch the rest of the show. Dwayne stood behind Reggie, listening to every word but trying to look like he wasn't.

Danielle used to scamper down the aisles of Barney's, her left hand rubbing against the racks of flannel, tweed, and wool suits. Then she'd hear her father call out to her and would dash back. He'd be in front of tall mirrors, fingering a stylish suit. "What do you think?" he'd ask her reflection. With the precociousness of Shirley Temple but with tons more charm, Danielle would circle her father, feel the material, and study how it looked on his broad shoulders. In a small voice that both echoed and mocked her mother's high-pitched delivery, Danielle would give her opinion on Dad's clothes. Part of the glue for this father-daughter relationship was that he took her opinions very seriously. It was a yearly ritual for her to accompany him on his annual Easter suit purchase. Daniel Embry had few extravagances. He didn't smoke. Drank vodka on rare occasions and didn't enjoy going out—Danielle had many fondly amused memories of her mother dragging Daddy off to parties. The irony was that while he was no party animal, when Dan Embry went out he was always "clean." He loved well-tailored suits as much as he did well-constructed homes. So, like clockwork, two weeks before Easter Sunday, he'd travel to Barney's at Seventh Avenue and 17th Street for one new suit. Maybe two, if he'd had a good spring. He had linen. He had seersucker. Gabardine. Even a couple of flashy silk numbers.

And it was Danielle, as an adolescent and teenager, who stood behind him watching and commenting as her father wore out Barney's salesmen. He saw clothes as he saw carpentry; good material plus solid structure equals durability. So he picked over the buttonholes and the stitching for flaws just as he did wood and concrete, which, Danielle supposed, is why she was always nitpicking her way through life.

Ironically, a squabble at the Embry residence had led to this harmonious father-daughter ritual. Jean Embry had been enraged by her husband's laid-back reaction to son Jack's decision, at seventeen, to leave home and preach the gospel at a storefront church. "Lord or no Lord," Mother shouted one evening, "he is still underage and still hasn't gone to college. I didn't raise my son to be an ignorant, undereducated preacher. At least send him to seminary school. Maybe he'll turn into Dr. King." But her husband, in one of those decisions that delighted his children and gave his wife indigestion, said, "If God wants my son's service, then let the boy go to it directly, humble before his maker and not as a seminary-school slickster."

In the weeks that followed that decision, Danielle heard no late-night lovemaking sounds through her closet wall.

Jack was to give the Easter Sunday sermon at the storefront temple, the Church of the Divine Guidance, and he wanted the family to be there. In protest Jean Embry refused to go Easter suit shopping with her husband. Now it was Dan who was mad. In his eyes, this was an important moment in the Embry family history. Mother thought so too, but not for the same reason. She suggested he take the hyperactive Danielle shopping with him, hoping to annoy him. As it turned out, Mother Embry was the one who'd suffer, since her husband found shopping with Danielle a pleasure.

The first Barney's excursion led to other father-daughter expeditions and to a special bond between them. Watching men shop, listening to the comments they made to wives, mistresses, and each other, Danielle came to appreciate men. Over time she even felt she understood men better than her mother did. In college she would encounter other young sisters, women with stores of abuse and hostility aimed at black men. To their disgust she would react with amused incomprehension. Did men and women really do things like that to each other? Were black men that rotten? Weren't all men prone to betrayal? Eventually she too would have her painful run-ins with brothers, but it never calcified into generalized bitterness. At Barney's, Macy's, the Stag Shop, and the other stores her father frequented, Danielle had heard angry exchanges between couples of all colors and classes. If the sister felt the brothers were so uniquely wicked, perhaps it was just because they didn't know white men very well.

At Yale, Danielle's blackness definitely got questioned. *For Colored Girls Who Considered Suicide When the Rainbow Is Enuf* was on Broadway, and anti-black-male hostility was being loudly voiced by many black women. Not an easy time for a suburban Connecticut girl who'd never even walked through Harlem to buck well-documented stereotypes.

The comments stung, but Danielle was too stubborn to back down. At a forum on "Black Male–Female Relationships" she stood up to say, "If being black means nurturing a patently pathological hatred of black men, then I'll just stay a naive suburban girl." This stance didn't make Danielle very popular, for it suggested a pride in being middle class which, while secretly shared by many black classmates, few had the guts to voice. Danielle frowned at these memories as she walked down Barney's aisles, caressing the stylish suits. *Should I buy him a suit?* she wondered. Dwayne definitely needed a wardrobe upgrade. Yet somehow a suit, a sweater, or a shirt didn't seem the right gift for him. Her eye settled on a fiftyish black man who had just asked his companion, a black woman in her twenties, for her opinion on a cashmere sweater. Danielle smiled. Father and daughter revisited? Then she pinched his right cheek and he, with considerable gusto, stroked her thigh with his left hand. Her Barney's sojourn, nice memories and all, was unnecessary. The best gift she could give Dwayne Robinson, she realized, was one she could enjoy herself.

The New Haven Line commuter train rolled past Co-op City, and Danielle knew it would soon be moving through White Plains. Then New York's city limits would have been breached, the Metro North vehicle would pass through Westchester, and not long after that she'd be back in Connecticut. Dwayne had joked back in Grand Central Station about how many black people came from Connecticut. "No," she told him, "there are a lot of us." New Haven, in particular, had a substantial poor working class community that serviced Yale, and to which the university, with the high-handed snobbery of the anointed, paid crappy wages and then ignored. Arthur was the black haven outside of town for black folks who, through luck, hard work, or both, had escaped Yale's economic domination. It wasn't a bourgie town, she thought, but it aspired to bourgiedom. Nothing wrong with having upwardly mobile dreams. That's what Connecticut was about. It was conceived to be comfortable, dull, polite, and tidy. The train would amble through Stamford and Greenwich and Milford and past the prissy homes and the private schools, engulfed in a smugness that a sagging economy had yet to wipe away.

Danielle squeezed Dwayne's hand and smiled at him, but said nothing. She wanted to comment on the passing landscape but realized that she could find nothing to say about it. Her life in Connecticut, apart from her studies at Yale and the family's early years in New Haven, had been confined to Arthur and a few nearby malls. *What do you tell a young, single New Yorker about Connecticut, anyway?* she wondered. They were only curious about Connecticut later, after the job and the marriage and, most certainly, after the babies.

It really didn't matter, since Dwayne wasn't asking any questions anyway. He was very nervous. She could feel it when she squeezed his hand. *You should relax, baby,* she thought. *My family isn't scary. Well, maybe Ma is a little eccentric.*

"So, Dwayne, my daughter tells me you're writing a book." Jean Embry said it in a tone that suggested a prelude to an uncomfortable question. They were sitting in the Embry's tastefully furnished living room.

"Well . . . yes and no. Yes, I want to write a book. But I haven't found a subject yet."

Mrs. Embry nodded. Dwayne felt she was gearing up for something else. He was right.

"Is writing how you plan to make a living? It seems to me that the real money is in television. Isn't that right, dear?" Danielle had just walked past with a glass of grape juice in her hand.

"Is what right, Ma?"

"That there is more money in television than in writing."

Dwayne detected a subtext here. "The earning power of a television producer or reporter," he said smoothly, "is a lot more than that of most print journalists. Or, for that matter, a book editor. Danielle's very shrewd to shift into that area. Did you advise her to do it?"

Mrs. Embry fell for the ploy and smiled yes. Dwayne, pressing his advantage, leaned forward, and with as much sincerity as he could muster, cooed, "As for me, well, I'm a born writer. I've managed to build a reputation for myself, and I've gotten pretty good at it." *Now,* he thought, *for the punch line.* "I mean, my dream is to contribute—like Alex Haley has.

Write books like *Roots* that help us understand our history better."

Mrs. Embry was enchanted. There wasn't a black mother of her generation who wouldn't have been. "Have you attempted to trace your family's roots, Dwayne? We have."

"Really." Dwayne leaned farther forward, bracing himself for the inevitable boring tale of Aunt Emma and Great-Grandpa Jack and all the cousins and nephews that the Embrys had discovered since Kunta Kinte had hit prime time. The book and miniseries of Haley's familial odyssey had remained, years after the telecast, a prime conversation topic at black gatherings. The only problem, as Dwayne could testify, was that if the tracing hadn't been done about your family, who cared?

Dwayne struggled to look engaged. He had to admit that Mrs. Embry could spin a yarn. Her father was Jamaican, and her mother was from Antigua. She'd met Dan Embry at a house party on the Bronx's Gun Hill Road. Love at first sight, she said with pride. Mrs. Embry discovered her father's family had resided in St. Ann's Parish since the eighteenth century, and that their great-great-great grandfather Isaiah Dalton had been a preacher who converted slaves to Christianity. To Dwayne that meant he was an Uncle Tom for English imperialism. "It was he, I believe, who set a standard for responsibility that my family has always lived up to."

When is Danielle going to come out of the kitchen and save me? Dwayne wondered.

"You believe family behavior patterns can be traced that far back?" he asked.

"Oh, yes, Dwayne. Families have character traits. Our family has a long history of being hard workers and good providers. Isn't that right, Danielle?" Jean asked in a loud voice.

"What, Ma?" Danielle was now setting plates and bowls of food in the dining room.

"I said that we found our family has always had a strong work ethic."

"You're not talking about *Roots* again, are you, Ma?"

"Dwayne brought it up. Isn't that right?"

"Yup," Danielle said, rolling her eyes. "Listen," she added, "if you promise to change the subject I'll feed you."

"Shouldn't we wait for your father?" Dwayne asked.

"You don't want to delay eating my cooking, do you, Dwayne?" Danielle joked.

"Is that all right Mrs. Embry?"

"It's sweet of you to ask, but you two go ahead—Danielle sounds like she's out to prove something." Danielle ignored her mother's comment. Dwayne was taken aback by the remark but said nothing. He stood up and went into the dining room. Danielle placed a plate of smothered pork chops, cabbage, and yellow rice in front of him.

"Thanks," he said and sat down.

"Can you keep up the good behavior?" she whispered.

"Only if the food is good. If it's lousy, who knows what I might say."

"Guess you'll be a choir boy the rest of the night."

"Oh, it's like that, is it?"

"Food," she said confidently, "speaks louder than words."

Out in the living room, Mrs. Embry sat flipping through a stack of *Jet* magazines.

"Does she always sit there and wait for your father?" Dwayne whispered.

Danielle smiled and said "Not always" in a way that suggested more often than not. She got a plate for herself and sat down next to him. The phone rang. Danielle was closer to the kitchen phone, but her mother moved like a shot toward it. "Dan? Where are you? You know your daughter has company? . . . Yes, the writer from Brooklyn . . ." Danielle looked at Dwayne and giggled. There was a long pause as Mrs. Embry listened. Then she said, "Okay, but hurry up" and hung up.

"He went over to Malik's house," she said, walking into the dining room, "and as usual they got into it. This time it was over the quality of the materials being used in putting on the extra rooms."

"Malik is being frugal?" Danielle asked nervously.

"You mean *cheap* and the answer is yes. Your guru is cheap."

"Daddy Dan and Malik have a love-hate relationship that goes back twenty years."

"The hate part is because your father didn't like the influence he had over you when you were a child."

"Malik never made a lot of money, and Daddy uses only quality materials," Danielle said.

"He says your father overcharges," Mrs. Embry said.

"Isn't Malik the guy you told me about? The community activist–role model superbrother?" Dwayne asked.

"Yes," Danielle said.

"Old Malik can do no wrong in Danielle's eyes," Mrs. Embry said prior to swallowing a forkful of cabbage.

"He's just a man with integrity," Danielle asserted.

"You mean hardheaded," Mrs. Embry replied.

"Sometimes," Dwayne said, "having integrity, or at least a firm belief in something, makes you hardheaded because you struggle for your ideas."

To the surprise of Dwayne and Danielle, Mrs. Embry laughed heartily at his comment. "No wonder Danielle likes you. That sounds just like her."

"Thank you—I think," Dwayne said. Danielle was not amused.

Then her mother added, "Danielle and her men are always agreeing," which made her daughter's face flush with anger.

"Ma, please don't start that again."

It was an old dispute. Mrs. Embry thought Danielle was far too susceptible to men who said what she wanted to hear. "Too trusting" was her mother's observation-condemnation. Dwayne couldn't decipher the subtext, but he felt the tension. He put some rice into his mouth to avoid having to say something.

Daniel Embry entered his home through the kitchen. Dwayne heard water running in the sink. Then Mr. Embry came into the living room—a smallish, smiling man in blue overalls, dingy brown work boots, and a red plaid work shirt. His face was a hairy facsimile of Danielle's. But his hands! Daniel Embry's hands were enormous—long and thick, the hands of a linebacker or power forward. Or a carpenter. He wiped them with a towel and then shook Dwayne's hand.

"Nice to meet you, Dwayne."

"Same here, sir."

Dwayne gave his best firm handshake, yet felt engulfed in the older man's fingers. The grip wasn't at all aggressive; nonetheless Dwayne felt Mr. Embry could have mashed his fingers like pretzels. It was actually comforting to shake his hand—like he was hugging you. Dan Embry kissed his daughter and wife, who'd brought him a plate heaped with food.

"Hope my wife didn't tell you too much about my family's roots." His smile let Dwayne know it was okay to laugh—laugh lightly, but laugh.

"Just a little, sir."

"She's just a little prouder about things like that than most people," Mr. Embry said. Then he yawned. "Excuse me. I'm gonna go change. Be right back."

"Why don't you sit down, Dad?" Danielle said. "You know how you are."

A little irritated by her comment, he put down the plate and said, "I'll be right back," with an emphasis on *right*.

When he exited, Dwayne whispered to Danielle, "Looks like you dripped right out of his penis."

Danielle hit him hard on the shoulder. "Lower your voice. If my mother heard you . . ."

Mrs. Embry came in from the kitchen and asked, "Where'd your father go?"

Danielle motioned with her thumb toward their bedroom. Mrs. Embry shook her head slowly. "At least he met Dwayne."

"Ma, I'd hoped for a longer conversation."

"Maybe if Malik hadn't argued with him—"

"Ma, that's not the problem."

Dwayne was a little bewildered. "Isn't he coming back?"

"It's not that he has poor manners," his wife said, "he just falls asleep quickly."

"Especially after working," Danielle added as her mother

disappeared into their bedroom. "He sits on the bed to take his boots off and the next thing you know he's asleep."

"Sign of a man who earns an honest buck. My father never fell asleep after work. Usually his day was just beginning."

"What do you mean?"

"Well, he was always working with his friends trying to throw parties. He and two friends back in the sixties had a company called Afrodelica. They all used to dress in sharkskin suits, with matching ties, white shirt, and wrap-around shades."

"I don't believe my father ever owned a sharkskin suit."

"Why would he need one? Loving wife. Kids. Suburban lifestyle. Self-employed. For a black man of his generation your Daddy was da joint."

"What about for a black man today? Is he still doing well?"

"Do his kids still love him?"

"Of course."

"Then he's a very big winner."

"You do love your father, Dwayne—I can feel it." He ignored her comment. Instead he took a bite out of a pork chop and smiled.

"My only true love is for your pork chops."

"Does that mean less eating out?"

"Of course not."

"Thought so."

"Dwayne, please excuse my husband." Mrs. Embry stood in the dining room doorway.

"I totally understand. I respect hard work," Dwayne said, and Danielle pinched his leg under the table.

"Good night, then." Mrs. Embry smiled apologetically and went back to her husband.

Danielle got right in Dwayne's face. "My mother is not that corny, Dwayne."

"Yo, I thought I was saying all the right things. Mothers always love me. Bet she'll sing my praises tomorrow."

"Nope. She doesn't like you that much."

"How do you know that?"

"*Roots.*"

"*Roots?* We talked about *Roots?*"

"Notice she didn't ask about your family?"

"She didn't, that's right. Is that real bad?"

"Well, I told her a lot, but let's put it this way. You didn't even get to the part of her *Roots* talk where you hear the similarities between our family and Kunta Kinte."

"Oh, that sounds major. So did I at least get to second base?"

"Bunted your way onto first."

Dwayne sighed. Then his eyes began to twinkle and he shifted his body toward hers. "Since," he said in a low voice, "I'm already held in such low esteem by your family that your moms held back on her polite conversation and your pops fell dead asleep after exchanging two sentences with me, I might as well be a total nigger and seduce you in the dining room."

"Sorry, but tonight's romantic highlight will be you helping me wash dishes."

"Just like a real married couple."

Danielle smiled so beautifully Dwayne didn't want to blink. He didn't want to miss one single microsecond of whatever this lady was radiating.

"You know, you really didn't do that bad with my parents, Dwayne."

"Really?"

"No. I'm lying. You did terribly."

"Kiss me then or I'm gonna be real depressed." And so she did, even as Mrs. Embry stood watching from the hallway, shaking her head. *Can't this child go three days without a man?* she thought, and returned to her bedroom.

On October 4, Dwayne's birthday, Danielle drove him up to the Poconos, where Ernest and Von time-shared a home with several friends. Outside the car windows was a rainbow of tree leaves. Red. Purple. Hazel. Orange. Waiting by the fireplace was Moët on ice and a chocolate cake with twenty-seven candles waiting to be lit. For his enjoyment she slid Marvin Gaye's "Let's Get It On" on the turntable and read aloud her favorite passages from *My Secret Life*, a bawdy book of Victorian pornography. After having cake and champagne in front of the fireplace, she announced, "I have another present for you."

"What else could you give me?" he said. "This is so nice I might convert to bourgie."

She made the sound of a racetrack trumpet and announced, "I am now safely and affectionately on the pill. No more diaphragm. No more plastics."

"Damn."

"Let's see if it works."

Later that night Dwayne vowed to do the right thing. Get up early. Cook breakfast. Serve Danielle in bed. Some payback was needed for all the glorious gifts on his birthday. But her loving had been too good. The bright mountain sunlight was already strong by the time he peeped at the old clock on the nightstand the next morning. He grunted despondently. His head flopped back against the pillow.

Dwayne smelled the aroma wafting up from the kitchen. *Damn, does she have to be this good? Another breakfast in bed. What did I do to deserve this?* Danielle, carrying a tray of food and looking innocently sexy in a loose-fitting robe and a set of her father's old pajamas, came in and walked over to the foot of the bed. "Bet you're hungry."

"I was going to make you breakfast."

"I'm waiting."

"Maybe dinner."

She placed the tray on the nightstand and sat down next to him. "No, you won't. One, it's your birthday weekend, and, two, your cooking has a long way to go."

"What?" He grabbed her and pulled her against him. "How could you say that to a birthday boy?"

"My journalistic integrity cannot be compromised."

Between kisses to her neck and breast Dwayne said suavely, "You have your price. Everybody does."

"Not when it comes to your cooking."

Dwayne stopped his kisses, sat up, and planted a serious look on his face as he stared at her garments. "Are you sleeping with me in another man's clothes?"

"My father's.

"He's a man. Isn't he?"

"It's a family tradition."

"Okay, tell me about it."

"On my parents' wedding night, my mother found that she'd somehow forgotten her camisole and negligees. She was crushed. My daddy, however, thought it funny and suggested she wear his pajamas. My mother, the type who'd kept her virginity until marriage, felt she hadn't waited all these years to lose it in baggy blue pajamas. But daddy convinced her by saying, 'You can make anything you wish romantic.' That's what my mother says. Must have worked. Nine months to that night their oldest child was born."

"Deep. Kind of romantic too."

"You think so?"

"Yeah."

"Good. I made it up. I just wore these because it gets damn cold up here at night and sexy stuff is impractical."

"You can't build a relationship on lies," he said, chuckling. "But that one was *good*."

"Good. Now give me a back rub." She stretched out on the bed. The romantic story about her parents was true. But, since it was also slightly hokey, she didn't feel totally comfortable telling Dwayne. So she had told him and then she hadn't.

"Getting a little bossy, baby."

"Who got out of bed, in the cold, and cooked breakfast?"

He tapped his hands on her back a little harder than he had to.

"What do you guys do at your apartment?" she asked.

"What do you mean?" Dwayne replied, though he had an idea where this was going.

"I mean, 'I was recently invited to a party where I spotted a charming mahogany cherub in red patent-leather heels and ruffled white blouse.' What is that?"

"That sounds familiar."

"What about, 'I'm convinced I'll end up married to some

warm, charming African queen who will spoil me rotten and send my cynicism to its grave'?"

"Cute, isn't it."

"Did you help Reggie write this?"

"Reggie can write."

"This sounds like Dwayne."

"What?"

"Didn't you write, 'My romantic life has been marked by a never-ending conflict between my romantic side and my cynical side'?"

"No. I did not."

"That is your voice."

"Before he began making records, Reggie used to write quite a bit and quite well. The man has no problem manipulating words, believe me, as you've obviously noted from his 'Say Brother' piece."

"How come you didn't tell me this piece was coming out?"

"It was no big deal. Reggie felt he had something to say of relevance to all black women. Besides it was funny."

"So how many letters has he received? I know that's why he wrote it."

"About fifty," he said, still rubbing her back while trying to stifle a laugh. She twisted around to face him.

"Just tell him to keep those letters to himself. He wrote the article himself; he can answer the letters by himself."

"Look, Reg is so happy he barely lets me read them. I won't tell you what they write because I know you wouldn't be interested. And I certainly won't bother describing the pictures they've sent."

"Dwayne, I know how horny some women are. And this picture of Reggie makes him look almost handsome. Put it all together and you have a dog receiving undeserved attention."

"You know you want to know what the letters say," he teased.

"Just rub my back."

"So you don't want to know about the pictures from lonely

ladies in D.C., Detroit, and Boston? What about the perfumed letters from Gary and Fort Dix?"

"No."

"Okay. You win. But you brought it up."

A hammer was ready to fall. "I brought it up because I know it was your idea for Reggie to write that trash. And I'm almost positive you helped encourage him to write it in a way that would entice women. It bothers me to think you concocted this strategy to get Reggie laid."

"Danielle, wait. Sure, Reg may meet some women. May even have sex with one or two of them. But honestly: the 'Say Brother' article was intended to help him find a good woman."

Dwayne sounded semi-sincere, but Danielle wasn't buying it.

"Maybe," she snapped, "if he hung around some mature women and not Joint-ski's groupies, his life would be different."

"Maybe you're right," Dwayne said. "For whatever reason, I told Reggie to write a 'Say Brother.' Since then he's been contacted by women, and just maybe he'll find a wife through this piece. Okay?"

Danielle sat up and kissed Dwayne on the cheek. "Maybe he'll be lucky, like you, but I doubt it."

Two weeks later Dwayne sat in the lobby of D.C.'s Ambassador Hotel, eyeing the crowd attending the Black Music Association conference. Seminars on the international market for black music, programming of urban radio, saving mom-and-pop stores, etc., were the backdrop for storytelling, casually serious sex, giving and/or ingesting cocaine. All of it done in the name of record promotion. While the far-sighted, successful record executives who organized the conference already had deep pockets, the label staffers, radio deejays, and musicians who comprised the bulk of B.M.A. registrants were still scheming and dreaming.

Watching them, Dwayne concluded that the record business consisted of equal numbers of cynics and dreamers. They all participated in the corruption of getting radio play, and viewed black music (which the conference program hailed as "the soul of our people") as "product," much like shoe polish or toothpaste. Yet, behind the phoniness and payola there were often dedicated people who supported great musicians in making great music. Detached from the hustle, Dwayne watched the moving tongues of commerce, detesting and loving these folks depending on which one had last bought him lunch.

Reggie called his name. Turning and looking up, he saw his roommate, with a huge grin spread across his wide face, crossing the lobby. Reggie had come to the convention partially to promote the release of "Break It Down" on B.C. Records, but mainly to check out four D.C. women who had responded to his *Essence* article. So Dwayne wasn't surprised when he saw that Reggie had a woman in tow. And what a woman this one was! She was tall—almost Reggie's height—and had very long, dark brown hair; luscious, lemon-colored skin; a wide smile; and a perfect Coke-bottle figure. She was wearing a well-tailored pink dress and a single gold chain. Her spike-heeled shoes matched her dress. Dwayne stood up.

Kelly Love Chase was her name: divorced, late-thirties; son eleven, daughter eight; supervisory position in a computer programming division of the IRS; duplex in Silver Spring, Maryland; proud owner of a cherry-red, vintage MG. Her letter to Reggie had read as follows:

Dear Mr. Olds,

We've only met through a recent article in Essence, "Say Brother." Your portrait struck me first, but after reading your article I was touched. You are truly talented as well as sensitive. These paragraphs rang with familiarity, as though for a moment you had walked through my thoughts. I appreciate your allowing this intrusion on your time and have no desire to disrupt the order of your day.

Mr. Olds please be kind with me. I'm rather a neophyte when it comes to these things. I have no explanation but it's important to me that I hear your voice, if only to say "Hello" and "Goodbye." Realizing this may seem corny, you'll more

than likely disregard this request. If this is the case I understand and will trouble you no further. Otherwise, please
say hello and complete this picture your article etched in
my mind.

P.S. Consider me a fan.

Very sincerely,
Kelly Love Chase
(301) 555-7777

After that meeting in the lobby Friday afternoon, Dwayne
didn't see or hear from his roommate until late Monday night,
when Dwayne was back in New York.

"So where the fuck are you?" Dwayne shouted into the
phone. "I had to pay all the hotel bills myself, and I ain't got it
like that."

"A little bill paying is good for the soul, Mr. Robinson. You'll
get used to it. Maybe sooner than you think."

"I take it you are in the company of a very tall woman."

"You mean Kelly Love? That beautiful, sensitive sample of
Afro-American architecture?"

"Did you just finish or are you about to start again?"

"We haven't stopped yet?"

"You in love yet?"

"Way past that."

"You know you left three women hanging? You'd made ap-
pointments with these ladies for brunch, lunch, and dinner. I
was so busy covering for you I missed some seminars."

"A tragedy."

"One of the promotion executives from B.C. was looking
for you. Wanted to take you around to some radio stations.
Heard the record on WOL while the convention was on. Great
exposure."

There was some background noise and Reggie was slow to
reply. Finally he said, "That's good."

"Sounds like you've been living *The Quiet Storm*."

"Something like that, Mr. Robinson. Something like that. Listen—I've got to go. Take messages. I'll be back tomorrow. Or maybe the day after."

"Dammit, Reggie. Remember you're an old man and remember it was *my* idea that you write the *Essence* piece."

"My glands will be eternally grateful."

Dwayne hung up and decided not to read too much importance into the conversation. Reggie often observed, "Pussy ain't nothing but skin and bone, you can fuck it, you can suck it, you can leave it alone."

FOUR

When he was a kid the IRT train ride home always seemed end-
less. Stop after stop. Franklin. Kingston. Utica. Then rattling
out of the tunnel into the sunlight. Past his elementary school,
PS 189, and into the Rutland Road station. Saratoga. Then
Rockaway and past his childhood home, the Tilden Projects.
Get off at Pennsylvania Avenue. The neighborhoods covered
by the elevated subway—Crown Heights, Brownsville, and
East New York—once had constituted Dwayne's whole world.
Now, riding on the IRT's New Lots Line brought a rush of images: Bobby Carter being pushed into the side of a subway entering the Rutland Road station by Ronnie Jones and then
bouncing along the platform; meeting big-chested Vanessa at
Rockaway Avenue one spring afternoon after being scared to
speak to her all winter; leaning over Pennsylvania Avenue's
elevated platform to unleash mushy yellows spit bombs at innocent passersby.

   While Dwayne mulled over the past, Danielle held his hand
and watched the sampling of Brooklynites who occupied the
subway car. She thought that the urban poor probably looked
much the same everywhere. Sullen young men with hardened
faces. Girls with the breasts of women and the bounce of children, chattering about so-and-so's doing whatever to whoever
whenever. Distraught young mothers smacking their kids into
tears with the harsh discipline born of impatience. Men her father's age but with weathered, exhausted faces and dull eyes.
My parents didn't want me to see this. That's why we left New

Haven. That's why we never went to Harlem. She squeezed Dwayne's hand so hard that he jumped.

"You okay?" he asked.

"Sure."

Pennsylvania Avenue is a long thoroughfare that forms the heart of East New York. At its northernmost tip Pennsylvania disappears into the Interborough Highway. At its southern tip it feeds into the Belt Parkway, a highway that rims the outer edge of Brooklyn at the Atlantic. Crumbling tenements and stubborn, embattled two-family homes testify to the struggle of black and Latino working-class families to survive in a city that neither valued them nor catered to them. As they walked toward Dwayne's home, Danielle tried to take in as much as she could of East New York, yet not be caught making eye contact with its residents. *It's like New Haven to the ninth power,* she thought, which was no compliment.

"I used to walk down this street every day and night," Dwayne told her. "Over and over. It didn't seem that bad then. The more I saw of the world, the more I knew better."

"Everybody feels the need to break away from their old neighborhood or town."

"But look at you. Living comfortably back home. The Parson's Penthouse isn't much, but it's better than walking through here every damn day."

His mother's house was nestled on a side street just off Pennsylvania Avenue. The street was lined with row houses that ran the gamut from immaculate to garbage-littered.

"The old homestead." He pointed to a nondescript white two-story stucco building. Entering, he shouted, "Ma, your shining black prince is home!" There was no answer.

The living room was filled with knickknacks: a die cigarette lighter, multicolored drink holders, porcelain ashtrays shaped like lobsters and maple leafs, two small stuffed animals won at Coney Island, and a poster bearing the likeness of the sixties martyrs, the Kennedy brothers, and Martin Luther King. On the wall over a gold, plastic-covered sofa was a medley of family photos as well as snapshots of Mrs. Robinson teaching.

Danielle studied them as Dwayne sought out his mother. There was a baby picture of Dwayne cradled in his mother's arms and photos of a toddling Dwayne laughing at the urging of a man who was surely Dwayne's father. There was buck-toothed Dwayne, his parents, and a beautiful Canadian husky. There was a polaroid of Dwayne, with an orange stickball bat and his father holding a pink rubber ball. Then Dwayne's father disappeared. Dwayne and his mother in a stern-looking portrait, probably when he was in high school. More recent photos had Dwayne and his mother solo or in tandem. It was as if the father had been erased from all Dwayne's postadolescent pictures, yet his outline remained faintly discernible in each.

"Danielle!" Dwayne appeared in the hallway. "She's out in the backyard. We're lucky she's barbecuing, 'cause she's a so-so cook."

"She's barbecuing in the winter?"

He replied, "I come by my craziness honestly."

They walked through a kitchen cluttered with "things"—calendars, coupons, shopping lists, pharmacy slips, and at least three different kinds of salt and pepper shakers. A handwritten sign tacked to the cabinet read, **THERE IS NEVER ENOUGH TIME IN THE DAY FOR THE BUSY AND NEVER REST FOR THE WEARY, BUT A LAZY HEART CAN ALWAYS FIND TIME FOR NOTHING. DON'T ALLOW YOUR HEART TO GROW LAZY.** Dwayne caught her eyeing the bric-a-brac and chuckled. "My mother never met a salt shaker she didn't like."

Out in a small concrete backyard a petite woman who looked like Dwayne's diminutive twin shifted chunks of meat on a grill. She looked up and smiled.

"Hi, I'm Miriam Robinson. Come on down here, Danielle, and help me finish this meat."

"Sure."

"That son of mine knows nothing about cooking," she said with a wry smile. "I know a little bit more. So I'm hoping you know how to do this, 'cause I'm going to go sit down inside and have a cigarette."

Mrs. Robinson started laughing, an infectious clucking that started in her lower belly and then flowed out like a bird, high and lyrical. One minute after meeting Dwayne's mother Danielle was laughing along with her and barbecuing in the winter cold.

"Don't burn those," Dwayne said.

"Dwayne, leave that girl alone," his mother reprimanded.

"Is this how you talk to kids in your classes?"

"Of course, son. You have to motivate them."

"You call that motivation, Ma?"

"Listen. Can you walk and talk?"

"He can talk," Danielle commented.

"Sure I can," Dwayne said.

"Then my motivational techniques work."

"Work too well," Danielle said.

"That's too true," Mrs. Robinson said. "Too true."

"Hey, don't gang up on me," Dwayne said, though he was loving it all.

"This chicken's ready," Danielle said and then blew on her hands.

Mrs. Robinson stood and studied it. "Looks good," she said approvingly. Turning to Dwayne, she said, "Glad you brought her along."

They sat in the kitchen and talked. When Danielle talked of her family and her dreams, Mrs. Robinson listened closely, said "Uh huh" at regular intervals, and in general interrogated her son's girlfriend without seeming to. When they moved to the living room she sent Dwayne to the store for some cigarettes, which he was reluctant to do, but she was his mother.

"Glad we got rid of him," said Mrs. Robinson as they sat on the living room sofa listening to Gladys Knight and the Pips' *All the Great Hits* playing in the background. "Sending him for cigarettes guarantees he'll take his time."

Danielle said, "He's very much against smoking."

"Well, good for him," his mother said, laughing. Then her face turned serious and she took a long puff. "Dwayne's really become a good man," she started slowly, "but there are things about him that bother me." Danielle was surprised and pleased by this sudden intimacy. "He's never really gotten over the way his father and I broke up. It turned him inside in some way. Won't talk to his father. They were close when he was a boy, but Dwayne felt betrayed." She took a puff. "I was the one betrayed. He always loved his son, though. But Dwayne just doesn't respond to him anymore. There's a coldness in him now you might feel sometimes."

"I've felt it."

"Don't blame him. Be patient." Another puff. "But at the same time don't take any unnecessary shit from him." Then they laughed together, a warm sisterly laugh.

The front door opened and Mrs. Robinson shouted, "You got my cigarettes?"

Dwayne entered the living room and held out a box of Parliaments at arm's length. He made a face.

"Cancer, anyone?"

"It keeps me from eating," his mother said.

"I hear cancer is good for that too."

"Does he give you a hard time too?" she asked Danielle.

"All the time."

"Good," Mrs. Robinson said.

"Good?"

"My son has no double standards—he irritates everybody. Now, Danielle, could you hand me the snake-eyes lighter?"

"When he screamed, the windows used to shake," Jacksina said in a low voice.

"He must have had one hell of a voice, Jack."

"When I was little he used to scare me. I'd just start crying at the first word out of his mouth." The Judge caressed Jacksina, moving his arms around her shoulders, tucking her even more snugly against his body. "But he changed. My mother got him to stop drinking. She just managed to turn him around somehow. He started going to AA meetings. He got to work on time. He stopped screaming. He just turned his whole life around."

"And seems like he turned yours around too."

"Yes," she said. "He did." She raised her head and kissed him
lightly on the lips. "And you have too."

"Don't compare me to your father." He said this much more
sternly than he'd intended. Still, this was sensitive ground and
he couldn't help it. "I didn't mean it that way, baby. All I meant is that you have
brought something special into my life. That's all, but that's a
lot. You understand, don't you?"

The Judge said "Yes," but the comparison to her father still
rankled. "So your father's been clean since you were, what,
about eleven?" He wanted to go back to the original subject.

"Yeah. It's been like night and day. To see someone fight and
win. No, to see someone fight and win for you. That was so special." Jacksina's body tensed. A tear rolled out of her eye onto
his chest.

"Don't cry, baby."

"No," she said, wiping her tears. "It's good to cry. It was that
deep, you know." She sat up, resting her head in her left hand so
she was looking down at the Judge's face.

"Don't get mad when I compare you to him. It's not about
age at all. It's about love. I've been with a lot of men."

"Stop bragging," he said, smiling.

"So," she continued, "I know the real thing. The real thing is
about sacrifice as well as pleasure. I know that my father sacri-
ficed for my mother and me. I know what you're risking being
with me." The Judge sighed and then frowned. "What did I
say?" she asked.

He looked up at the ceiling, the blanket, the wall, everything
but her lovely face before he could reply. "I'm embarrassed.
For you to say these things to me. I feel unworthy, that's all. It's
like you're making me seem like a character in a play. In reality
I'm an arrogant, stubborn old bastard."

"You sound like the *Post*."

"That paper may be racist, but a lot of what their columnists
say about me is true."

"That's a lie."

The Judge knew it wasn't, but Jacksina would be the last

person to admit it. Though defiance was his media specialty and trademark, there was doubt in his soul. He watched as she walked naked over to the cassette player and slipped in Rick James' *Street Songs* and cued up to the ballad "Fire and Desire," an erotic duet with Rick James and petite white singer Teena Marie shouting ecstatically at each other for five minutes.

Jacksina headed for the bathroom; the Judge wondered what his wife was doing. Probably at the word processor, writing the *Links* newsletter for dissemination at the weekend meeting out at Sag Harbor. That organization of monied, concerned, light-skinned black folks was taking up increasing amounts of her time—time that had once gone to her three grown children and her husband.

Harriett had never really challenged her husband on anything. She had been trained in Nashville, like all good female products of the fifties black Southern aristocracy, to support their men without reservation. Backing their men against the machinations of a segregated, racist world had for the most part been easy. During the years of financial hardship, the Judge had loved her deeply. She was always there for him. She'd been there when he was a poor Harlem lawyer. She'd worked for the Board of Education when he was earning the meager salary of an assistant D.A. Harriett was present and beaming proudly the day Alvin Peters was sworn in as a jurist.

After that triumph came change. Harriett, by then a comfortable member of New York's black bourgie establishment, grew chubby and matronly, while he became increasingly obsessed with his physique and his sometimes flagging virility. His one-man battle against the court system made him feel isolated, and caused him to be irritable and withdrawn at home. Harriett, through no fault of her own, reminded him of a past which he no longer took pleasure in recalling and a future that promised only his mortality. To the Judge, his wife's weight gain, his punishingly rigorous workouts, and his outspoken pronouncements from the bench were all factors that were pushing him toward change.

Jacksina, in loving contrast to poor Harriett, always made

him feel contemporary, like a vital part of 1982, not 1972, or, God forbid, 1962. This, of course, did not justify cheating on a wife of so many years. He knew that. When she and the kids found out—as they inevitably would—they would, of course, hate him. But he had his reasons, and he knew what they were, even if no one else seemed likely to understand them except Jacksina. The Judge sighed. *All truly great men are rife with contradiction,* he told himself. That thought, which occurred more and more often now, usually soothed him for a while.

But as surely as the digital clock read 8:54 p.m., the Judge was aware that morally he was dancing on the head of a needle. *I chastise the system for its injustice toward black people, yet look how I treat my women.* By now "Fire and Desire" was near its end, and the voices of James and Marie were entwined like the thrashing limbs of two lovers, like the legs of the Judge and Jacksina had been just moments before. The song seemed to stir up all the latent turmoil in the Judge. Jacksina emerged from the bathroom, still naked, and asked, "Do you want to take a shower?" Peters ignored her. He sat on the edge of the disheveled bed, his silver hair flowing over his closed eyes and his body bowed in supplication to the music.

Queens was all right. Lots of well-mannered women and neat little black-owned homes. Still, it wasn't Brooklyn. Jogging past McDonald's, he slowed to see if Sandifred was working (she was) and then sped up so she wouldn't see him. Dinner tonight was takeout food from the local Chink-a-Rican, aka Chinese-Spanish, joint, an establishment Reggie called "trilingual nausea" since its employees spoke some weird English-Spanish-Chinese hybrid. The food wasn't good. It was, however, cheap and fast. Dwayne sat at the counter, waiting for his ribs with shrimp fried rice and watched the residents of Hollis, St. Albans, Springfield Gardens, and Far Rockaway step into brown buses.

Instead of jogging back up Parsons Boulevard, Dwayne walked down a side street and then up past St. Mary's Hospital and King's Park. The soccer players were gone. So were the mothers with the carriages, and the handball players. Even the methadone junkies who crowded daily at the battered bandshell had called it a day. Almost dark now. Only a solitary nurse, perhaps late for the six o'clock shift, hurried through. The wind rustled the leaves. A few crunched under Dwayne's feet. Autumn air made everything so sharp, like watching life through RCA Select-a-Vision ads. He turned the corner onto 90th Avenue, jogging through the courtyard and into the building.

Reggie and Joint-ski were in the living room, listening to remixes of "Break It Down" when Dwayne entered.

"Yo, man, still working that cute baby doll?" Joint-ski inquired.

"Word."

"Whenever you get up off, let me know, man."

Reggie asked, "You don't really want to go behind Dwayne, do you?"

Joint-ski responded, "Man, I carry a bottle of penicillin with me, so when I got to have it, I don't have to crab it."

"Later, gents," Dwayne said. "I have to write something."

Reggie smirked. "I think you hurt his feelings."

"Good night, gentleman, and other," Dwayne said, and he went into his room. He pulled out a yellow legal pad from his desk and placed it next to his meal, then scooped up rice and ribs with his left hand and wrote with his right.

Danielle, you have been so good to me I am almost embarrassed by the attention. I'm just not used to it. You told me you love me and I didn't answer you and you have never said it again, but you have certainly backed it up. I am not used to that either. Yes, women have tried to love me. I just never let them.

A page later he concluded:

You have helped me so much with your gentleness and sweetness. When I am with you, I have no past. I do not contemplate the future. I just exist, suspended alone with you in a city of many. Hang with me, Danielle Rainey Embry, and I think it will be okay. I really do.

It seems like I should be saying more, he thought, though what he didn't know. Then, afraid he'd change his mind, Dwayne slipped the letter into an envelope, licked it, and dropped it into his briefcase to mail. The living room was empty. Reggie and Joint-ski had split for an all-night studio session.

From the pile of records that lay stacked haphazardly against the living room wall, Dwayne dug past albums by Chic, Monk, and Parliament in search of the proper mood. It was an obscure cut on Otis Redding's "Greatest Hits" collection called "Cigarettes and Coffee." Though Dwayne indulged in neither, he found Redding's song an amazing rendering of the mood that followed satisfying sex. When Dwayne was young and his mother played it, the nuance had gone over his head. He'd preferred Otis' "Satisfaction" and the frantic "I Can't Turn You Loose." Now Dwayne fully understood the song's poignancy, and on this night, Otis' voice—tender, strong, masculine, vulnerable—made him cry.

Danielle read Dwayne's letter on the IRT local on the way up to Columbia a few mornings later. *Don't get upset,* she vowed. *Too much to do today.* At nine a.m., her first class was "Ethics in Journalism." Taught by former CBS big shot Fred Friendly, also known affectionately and otherwise as "Ed Murrow's boss," it was a fun class spiced with the veteran journalist's anecdotes about television in the fifties and sixties, and his blasts at lapses in craft and conscience in contemporary TV news. It was good stuff, but Danielle was mentally still on the IRT, trying to decide if Dwayne just wanted to play with her mind or whether his family background and perhaps his neighborhood had conspired to somehow block his emotions.

When class ended, Danielle sped up the J School's winding staircase to the third floor's bank of telephones and typewriters, where she focused on her term project. In the two months she'd been at Columbia Danielle found that the name of the prestigious journalism school opened lots of doors. Today's first calls were to the Frederick Douglas Democratic Club, Harlem's leading political organization.

She set up an interview with Hilton Clark, son of *Dark Ghetto* author Kenneth Clark, who was building a reputation as a pollster of minority communities and momentum for a possible run for the city council or the assembly. Following on the Judge's recommendation, she spoke with Dan Winfrey's office. Winfrey, an ambitious black neoconservative whom the tabloids loved to quote attacking black Democrats, would provide balance to her piece. And, she had to admit, she wondered if he looked as fine in person as in the papers. An appointment was made for next week. Finally, she chatted with Peter St. Ann, the *Amsterdam News'* chief political reporter, a sometimes irascible Jamaican who'd been quite helpful once Dwayne invited him out to a dinner and stuffed him full of roti and jerk chicken.

As Dwayne had predicted, St. Ann was more helpful as a telephone number source than for any insight. The meeting with St. Ann confirmed Danielle's long-held feeling about the black press—that its members knew where the bodies were buried, but lacked the will and/or the skill to criticize black figures with the zeal needed to hold them accountable.

It was just this kind of analysis that was to be the engine of Danielle's thesis—a critical study of Charles Rangel's succession to Adam Powell's congressional seat. Her position was that this was a classic case of establishment politics being misinterpreted as leadership.

Danielle saw this ambitious and potentially controversial piece as her calling card. Talking with politicians excited her, and Danielle felt she was finally getting plugged into a world she'd studied for too long from outside. Von, Ernest, and Danielle had spent many nights talking about Rangel, Jesse Jackson, Martin Luther King, Jr., Malcolm X, Andrew Young, etc.—the whole panorama of black politics. Now it was time to test her theories.

Danielle was greatly disappointed that Dwayne wouldn't
dive in with her. He *was* interested in politics, yet was always
frustratingly ambivalent. To Danielle, Dwayne too often failed
to challenge his mind, slipping into the "easy" world of entertainment as if being an expert in one area was enough. Yet,
being around Dwayne reminded her of a Sag Harbor party two
years ago where she sniffed cocaine and couldn't sleep for two
days, except that Dwayne was more addictive. *I want Dwayne
to love me, to tell me right out that he does,* she thought, while
slipping notes under her clipboard. Yet the letter made it clear it
might be a while before those words would slide through his
lips. Beneath the romance and the Hitchcock movies, Dwayne's
resistance to unconditional love nibbled at Danielle's self-
confidence. Before going upstairs to meet with her adviser,
Danielle called Dwayne, catching him just before he headed to
Billboard's Manhattan office.

"Let's have dinner," she suggested. "My treat."

"College student treating freelance journalist to dinner.
Sounds like the poor leading the starving. How could I refuse?
And I have just the place."

"Where?"

"Deep in the heart of Harlem. It is time you got up close and
personal to the world that fascinates you, Ms. Embry."

"Sounds good," she said trying to camouflage her sudden
anxiety. "Meet you in front of the J School at about six. Is that
okay?"

"Perfect. I might have some good news," he said.

"Me too."

Danielle camped out in the Columbia J School library for the
rest of the afternoon, sifting through back issues of the *New
York Times, Amsterdam News,* and even the *New York Post*
which, to her surprise, had once been a very liberal newspaper.
When she looked up again it was 6:15. She hustled down the
stairs where Dwayne, reading *Billboard*, stood waiting. They
kissed and then Danielle started talking—gushing really—
about interviews arranged, information gathered, and how fulfilling the day had been.

"Sounds great," he said quietly.

"It feels that way to me. It really does. So where are we going to eat?"

"A place I know just a little ways from here."

"Okay . . . let's go. Let me tell you what my adviser said."

Danielle grabbed Dwayne's left arm and together they walked across Columbia's campus, past the library, and the lawn, and through the old black gates onto Amsterdam Avenue. Past the law school and the Columbia-owned tenements that served as dormitories and the book stores and the student-frequented diners. As they walked, with Danielle recounting her day, Dwayne listened, saying little. So engrossed was Danielle that at first she didn't notice the change. Past the elementary school at 122nd Street and the projects at 124th they walked, and, as if she'd clicked her heels, merry old Morningside Heights disappeared.

Now they stood at 125th Street, in the shadow of public housing, with Columbia well behind them.

"Dwayne, I've never walked this way before."

"Wild, isn't it? It is as if someone switched the lights off and then told the garbage collectors it was all right to turn back."

"Columbia really is in Harlem, isn't it?"

"Don't tell your classmates from out of town, but, yeah, it is. Harlem. Morningside Heights. Words. They don't mean shit."

Danielle recalled Dwayne's letter, thinking that his remark related to it. She looked at his face, *really* deeply at his boyish face, for the first time that evening. His jaw was tight; his eyes narrow. She was about to ask about his day when Dwayne pointed out a store on 125th and St. Nicholas Avenue where black men with picket signs marched in front of an Arab-owned grocery store. The signs accused store personnel of sexually harassing black women.

Dwayne said, "It's a shame that they've been able to come into our neighborhoods and open up business, taking money right out of the community."

"We need to get organized and open our own."

"One, the banks won't lend us the money needed to start, and two, the old Jew merchants who previously controlled these stores aren't crazy about giving anything up to niggers."

"Dwayne, that does sound unnecessarily anti-Semitic."

"If you had grown up in the ghetto, you wouldn't think so."

Danielle let go of his arm. "And what is that about?"

"Reality, Danielle. Reality. You want to cover black politics. You have skills. Look how quickly you're moving ahead with your paper. But there are things about attitudes on this street you have to understand if you're really gonna help people. That 'Jew' crack was probably simpleminded, but it was from the gut. You gotta know what their rage is about. Otherwise you'll be just another pretty lady on tv."

They turned up Lenox Avenue, walked through the outdoor clothing mart between 125th and 126th, and then crossed over to the east side of Lenox before Danielle spoke again.

"I understand what you're saying, but why be so nasty?"

"Am I being nasty?"

"Dwayne!" Danielle was hot now. She just stared at him, her look demanding an apology. After looking into space and sighing, Dwayne said softly, "I'm sorry, baby. I'm sorry. Here we are."

"Here?" Danielle said, looking at a dark, poorly lit shack of a storefront where the running of numbers and procuring of controlled substances were routinely handled.

"No." He smiled. "Here." He pointed next door.

Sylvia's restaurant was a Harlem landmark, though fans of Copeland's on 145th Street and Wilson's on 154th Street would argue that those establishments had superior soul food. One side of Sylvia's had the look of a greasy spoon—a long, crowded counter, a blaring jukebox, and tables with booths. The other had smaller tables, no counter, nice wallpaper, and a space for an organist, drum machine, and vocalist who was warming up for the evening's set. Dwayne preferred eating on the funkier side, but knew Danielle would have none of that.

After sitting down and ordering smothered chicken, greens, potato salad, and yams, they looked at each other. There was a lot of ground to cover and Danielle, now fully discerning

Dwayne's gray mood, was afraid to start. *A neutral question, perhaps?*

"I've told you about my day, now tell me about yours."

"I was told that my writing was too black and needed upgrading." His voice was flat and bitter.

"Who said that?"

"The managing editor of *Billboard*."

"How could he say that? I thought they wanted to hire you."

"The New York office does. But the managing editor is in L.A. and apparently has his own candidate for the spot."

"Dwayne, that man obviously cannot read. You are truly a fine writer and *Billboard* is probably the worst-written magazine you contribute to."

"Yeah, well, I guess I should have told you I wasn't in the greatest mood. It is not every day I'm told I can't write. Or that I write 'black English.' You know—slang illiteracy."

"What happens now?"

"The New York people are going to fight for me and see what they can do. If they bring on a person to cover black music full-time, it means a lot fewer freelance assignments and a significant cash flow decrease." Dwayne sighed. "You won't be able to stop by my place tonight, will you? What am I thinking? I know you have a lot of work to do."

"Basically, yes I have a lot of work to finish. But this weekend we'll hang out." She reached her hand across the table taking his. "I promise."

"Did you get my letter?"

For a moment she thought about lying. Then she heard herself reply, "This morning," and knew they'd have to discuss it. As sensitive as Dwayne was now, Danielle was worried where this talk might lead. "I read it on the bus and train to school. I was glad you felt you could open up to me. It must have been so hard to write. I admire you for it."

"What about what I said?" he asked quickly.

Just then their meal arrived and there was a brief moratorium on serious talk. As soon as the waiter turned away, Dwayne said, "I know you're disappointed. You don't have to tell me that. I just want to know that you'll bear with me."

"Of course I will," she said, smiling. Danielle squeezed his hand and locked eyes with him. "Whatever you want I will give. I just want the same from you." With a sweet smile she added, "Just a fair exchange of affection. It's not so hard."

"Baby, that is really what it is all about," Dwayne said. He then quickly dipped the back of her hand into his smothered chicken and licked it.

"Dwayne!" she laughed and snatched her hand away.

It was 3:13 in the morning and Rahiem sat silently behind a long table where his turntables and beat box rested. He took a long drag off the fat joint in his right hand and then closed his eyes. Smoke flowed out his open mouth. Then he mouthed a beat. "Bop-bop-bop-baba-ba-ba-ba-ba!" Rahiem did this a couple of times. Then he stood up and stuck the joint in his mouth. Using his two index fingers, he tapped out that rhythm on his beat box. He closed his eyes and began to fall inside the groove as if the groove were a dream and he were dead asleep.

The door to Joint-ski's bedroom opened and the rapper, looking drained and smelly in a tank top and Georgetown shorts, stumbled into the hallway. Rahiem opened his eyes briefly to acknowledge Joint-ski and then closed them again. Joint-ski walked into the living room, past the sofa, and over to Rahiem, where he plucked the joint from his deejay's lips and stuck it between his.

Joint-ski stood there, puffing and listening for a while, before he flopped onto the sofa. He tossed his rhyming dictionary to the floor and pulled a Mead composition notebook from under his butt. Sliding his hand into the sofa's folds, he liberated a blue felt tip pen. He listened to Rahiem, then said, "Keep it right there." Rahiem didn't reply but kept the rhythm steady. With his mouth Joint-ski made percussion sounds, not words, as he searched for a cadence that would complement Rahiem's groove.

Out of Joint-ski's bedroom came Latonya, wearing Joint-ski's number 36 basketball jersey from Clinton High School. She walked barefoot into the living room and sat on the other end of the sofa from Joint-ski. She yawned, yet was keenly aware of what was going on. Joint-ski's words were now becoming audible. "Rap is my religion/and it's not a split decision" he intoned.

From inside Joint-ski's bedroom another girl emerged. Sixteen-year-old Trisha, garbed in jeans and a pink t-shirt, looked around evilly, as though a party had been planned and nobody invited her. She walked into the living room and demanded loudly, "So what the fuck is going on?" Interrupted in midsentence, Joint-ski turned toward her and shouted, "Shut the fuck up or get the fuck out!" Surprised and hurt, Trisha cursed and then retreated to the bedroom, slamming the door behind her.

Latonya giggled. Joint-ski smiled at her and then made a "Shhhhh" sign by putting his hand to his mouth. Rahiem ignored the whole thing and literally didn't miss a beat. He continued his pattern, occasionally adding slight modulations to it for flavor. Latonya, a Dance Inferno regular, nodded her head in time to the beat. She could feel it was gonna be a good one.

Joint-ski sat rocking to the beat on the sofa, mumbling under his breath and scribbling madly in his Mead composition book. "Rap is my religion/And I'm a soldier on a mission." It was another variation and he said it over and over again. And there Joint-ski and Rahiem stayed, working on and on well past the break of dawn.

Of all the politicians Danielle wanted for her paper, Dan Winfrey had been the easiest to get to. Part of it was that he didn't yet have an elective office; part of it was that he was a press hound. His assistant, Phyllis Cole, got back to her the day after Danielle called and set up an early evening meeting for two weeks later. A couple of days after that phone call his biography, along with news clips and position papers, were express-mailed to Connecticut. Clearly Winfrey was a man who sought as much press as he could get. Danielle loved it since she desperately needed a counterpoint to the Democratic Party boilerplate she'd gotten from Rangel, Clark, etc. And, after all, countering black Democratic rhetoric was what Winfrey was all about.

As New York's only visible practicing black Republican and a candidate for the Bronx's at-large city council seat, Winfrey was one of the most-quoted people in town. With the exception of CORE's born-again neoconservative Roy Innis, Winfrey was one of the rare sepia-toned politicians to attack Rev. Al Sharpton, oppose Jesse Jackson's presidential ambitions, criticize quotas, and have Ronald Reagan mention him at a presidential press conference as his favorite New Yorker.

Winfrey was viewed as a charming aberration by the local press. However, his positions were no surprise to Danielle, who knew most black families were quite conservative on a wide range of issues. Her parents both supported the death penalty, law and order, getting folks off welfare, and private jobs creation. And these were the issues Winfrey's literature emphasized. That the Republican Party dragged its feet on South African divestiture, drug rehabilitation services, and a number of other potentially tricky issues were matters he finessed by distancing himself from the national party when convenient. None of this would have flown in New York, however, if Winfrey hadn't been tall, slim, handsome, and elegant. In fact, the physical resemblance to Dave Winfield, the Yankees' star right-fielder was striking—it was as if the politician were a more compact version of the ballplayer.

Following up on the Judge's backhanded endorsement, Danielle had begun a clip file on Winfrey and gone from vaguely interested to actively intrigued. Enhancing her anticipation was his suggestion they meet for drinks at Jezebel's, a posh, black-owned Creole restaurant on 46th Street and Ninth Avenue. Its decoration was as ornate as a New Orleans bordello. Flowers of every description overflowed beautiful vases. Elaborate lace dresses dangled on nylon strings from the ceiling. Antique jewel boxes and books were carefully arranged on small glass night tables, while huge Warhol silk screens of Muhammad Ali and Miriam Makeba hung next to French caricatures of Negroes and Negresses from the thirties. The gauzy pink lampshades and the candles atop each table gave Jezebel's a cozy warmth that always transported Danielle. Ernest and Von had first taken her there, which gave her one more reason to love them.

"Miss Embry?"

"Yes, I am. So nice to meet you, Mr. Winfrey."

He said, "Nice to meet you too," and then laid on that telegenic smile. She quickly took inventory: Black loafers. Blue suit. Red tie. Briefcase. Burberry raincoat. Thick mustache. Long eyelashes. The Moynihan Report under his arm. *Lovely,* Danielle thought.

"I'm sorry I harassed your secretary, but I felt I really needed your input into my piece," she said rapidly. "I mean, I know your schedule is packed, so for you to meet me, especially in the evening, was generous—"

He cut off her babbling with a firm hand on her forearm. "Ms. Embry, I respected your thesis about politics in this town post-Powell. Besides, my wife and I always come here when things get thick."

Danielle's disappointment registered so nakedly on her face that Winfrey said, "For the next hour I'm all yours." He laid the smile on her again and she got goose bumps.

He reached inside his suit and pulled out a yellow button with red words in black letters. "Wear this at your leisure." It read, **"WAIT! I'M A REPUBLICAN!"** "Everybody assumes a black politician has to be a liberal Democrat. People—white people—used to walk right past me. This button stops commuters in their running shoes. Who says conservatives have no sense of humor?" *Not you,* she thought.

They sat down at a small table in the lounge area. He ordered a gin and tonic; she had a Chardonnay. When she pulled out a tape recorder Winfrey scowled. Then the smile. Then he said, "No taping, all right? Just notes. I thought my secretary told you." He lied. She could feel it, but there was no need for a fight.

"I'm just happy you made time for me."

"Thank you."

A half hour into the conversation Danielle realized why Winfrey didn't want the interview recorded. Underneath his neoconservative clothes were quite a few liberal attitudes—slash the defense budget, aggressive civil-rights-law enforcement, and less skepticism about the ability of the government to alter social conditions than a Republican candidate should admit.

For the purpose of her paper, however, Winfrey was right on time: "The basic problem with Rangel, as well as Dinkins, Patterson, and Sutton, is not liberal conceptions of social engineering, but pisspoor management skills. These brothers, like the entire Democratic party, have not shown they know how to run anything well. I say to black New York, 'Don't listen to what they say. Look at what they do.' Republicans have always been better at making the trains run on time which, for example, is the difference between Rockefeller and Carey. New York began falling apart when Carey was governor and Carter was president."

"Mr. Winfrey, 'New York: Drop Dead' came about when Ford was in the White House. Right now you sound more like an old-line Rockefeller Republican than a now-fashionable neoconservative."

"If you're black and Republican these days, the more associated with the right you are, the more it sounds like you have a fresh idea. I always attempt to be fresh."

"That's very pragmatic."

He just aimed and fired the smile.

"How'd you wind up in politics?" she continued. "Up until the last few years you'd been a surgeon."

"My wife," he said. "I always liked people. Was always talking politics in the office. She said I did more talking than cutting."

"I believe I read that you and your wife practiced medicine together."

"Yes, it was wonderful. I really miss medicine. There's a satisfaction in helping one person at a time and seeing the direct result that's hard to beat. But this city is crying out for a critique of black leadership. I just started opening my mouth and people noticed."

"Some suggest you'll eventually challenge Rangel."

With a grin that belied his words, he said, "A campaign against Rangel is too far in the future to contemplate. Now, can I ask you a question?"

"Sure."

"Your writing samples and thesis topic are very critical of the Democratic Party. Does that mean you don't automatically hate Republicans?"

"Why do you ask?"

"I'm trying to build an organization." He was very serious. There was steel behind that smile. "I'm not looking to the old hacks or the old ideas. I'm trying to find a new direction for the hardworking black folks of the city. It may not work. This neocon philosophy has lots of flaws, but look what liberalism has produced—hacks, poverty pimps, and tired old men still dreaming of bus boycotts and sit-ins when we need to build skills in our community. Doors are open but we can't walk through."

"Are you trying to procure me?" she said mischievously.

The smile was back. "No, Miss Embry, not procure. Recruit. Someone with your analytical and writing skills would be a dynamite congressional aide."

"Congressional aide?"

"You know, down the road."

"Oh."

Despite the threat of snow, Dwayne attempted to recapture the magic of their first date on Danielle's twenty-seventh birthday. This November night they had dinner at a small Hunan-style Chinese restaurant on the West Side, saw a lousy play at the Negro Ensemble Company, and checked out the Ron Carter Quintet at the Village Vanguard. Danielle observed approvingly, "This has been a very bourgie evening, Dwayne. I hope you know that."

"It's not over yet, Ms. Embry."

He let Danielle walk into his apartment first and didn't turn the lights on when he followed her in.

"What's going on?"

"Just walk into the living room."

In the darkness two Day-Glo graffiti posters hung on the walls. One was marked "Dwayne-ski!" The other "Danny-Dee!" Danielle laughed. "Who did this?" Dwayne wasn't behind her anymore. "Dwayne?"

She started to walk toward his bedroom when she heard a drum machine beat. Now carrying a huge portable cassette player, Dwayne entered the living room with the volume pushed to ten. Over the instrumental track to Herman Kelly's "Dance to the Drummer's Beat," Dwayne started rapping.

The Buppies Rap/uh uh/ uh uh uh!
A Buppie is a Yuppie/Only they are black,
I wear Brooks Brothers suits/she wears Ann Klein slacks
Together we dance/but we never sweat
And these are the things that Buppies do

The Buppie Rap/uh uh/uh uh uh!
Sag Harbor days/Bristol Cream nights
We don't wanna talk black/we sure ain't white!
To meet a Buppie girl/all you need to do
Is wear a nice wool suit and Gucci shoes
Engineer/lawyer/is on the one
But if you're a sanitation man/you won't get none
To date a Buppie man/just like me
Talk quiche/talk sushi/talk going down
'Cause we Dudes/uh uh/like to eat out
Buppies learn early to do right, not wrong
We learn it from Jacks/we go greek all the way
Sigma/Delta/AKA

Buppies think preppie/Buppies work hard
Buppies think profiling's part of the job
BMWs are our car/Izod shirts our calling cards
Howard/Morehouse/Spellman/Cheyney State
Are our schools/At these institutions
Buppies learn the rules

One! Buppies aren't funky/though we may be cool
Two! Buppies get horny/but we never drool
Three! Buppies support black charities
Especially if it's noted in *Essence* magazine!
That's the end of my Buppie tale
Except to say uh uh uh.

Danielle was on the floor laughing. Dwayne stood over her with a big grin and held out a gold chain with a small sign that said, **DANIELLE.**

"You my baby doll or what?"

"Only if you give me some of that slick b-boy tongue."

He said, "How vulgar," and leaned over her with his chains dangling just above her head.

"Come on down here and see if you can turn me out."

"So it's true what they say about suburban girls."

A few hours later Danielle woke up and saw Dwayne staring at the ceiling with one arm stretched across his forehead. It was about 3:30 a.m. and snow was falling softly from the sky.

"What are you thinking about?" she asked.

"You won't believe this, but Billy Joel."

"You aren't lying in bed with me thinking about Billy Joel?"

Embarrassed, Dwayne said, "He has this song called 'Allentown.' It's probably the best thing he's ever written."

"That song's about unemployment in Pennsylvania."

"That's right."

"There was a piece about it on the 'CBS Evening News.'"

"Really?"

Proud that she knew something about music that Dwayne

didn't, Danielle continued, "The mayor of Allentown invited him to do a concert there and Joel accepted."

"Well, I was thinking about this line where Joel sings about our parents never telling us what the deal was in life. How things like diamonds and coal and the battle over natural resources could control your life."

"Why are you thinking about that?"

"Because Joel's talking about how schools fill your head with dogma. But you don't learn a thing about the real world, like natural resources and tax returns."

Now intrigued, Danielle asked, "How do you work tax returns into this?"

"We spend hours on algebra in school. But when we graduate from high school we can't fill out income tax forms, so we spend the rest of our lives slaves to H and R Block."

"True."

"You know when I realized what we're taught is a joke?"

"Tell me." As he talked she rubbed his back and thighs.

"The gas shortage, back when we were in high school. The country's in chaos. No gas. No transportation. No basketball games. No shopping. People shooting each other over a space in line. It hit me that America did not rule the world. Natural resources did. Without resources, and the goodwill and/or bribery of the world, America was brought to its knees."

"Preach, Brother Dwayne!"

"You have to control your own thing. You have to develop a resource—yourself—and work for yourself. Otherwise you are just another piece of this broken-down machine. The brightest of us are just part of the system, and look what it has gotten us: some nice clothes and a weekend retreat in the Poconos."

"I didn't see you complaining when we were making love in front of the fireplace."

"That was because of you." He kissed her. Then he was back to his rap. "My point is, is a house in the Poconos the end of that dream?"

Danielle felt the subtext and, never one to back down from a challenge, said, "It *is* part of the package. I haven't heard you volunteer to move back to the projects. You are not a b-boy."

"I *am* a b-boy intellectual."

"You're a buppie in development."

"Then I say you don't know me."

"You can fight it but one day you're going to be like Ernest."

"You wish," he answered quickly.

She said, "I know," just as fast and stopped rubbing his body.

"Is that our future? A place on the West Side, a place in the mountains, brunch in the morning, and Sag Harbor weekends?"

Danielle cut him a dirty look. "You won't make me feel guilty about wanting to enjoy life. I know what I want. So do you."

"Danielle, I'm not sure what I want."

"You just want an argument." Her face was getting red.

Way too vehemently, he retorted, "No—I just want you to accept our differences and not talk yourself into seeing things that aren't there."

"Okay. You win."

Danielle jumped out of bed, stomped into the bathroom, and slammed the door behind her. Dwayne sat on the edge of the bed and stared out the window. On occasion he scratched his beard.

When Danielle re-entered the room, she snatched up a pillow and took the top sheet off the bed.

"I'm sleeping on the sofa."

"Why?"

"Because you are being cruel and I don't deserve it. When you explain your nasty attitude I'll come back."

"I was just thinking out loud," he said sheepishly.

"Your brains are for thinking. Not your mouth."

Danielle went out into the living room, dropped onto the sofa, and fell asleep. Dwayne stood over her. *Why did she get so worked up? I didn't mean it as an attack on her character or an insult or anything like that. Wait until Reggie sees this. My girl-friend on the living room sofa.*

When Dwayne woke up the next day, Danielle lay beside

him, her face moist from crying. He'd meant what he'd said but as usual his delivery sucked. He stroked Danielle's hair. Honesty was great for reviews, but caused terrible trouble in real life. But he was surprised she was so sensitive. *Just say "I love you" and everything will be cool. Like Ernest and Von. Like Reggie and Kelly Love Chase. Like half the world. I should be able to say the words to Danielle,* he thought. He felt like shouting "I love you" five times into her face, but it was just an urge. It passed.

Inside Danielle's head was unfolding a nightmare in 70mm with Dolby sound. Hitchcock was behind the camera. Danielle stood at the center of a large party, only no one seemed to know her. Her loved ones—mother, father, Dwayne, Jacksina, T.J., Morris, everybody—ignored her and then disappeared into the crowd. She passed one mirror. Then another. Then another. She stopped and saw herself in profile. Her stomach was swollen, huge and round and gently throbbing. Danielle's eyes opened, but her mind was still at the horrible party. She awoke as agitated as when she'd fallen asleep.

He said, "Hello."

"I'm not talking to you."

Working hard at being upbeat, Dwayne said, "We are young and in love. Christmas is coming up. The world is white with snow. Look at it." She sat up and looked out the window over his shoulder. He continued, "Danielle, I'm sorry about last night. I really am."

Her eyes stayed focused out the window. "I haven't been feeling well. Thinking about seeing a doctor."

"Tension, baby. Papers due. Working on your Rangel epic. You made major changes in your life this year. It's all just coming down on you at the end of the year."

Danielle felt dizzy. She got up and wobbled into the bathroom. Dwayne came in and patted her back.

"Baby, what's wrong?"

It was a "magic week." That's what Dwayne called the days between Christmas and New Year's, a time when New York was full of the excitement the mayor always talked about. Red, green, orange, and yellow lights flickered on every midtown street. The department stores were concrete Christmas trees. Dressed in furs and leather boots, arms filled with bags labeled Macy's, Bloomingdale's, Orbach's, New Yorkers marched on shopping missions. The latest movies filled Times Square, and the children of the city packed theaters and fast-food establishments with dates, schoolmates, and pockets stuffed with rolling paper. Walking up Seventh Avenue, his eyes taking in all the rituals of celebration, Dwayne wished he could partake. Usually this was his favorite week of the year. Moments of freedom to savor before the grimness of January.

But as 1982 approached 1983, Dwayne's life was out of control. Danielle was pregnant. She'd found out two weeks before Christmas and told him in her parents' basement.

Dwayne had reached 57th Street, next to Carnegie Hall, but all he could see were Danielle's eyes and lips. No city sounds penetrated his mind. Only the large sound of her announcing she was pregnant.

"I have something to tell you." He had finished her sentence. He hugged her. And then, he didn't know why, started laughing. It was a laugh of nerves, an explosion of anxiety, a giggle of despair. Danielle was initially relieved by Dwayne's strange good humor. She had dreaded this moment since leaving Dr. McCabe's East Side office and walking into the coldest night in her memory. Despite his laughter, Danielle grabbed Dwayne and held his head against her breast like a baby. Then he began sucking her breast through her t-shirt and, though Danielle's mother was hanging pots in the kitchen, they made love with eerie abandon.

The other times had been accidents. Popular lore says black men—cold, horny, heartless bastards—are cavalier about the question of pregnancy. Dwayne could have told you differently. He sat stiffly on the E train, staring into space as the subway rolled toward Queens. Simple teenage stupidity. He didn't even remember the first girl's name, only recalling that she lived on 140th Street in Harlem. They met at a disco on 56th Street. Lust at first sight. A few days later that lust was consummated clumsily in his mother's basement. Just one of those mistakes. They give you condoms in sex education class. Who shows you how to put them on? After some days of panic, Dwayne scraped up the money for an abortion. He assumed she'd had it, since he never heard from her again.

Then there was his high school sweetheart, Candi Bailey. She'd gotten pregnant the summer after he graduated, but Dwayne didn't know it until after the abortion. Candi had just gone over to Planned Parenthood and, in her own words, "Had it taken care of." Dwayne was hurt that Candi hadn't asked for money, comfort, or advice. It was as though she felt Dwayne couldn't have handled the pressure.

As he walked up Parsons Boulevard he knew the heat was on, and he hoped Reggie wasn't at a session. Sitting at the kitchen table, reading *Sports Illustrated* while his roast beef warmed in the microwave, Reggie received the news in silence. Finally, after he finished a piece on the Philadelphia 76ers, he said, "You are no longer in control of your fate, Mr. Robinson. Your future now depends on the attitude of the woman you foolishly injected with your sperm."

"But what can *I* do?"

"Nothing."

"There has *got* to be something."

"Okay. Does she want the baby?"

"She does not want the baby, but she isn't crazy about having an abortion either."

"That, my friend, is not good."

"I'm not sure if I love her."

"That's got nothing to do with this problem."

"Nothing?"

"If she thinks that you do in fact love her, it could push her into having the baby. She'll think, 'If Dwayne loves me, we could make it.' "

"No, we can't."

"If she thinks you can, Mr. Robinson, you'll be a daddy as

sure as you're not Hemingway. Might as well just begin saving up those dollars."

Dwayne slumped in his seat, thinking about changing diapers.

"Reggie, I'm scared."

"You are going to have to be pragmatic yet sincere. Tell her how you feel and then . . . That's it. After that, it's up to her."

FIVE

Water trickled down a sewer pipe, sending rats scurrying through garbage. It was 2:35 a.m. in Manhattan, and on the subway platform Dwayne's foot pushed an empty Budweiser can, first to the right, then to the left, then over onto the tracks. Across the tracks on the downtown platform a young white couple, wearing matching black boots, tight black jeans, and black leather jackets, fondled each other's private parts and giggled while Dwayne stared enviously.

Loud, laughing male voices echoed through the catacombs known otherwise as the Union Square subway station. At this time of night any laughter, especially young teen laughter, was not reassuring.

Immediately Dwayne considered the possibility of being a statistic in a Transit Authority crime report. He remembered an afternoon last winter. He was sitting in an empty BMT car when a posse of six high-school-age brothers passed by. They settled at the other end of the car, talking loud, acting young. Maybe a couple were "dusty," but Dwayne gave them the benefit of the doubt. One slim blood, wearing his Yankee cap sideways, Lee jeans, and unlaced Adidas, leaned back on a door and scoped Dwayne. Dwayne stared back. They made defiant eye contact. The blood whispered something to a friend. A pause. Then he received a cigarette. This reckless eyeballing went on for two stops. Dwayne watched him from the corner of one eye and he straight-out stared at Dwayne. Next stop Dwayne exited, and as the subway pulled out of the station, he heard laughter—that same chilling, young-boy laughter.

Except for a bag lady, about fifty feet away, curled up beneath a tattered pink blanket turned crimson by dirt, no one else was on the uptown platform. Dwayne cursed the TA as not one, not two, but three N trains rattled through the station, going downtown. The couple, apparently reluctant to shift positions, finally got on the third train. The young male voices disappeared too, as did the faint ripple of anxiety that accompanied them.

Dwayne remembered when he was seventeen, constantly horny, and every date was an adventure: long waits in damp, benchless and toiletless stations, cursing having no money, cursing the cold, cursing dating women who lived in the ass end of Queens, and cursing not getting "any" so that these trips wouldn't be necessary, or at least would be undertaken in a relaxed state of mind.

Of course relaxation on a subway was a dangerous luxury. Sleep on a platform or in a train? That was only for municipal workers, the ignorant, or the high. He observed that anyone who even closes his eyes on the IRT or BMT had to be profoundly optimistic. If it hadn't been a rainy Friday night, if he hadn't been wearing beat-down Adidas and a black Pittsburgh Pirates cap, the cab outside Pay Day might have taken him home. But that's how he was dressed and that was that. Dwayne was well past the point when getting ignored by a white driver bothered him. It was the drivers from Kingston and Seoul and Zaire who now irritated him. The cabbie who dissed Dwayne tonight was Asian. When Dwayne said his destination was Queens, the man refused to open the back door. Instead, he made a U-turn and stopped by two young white women strolling along under a plaid umbrella. *If I'd been with Danielle it wouldn't have happened. Or it still might have happened but the odds would have been fairer. Without her I'm just another b-boy. With her I'm a better risk. Hell,* he thought, *with her I'm a better everything.*

As he pondered this minor injustice, two TA cops marched up the concrete staircase that connects the N and R lines to the

LL. One was black, one was white, and both were rapping excitedly about the Mets. Their presence should have made Dwayne feel secure. Instead, images—bad images—flashed on his internal video screen. Last summer, dressed much as he was now, he was walking past the Guggenheim Museum when he noticed three pedestrians staring his way with bugged eyes. One of them pointed at him. Quicker than you can say "Bang!" a sergeant leaped from a van and grabbed him by the arm. Three of New York's finest surrounded him. The sergeant turned to a baby-faced black cop and asked, "Well?" The brother cop studied Dwayne a moment and nodded, "No." The sergeant let go of Dwayne's arm, said "Sorry," and they were gone.

By the time Dwayne awoke from his latest paranoid memory, the cops, who hadn't paid him any notice as they jabbered about the 1969 Mets, had disappeared. Dwayne began counting the number of rats he saw running across the tracks. *One . . . two . . .* Then the rumble of the uptown N chased them away.

Dwayne shared a car with a big homeless man cursed with charcoal-black feet, an Italian dude wearing "Saturday Night Fever" gear, asleep and stinking of beer, and a Woody Allen lookalike peering at the Sunday *News* through thick glasses. The train hit every local stop in Queens as time trickled past three.

Mrs. Embry was complaining that Danielle was disrespecting her. Whenever Jean Embry picked up the phone on this snowy late December Sunday Danielle was sure to be on it. She'd yell, "Mother, please!" and Mrs. Embry would hang up. *When is that young woman going to get off the phone?* Luckily she didn't know what her baby girl was talking about, for in making a crucial decision about her life, Embry's daughter was consulting a lot of people, but not her.

Jacksina's advice was blunt and graphic. "Have the abortion, Danny," she urged. "But know it will not be pretty." Jacksina admitted she'd already been through two, and that a doctor had told her one more and she could forget about children. "I wish my sex drive was as feeble as my uterus," Jacksina joked, a flippancy that didn't do much to lift Danielle's spirits. She now understood some of the price Jacksina paid for her lifestyle.

Next she rang Ernest and Von. They were kind, supportive, understanding, and vehemently opposed to her having a baby out of wedlock. Unless her relationship with Dwayne was rocksolid, and plans for the child made with the cooperation of everyone involved, especially her parents, it would be foolish to shoulder the demands of child-rearing alone. Moreover, it could totally derail her career. Which led Danielle to ask something she'd often wondered about: "Why haven't you had a baby?" After an embarrassed pause, Ernest told Danielle they'd been trying for the past three years. Which, in turn, led Danielle to feel guilty about the perverse sense of accomplishment that washed over her. She had accomplished something Ernest and Von hadn't. As with Jacksina, Danielle listened more than she spoke, not saying what she'd do, even when asked.

Her last call was to T.J., who could feel his stomach burn with anger, then threatened to kick Dwayne's no-good skinny ass.

"T.J., it was both our faults. He didn't screw me. We made love."

"Do you love him?"

"I didn't call for that, either."

"You should not have this baby."

"Why not?"

"Why not? Why not? What are you? Fucking crazy? I know you aren't ready, and even if you were, Dwayne Robinson is not the man."

"Okay. That's enough. 'Bye."

"What are you going to do?"

"Tell you later."

It was New Year's Eve and they were going to have fun. Dwayne met Danielle at the Port Authority at 8:30. They walked over to Video Shack at 47th Street and Broadway, where he purchased Hitchcock's *The 39 Steps*. On their way to the subway they walked past people wearing funny paper hats and blowing noisemakers and cops shifting barricades. On the ride out to Queens, Dwayne read passages from Ray Charles' "Brother Ray" into her ear as she snuggled up against him. At Parsons Boulevard they stopped at the Chink-a-Rican place for Dwayne and at McDonald's for Danielle. As they entered the apartment, Reggie was on his way out.

He smiled sweetly. "It's always lovely to see a family spend the holidays together. Happy New Year!"

Danielle dropped her bag on the table and sighed. Dwayne told her to forget Reggie's crack and went into the kitchen. With forced good humor they ate, watched *The 39 Steps*, and sipped from the first of two bottles of Freixenet's Cordon Negro. Dwayne, usually an aggressive nondrinker, was getting ripped, while Danielle's intake merely increased her anxiety.

"Except for you, Danielle, this has been a bad year."

"Your writing seems to be going well. You're always working on a piece for some magazine or another."

"I'm in a rut. I write articles. People seem to like them. But I have no strong book ideas."

"I don't understand why no one at Doubleday ever contacted you. I'll call again after the holiday."

"What's the use? I really don't have a solid idea." Using the remote control dial to flick from ABC to NBC to CBS, they watched the old year die. Pictures of Times Square. Pictures of digital numbers clicking away. Pictures of Dick Clark. Pictures of singers in cummerbunds. Pictures of middle-aged couples boogeying to big-band standards.

Glassy-eyed, Dwayne surveyed it sardonically. He turned to see that Danielle was staring at him from the other end of the sofa, her hands resting on her stomach. Dwayne smiled. Danielle did not.

"I can't wait any longer. I've been pregnant almost two months, and we haven't really discussed what we're going to do."

"Can we talk next year?" Dwayne said it lightly, yet inside he was aware of his own heartbeat.

"No. We cannot talk next year."

Danielle clicked off the television and sat back down, her hands folded on her belly. "I used to dream about being pregnant," she began cautiously. "I would listen to my sisters talk about it. Now I feel life inside me. Life we made. I would like to describe it to you. I would like to break it down, detail by detail, describe it—do all the things you do with words. I wish you could feel what I feel."

She watched him for a long moment. "There's no way you could want to have this baby. You are too selfish. You have too much to do. And I love that about you. All that energy and so little time. A baby would drive you crazy. But I could handle the fact that my friends would disapprove. That my career would be on hold. I could freelance edit. I could teach. I know I could make it. But not without you."

She moved toward him, her face filling his eyes until there was nothing else in the room. "I want to be in the middle of politics and on TV and all that too. But the lives my parents led weren't so bad either. A houseful of kids. Lots of love. Together we could do it." For the first time since she had started talking, Danielle smiled.

Dwayne licked his lips, then stood up and paced around the room. He looked at her. He looked at the walls. "You know me so well," he said. "So damn well. I had a nice speech too, but I can't remember it now. So where am I? I am standing in my living room at the beginning of 1983 about to justify something that I think is right. No, not right, but the right thing for us. Now it seems mean. You want me to prove you wrong. You want me to say, 'I'm *not* selfish. I love you. Together, baby, we will make it through.' All that shit. Danielle, I've been with you because you're smart. Now you're being devious."

She was furious. "Dwayne, how can you interpret my words that way?"

"What you said is that you want the baby and if I say 'Yeah' you will have it. That is what you said. Jerry Falwell couldn't have been clearer. How could you work me like that? I feel real bad that you could do that. You could have just said, 'I want it.' But, no, you had to critique me at the same time. On one hand this, on the other that. Bottom line: one, I wouldn't have a child without a father if I were you, and two, I don't want a baby by a woman I like a lot, but I do not love."

He stopped and let that last sentence dangle in the air. Now he had told the big lie, a lie as large and monstrous as any his parents had told him, a stabbing sick lie. But he knew it would work. He flopped onto the floor by the television, pushed the on button, and peered into Dick Clark's youthfully weathered face, seeking somehow to distance himself from what he had just said.

Danielle sat staring at the strands of black hair on the back of his head, wanting to kill him, then herself, then the birth-control-pill manufacturer, and then herself again, for getting involved with this selfish, silly little boy. *Fuck him—and don't cry.*

Nineteen eighty-three entered dressed in white. But by the end of the New Year's first week, the snow had been ground to thick gray slush. Even on the hills of Central Park it had lost its luster. Like January's sky, the park was now gray and dirty. Danielle looked at the sooty snow, then closed her eyes. T.J., driving carefully on the slippery street, was saying something about his insurance coverage helping her, but she didn't listen. When Joint-ski's "Break It Down" came on WBLS, Danielle didn't hear that either, even when her voice, saying "meow," came through the Volvo's speakers. *T.J. really cares about me a great deal,* she thought. *I mean, he has always gone all-out for me. Maybe he really does love me. And not as a friend. What a strange thing to realize now. Fascinating. The twists your mind makes under stress.* T.J. turned right on 92nd Street and Madison.

"Stop at the corner," she said. T.J. pulled over to the southeast corner of 92nd and Madison.

"Want me to wait?"

"No, don't."

"Where is he?"

"Inside. He's always early." She spoke flatly.

"Let me pick you up."

"No."

"Where are you going after this?"

"I'll call you later."

"I hate that motherfucker."

"No, don't hate him. Just love me."

T.J.'s face grew red. She reached over, hugged him, and then she was out of the car and down the block, leaving T.J. in his car with Joint-ski on the radio and the motor running.

The office of Dr. Jennifer McCabe was fronted by a small outer room with gray walls and gray furniture. Some *Interior Decorating* magazines were stacked neatly on a coffee table, and a mounted reprint from *Essence* magazine about Dr. McCabe hung on the wall. An owlish Jamaican receptionist glanced up from behind the front desk, but Danielle was looking at Dwayne Robinson sitting nervously on the couch. He wore the pained expression of a lost little boy.

"Hey."

"Hello," she said.

Danielle went to the desk and introduced herself, then turned and went over to the couch. She sat next to Dwayne as if he were surrounded by a wall of air.

"How are you?"

"Oh, I don't know," she replied.

"I could have picked you up."

"It was all right. My father dropped me off."

"You told him?"

"I told him I had an interview over here."

Why is she lying? Dwayne saw her get out of T.J.'s car. No time for that now, though.

"Dr. McCabe won't talk to me," he said.

"She isn't very warm to me either, and I'm the one going through with this."

"Who recommended her?"

"Friends."

"And *Essence* magazine," he said, gesturing toward the mounted article.

Just then Dr. McCabe, a stern-looking, attractive dark-skinned woman in her late forties, emerged from her office. The parents-not-to-be stood up.

"Let me speak to you, Ms. Embry," she said. She didn't even look at Dwayne. They entered her office. Dr. McCabe did not even ask Danielle to be seated.

"This is your last chance to change your mind."

"I understand that."

"It is *your* body."

Danielle bit her lips as the doctor continued. "I want you to walk over to the park and then back. Take your time. If you still want to do this, we will proceed. But let me tell you—I prefer to *deliver* babies."

Danielle slowly entered the reception area, put on her coat, told Dwayne "Be right back," and went out the door. She paused at the head of the steps leading to the street. *Am I ready to bring this child into the world or not?* She had only a few minutes in which to decide. In spite of the unpleasant scene on New Year's, Danielle was certain that if she went ahead and had the baby, Dwayne would eventually pitch in and do his part. *Yes, he is selfish and immature . . . The immaturity would probably pass. Probably . . . He does love me. I know it . . . Doesn't that count for something? But that cold, detached streak—it's real, too . . . As real as his love for me . . . Its nastiness would be part of having the baby . . . But he'd love that baby . . . Would he hate me? . . . I want the baby . . . I want Dwayne . . . I want both . . . I want love . . . Not love with resignation . . . I'm too young to settle : . . No.*

She turned around and went back into the building. The walk could wait.

Peering out between the window blinds, Dwayne watched slow-moving cars splash dirty slush onto the sidewalks. A postman was dropping off mail at a brownstone across the street. He could see an elderly woman in a nearby building removing Christmas lights. Then she pulled the shade. All he could think was, *The holidays are over now. They are over now. They are . . .*

Danielle walked past him as though he didn't exist. Dr. Mc-
Cabe was waiting for her at the open door of a small room, lit by
fluorescent lights, halfway down the hallway. "Well—what did
you decide?"

"Yes."

The door closed behind them.

As the Jamaican receptionist entered Dwayne's check in a
ledger book, he thought he could hear the hum of the suction
machine, but decided it was just cars going by.

Dr. McCabe's office gradually filled with black women.
Most were in their thirties. They were chic, and they spoke in
low voices about kids, clubs, husbands, and dinner parties
while ignoring his presence. Dwayne pretended to read a magazine while studying them, knowing that Danielle would be one
of them in ten years.

Each time the doctor appeared and called one of their names,
Dwayne looked up from his unread magazine and smiled at her
hopefully, expecting a status report, but an hour passed before
the receptionist finally motioned for him to follow her into the
operating room, then left and closed the door.

Danielle lay on the table in a knee-length surgical gown, on
her back. Her face was turned toward the wall. Dwayne sat on a
tiny low stool next to her, reached up, and took her hand. It was
cold. He kissed it and she turned her head and looked at him.
Her face was beautiful and drained-looking.

"We made it," she said.

"How are you?"

"Tired." She smiled. "No dancing tonight, Dwayne."

"You sure?"

She smiled again, and said, "Maybe I'll get my second
wind," which made him fell guiltier.

The receptionist knocked and entered. "Excuse me—the
doctor needs this room in five minutes."

Dwayne scowled at her back as she left, then helped Danielle
get off the table and dress. She noticed that his touch was more
gentle than she could ever remember. She had never felt so
weak, and wondered if there was any blood left in her body. As

Dwayne helped her button her blouse, she thought she would pass out, and had to grab the edge of the table. Dwayne held her tightly and whispered, "It'll be okay, baby . . . okay." But as they left the room she imagined that her body was hollow.

Dr. McCabe didn't help. After rapidly running down the best procedures for recovery and telling Danielle not to be concerned about bleeding, she said coolly, "And sexual activity should not resume for at least six weeks." Then she added with a nasty edge, "Though *some* people can't wait and begin in four." It wasn't the words, but the tone that insulted Danielle. *She said that like we're a pair of dogs anxious to start humping as soon as we go outside.*

"That tone was not necessary, Dr. McCabe."

"I'm sorry you're offended," she said crisply. "But I've been frank with you from the beginning. That doesn't stop now. See you in two weeks."

Outside, under a salt-and-pepper sky, Dwayne carried Danielle's bag in his right hand and wrapped his left arm around her waist.

"I got a surprise for you."

"What?"

"Right here."

Before them stood Joint-ski's long red Electra 225, aka the Batmobile. Behind the wheel was Joint-ski's driver/deejay, Rahiem. Gaudily appointed—someone had spray-painted the interior flaming red—the 225 was also spacious. Danielle was able to lie down and sleep all the way to Queens.

She stayed at Dwayne's apartment for three days. He carried her when she had to go to the bathroom. He watched her bleed. At night she held on to him, not knowing whether she wanted to fondle his chest or tear out his heart. Most of the time she slept, but she was able to dictate parts of her term paper to Dwayne, and he delivered it to school. They avoided all serious subjects, especially ones concerning their futures.

A week after the abortion Danielle was waiting at the Columbus Circle subway station to transfer to a D or A downtown express.

She noticed a Latino couple, both about twenty, standing near each other as an uptown train pulled in across the way. Their body language announced that they were together, or had been, though neither spoke and they were looking straight ahead. As the doors of the train opened, the girl stepped inside and darted over to a window. She leaned her forehead against it and stared out at the platform, her face without expression.

The doors closed. In the moments before the train pulled off, Danielle saw the man smack a concrete pillar with his open palm, hard, then turn away. There had been no eye contact between the couple, but across the platform Danielle could feel them—confused and wretched—calling out to each other through the space, through the pain, through the glass and steel and bodies.

The train pulled off, and the girl seemed to shrivel. She stumbled backwards into a seat, turned, and pressed her forehead against a window again, though now there was nothing to see. Then the train was lost to sight. Danielle didn't think the girl was crying at that moment, but she felt her own tears begin, and, embarrassed, wiped her eyes with a tissue.

A compelling mesh of young and veteran musicians stood on the stage of Avery Fisher Hall. Drummer Tony Williams, bassist Ron Carter, and pianist Herbie Hancock enjoyed many triumphs during their long careers as jazz improvisers. But they will be forever linked with Miles Davis, circa 1963–68, when they formed the rhythm section of, perhaps, the trumpeter's most cohesive band. Watching them, reunited for this tour, gave listeners a taste of history. The front men this evening, trumpeter Wynton and saxophonist Branford Marsalis, two twenty-something phenomena, were attending elementary school in New Orleans when Williams, Carter, and Hancock appeared on Davis' "My Funny Valentine." These two brash young lions, resplendent in well-tailored suits, had revived interest in traditional jazz with their style and talent. Despite the age difference between the rhythm section and soloists, all five players shared similar musical aesthetics.

For most of the 2,738 nicely attired patrons in this elegant beige auditorium, the onstage mix of experience, age, and youth was an engaging musical gimmick that guaranteed a concert of classic compositions played with vigor. But for one couple in orchestra center, Row F, the music wasn't about bridging generations, it was about them. Judge Peters and Jacksina sat holding hands as in unison Wynton and Branford played the opening bars to one of Hancock's most famous melodies, "Maiden Voyage."

This date was both soothing and unsettling for Jacksina. She was thrilled to be out in public with the Judge, to be brazen about their love, to hold his hand in a roomful of strangers— even if she did it only when the lights went down. *I have nothing to lose,* she thought. *But he does.* Jacksina wondered why the Judge would risk putting his business out in the street. On the way over, in his Lincoln Continental, she asked, "Aren't you worried that people will see us?" He'd just chuckled and said proudly, "When a man has a woman as fine as you, he'd be foolish not to show her off."

Jacksina knew there was more to it. He'd be noticed. This would have repercussions, both private and public. Again she asked herself, *Why?* But she wouldn't let these worries ruin her evening. They were together in public, and no matter what lay ahead, this was a beautiful, life-affirming moment.

He whispered, "You hear how Wynton's playing?"

"Yes, baby."

"That's very much in the style of Lee Morgan. Remember I played that 'Sidewinder' album for you?"

"Oh, yeah." She clutched his arm in affirmation.

The Judge smiled at her, a smile that clarified to anyone who cared to look that they weren't father and daughter. His look shouted "Lust!" and the Judge was happy to display it.

Branford was soloing now; his tone bold and passionate. The Judge much preferred him to the more celebrated Wynton, whose approach he found too stiff. Something less didactic about Branford's playing struck a chord in the Judge. Or maybe he just held Wynton's classical recordings against him—the

Judge viewed jazzmen dabbling in European music with the same contempt he had for a lazy or inept public defender.

As for being in public with Jacksina—*well,* he thought, *it's going to come out.* He'd heard that the PBA was snooping around the courthouse for dirt. Word was they planned to use Winfrey to leak it. So why hide in the dark tonight when the light feels so good?

Neither the press nor the gossips nor the fear of scandal bothered the Judge this night. His only problem was his own insecurity. He was not really that old, and he was, he felt, quite handsome, and obviously successful. People had described the Judge as a slim, clean-shaven Ed Bradley, and he didn't disagree. Still, Jacksina was half his age. . . . In his rare moments of honest introspection, the Judge wondered if he could hold her. Every day she grew stronger, smarter, wiser; every day he just got older.

That's why, as Hancock slid suavely into his solo, the Judge peeked left, down the row, and across the aisle at a lanky young black man writing in a spiral reporter's notebook. The Judge tagged him as a music critic from the way his right foot tapped in time to Williams' hectic cymbal work and from his body language. No regular street reporters know jack about good music and, as was well known, the *Post* had no black reporters.

But that wasn't what caught the Judge's attention. It was the critic's glances at Jacksina and the way, for one uncomfortable moment, the Judge saw their eyes lock when she finally noticed him. His deep-seated insecurities throbbed through him like Ron Carter's bass lines. Then it passed. Jacksina returned her attention to the bandstand and what the Judge viewed as her acceptable admiration for Wynton and Branford.

The Judge didn't know that the look his date and the critic had exchanged was far from affectionate. To Jacksina, the critic, aka Dwayne Robinson, was an unwelcome spectator: an obnoxious jerk with probing eyes and a facile pen. There were plenty like him. Reading the venom hurled the Judge's way by the press had made her in general contemptuous of reporters, no matter what their color, and Dwayne looked like just another sorry specimen of that miserable tribe. So when Dwayne's eyes turned her way, Jacksina hit him with a steely stare, then rolled her eyes. Annoyed, Dwayne turned his attention back to the stage. He'd first spotted the Judge and Jacksina walking up the steps to the main plaza. He'd been standing near the plaza's central fountain, leafing through a copy of Bill Cole's Miles Davis biography in search of choice jazz adjectives.

His journalistic curiosity overwhelmed his sense of decorum, and Dwayne followed them into the building, past the ticket windows, into the auditorium, and finally down Avery Fisher Hall's long, descending left aisle toward the stage where, to his delight, they sat down next to each other and held hands and hugged. He knew he was staring, he knew he was being indiscreet, but he couldn't help it. Then Jacksina cut him that hateful stare and he felt as dirty as a voyeur in a brothel.

At the end of "Maiden Voyage," the crowd stood, applauding appreciatively at this satisfying blend of experience and youth. The Judge and Jacksina stood pressed together, looking happy and very much in love, and Dwayne, who rarely clapped at concerts, yet this time wanted to be part of the crowd, stood and lightly tapped one hand on his notebook.

Danielle played catch-up with her ambition in the sexless weeks that followed her abortion. The term project took on new meaning now. At one point she'd viewed it as a way to satisfy her intense curiosity about Powell and set up her career, but now it helped her not to focus on the unpleasant present. In between classes she'd dash up to Harlem for interviews with local politicians, such as Congressman Rangel (albeit brief), Hilton Clark, Joseph Perkins, and sundry community organizers. Many evenings she'd stop by Dan Winfrey's office on 96th and Broadway to talk politics with him and his assistant/political adviser, Phyllis Cole. She'd read proposed papers and even did a little editing. Not that she supported all his actions—it irked her to see supportive faxes arrive from Mayor Ed Koch. But there was a sense of mission (and sex appeal) about Winfrey that excited her. They flirted lightly, but both also seemed relieved that Cole was always hovering around. They both thought about each other sexually, but clearly it was the wrong move for each and they both knew it.

Any wariness of Harlem had long passed. In fact, the thought of physical danger now seemed a joke to Danielle. She often thought that no mugger could do more damage to her body and spirit than she'd already done to herself. The possibility of being mugged no longer frightened her. Reflection did. In unhurried moments, ones in which tape, paper, and books escaped her eyes, Danielle searched for weaknesses in Dwayne, in herself, in her philosophy of life. These moments were painful, especially since she really wanted to have nothing to do with coming to conclusions about them. So Danielle filled up the time, using work to suffocate her anxiety.

Then one Sunday in late February Danielle attended service at the church Adam Powell, and his father before him, built into a national black institution, the Abyssinian Baptist Church, old and ornate, conservative morally and progressive politically. Abyssinian wore its history like a crown. In the faces of its dignified parishioners Danielle saw heroes of a revolution that had ended when she was a child. Before the service Danielle stood in front of a huge Adam Powell portrait. In his face she saw leadership. Or was it just sex appeal? She sat in the rear of Abyssinian listening to an outspoken sermon on black empowerment by the charismatic pastor Calvin Butts, who some whispered might one day challenge Rangel. A dark, feisty little baby named John Wesley Brown was baptized that Sunday. His parents held him proudly before the congregation. Danielle studied the Browns. She bowed her head to pray for young John, but instead started crying loudly. Two of the ushers, women in their late fifties, dressed in white suits, white shoes, and small pillbox hats, rushed to her aid. Sobbing uncontrollably as the churchwomen cradled her, Danielle seemed to feel God's hand reach into her soul and lift the shadow from her. A terrible pain flashed through her body and she fainted.

*   *   *

That night Danielle invited her father into her room, closed the door, and told him her story. When she finished he asked, "Are you all right now, baby?" and wiped away her tears.

"Yes and no."

"Talk to me." He wrapped her hands in his and locked eyes with his favorite child.

"It's Dwayne."

"Do you love him?"

"I thought I did."

"Does he love you?"

"I thought so."

"You're not sure now."

"Ever since the abortion he's been good. He really has. Still, he acts like he doesn't know what to say. Before my pregnancy we had some small conflicts. But it was going to be fine. Then when I got pregnant Dwayne was so horrible and so insensitive and cold."

"Did you want to have it, baby?" he asked and immediately felt stupid for his choice of words.

"Yes. I couldn't help it."

"It scared him. Probably still scares him. When play sex becomes serious it takes an extraordinary, mature young man to deal with the consequences. How old is Dwayne?"

"Twenty-six. Old enough."

"Doesn't seem to me either of you were ready. I hate to be stern and sound like your mother, but I've always indulged you, baby, and *you* have indulged yourself. This whole experience is a signal that you must re-examine your relationship, not just to Dwayne, but to yourself. You *have* moved around a bit. Maybe you just need to concentrate on yourself for a while."

"Have I hurt you, Daddy?"

"No. It's your life, not ours. But know this: with your ambition and brains, it'll be hard to find a man secure enough to support you and not be resentful. It's hard now. But later all this will make you stronger, and the man you need will be there. It'll just take some time. Have I been lecturing?"

"That's why you're a great parent."

"Good, because I'm through. Come out and play some cards with us."

"All right. Just let me make a phone call."

Dwayne wasn't home. Reggie answered and said he'd leave a message, but Danielle vowed to call back later, suspecting Reggie might not do it. Ever since Reggie's horrible "joke" on New Year's Eve, Danielle suspected a lot of Dwayne's problems relating to her (or anybody) resulted from Reggie's bad advice. *He probably brought over some of those tacky b-girls of Joint-ski's to entertain Dwayne while I recuperated.* Just as she started out of her room the phone rang.

"Can I stop by?" T.J. asked. "I'm in Connecticut."

"Sure. My parents and I were about to play cards."

"I'll be over in fifteen minutes."

"Where are you?"

"Not far away. See you in a few."

Sam Samson's publicist had mistakenly left Dwayne's name off the Bottom Line guest list, but the box-office manager let Dwayne in, joking that the writer should station a bed in the dressing room since he was in the club so often. A year before, Dwayne would have taken that as a compliment, a testament to his growing prominence in the music scene. Now he just saw it as evidence of his dead existence as a hustling black music critic. He spent his nights rushing from one smoky, beer-spattered joint to another in search of musical transcendence, a pithy phrase, and a free meal. It was only March, yet he was already tired of 1983.

I want to write books, I want to write books, his heart chanted. *Well, my man, came the reply, where is the grand idea that will impel you into the great world of literature?* His failure to develop a subject ate at his pride, and was rivaling his guilt over Danielle's abortion as chief inspiration for regular nightmares.

The unexpected cure for Dwayne's frustration walked on stage with Sam Samson's band. Samson, a smooth yet limited crooner in the white boy r&b direction of Michael McDonald and Hall & Oates, had hired as his one black band member a living legend, tenor saxophonist J. C. "Mississippi" Rivers. To Dwayne, it was as if the god of funk had risen from East St. Louis, Missouri, the troubled, feisty, predominately black city that Ike and Tina, along with a generation of obscure bluesmen, had called home.

Rivers would have been just another of those obscure houserockers if it wasn't for the five incredible years he led the house band at Chicago's Delux Records. Delux was a great, shortlived, black-owned record label of the early seventies, whose acts were national treasures: the glamorous Pammi Lewis and the Vibes, the mercurial love man Robert Ford, the fourteen-year-old child prodigy Shelton Lee, and the production team of Hudlin-Harrell-Hudlin, all created classics toiling under the manipulative motivation of Holis Mulray. Mulray was a visionary businessman who, before his mysterious drowning in a Beverly Hills swimming pool, threatened to overshadow Berry Gordy as black music's greatest mogul.

Rivers, legend had it, was one of the few to tell Mulray to kiss his black ass. After Delux's collapse in 1973, Rivers kept a low profile and, except for occasional gigs around the Midwest, reportedly spent his time acquiring East St. Louis real estate. His tenor, a honking, preachy weapon of gut-bucket soul that had propelled several hundred hits, easily overwhelmed Samson's wimpy falsetto. Dwayne shook off his attitude of professional detachment and was transported to rhythm and blues heaven.

Between sets Dwayne fought off Samson's publicist and slipped into the band's dressing room, where Rivers was guzzling a Rolling Rock. Hoping he didn't sound too golly-gee-whiz, Dwayne stuck out his hand and said, "My name is Dwayne Robinson. I'm a music critic and I just wanted to say it is an honor to meet you."

"Thank you kindly," the musician replied in a voice that was Mississippi by way of Chicago's Michigan Avenue.

"I have most of your solo albums and loved your version of 'Something That Will Last.' "

Rivers laughed and eyed him curiously. "I'll be damned." He

wrapped Dwayne's right hand in a firm shake. "A brother with a sense of history."

"Only about things worth remembering."

"Sit down, young man. Now, where'd you get my records? Your father?"

"A few were from his collection. He took me to see the Delux show at the Fox Theater in Brooklyn quite a few times."

"The Fox? You that old?"

"I have a great memory."

"That right?"

"I wish my friend Reggie was here. He loves your work too. He just started producing records. I'm sure you don't listen to rap records."

"Sure I do. Nothing but James Brown beat with a sped-up Rufus Thomas rap. It's the blues for kids with their caps on backwards."

"Where is James McDonald? Ben Hemingway? Carl Wright? The old rhythm section."

"You know who they are?"

"I read album covers," Dwayne said proudly.

"Shit, you had to read some real small print on Delux covers."

"You know it."

"Most of them live out near me. A couple of them even bought homes from me. Carl did. Ben too. That hard-headed McDonald? I don't know where that fool is." Then lowering his voice, "Speaking of fools, here comes Samson. You interviewing him?"

"Yeah."

"Son, if I wasn't making a king's ransom for two months' work, I'd be back home on my porch."

"I hear that."

Samson entered.

"Hello, Mississippi. You see a writer back here? The publicist said he's back here."

"Only writers I know are numbers runners."

"Love you, Mississippi," Samson said patronizingly.

"This is my nephew Dwayne."

"Samson, so nice to meet you. My uncle is happy to be with you. He respects you very much."

Afterward, Dwayne and Rivers chuckled at Samson's lack of talent and wealth of ego. Instead of going home, Dwayne called Reggie at the Greene Street Studio, where he was running an all-night session with Joint-ski. After sitting through the second set, Dwayne walked Rivers the ten blocks to the studio. Surrounded by Dwayne, Reggie, the musicians and engineers, Rivers told tales of rhythm and blues until morning. He even improvised a bluesy jam with them called "Long Ass Journey." At some point in the night Dwayne turned on a tape recorder to catch some of Rivers' stories. At about 8 a.m., on the E train, Dwayne looked at a notebook full of quotes and wondered if anyone would buy a book on Delux Records.

The Judge walked into his office, unbuttoned his robe, and then with a handmaiden's delicacy, placed it on its hook in his closet. He put on the jacket to his gray suit, then reached down to pull out his Fila gym bag. The phone rang. It was now against his policy to answer the phone after work—too many crazy threats had been coming in. But then he thought it might be his wife because of the dinner that night. He put down the Fila bag and picked up the phone. Mistake. It was that voice again—white, Irish, angry, surely employed in law enforcement by the City of New York.

"Hey, See-em, Free-em! Free any nice drug dealers today?"

"Don't you get tired of this, young man?"

"You don't, why should I?"

"Talk to you later, young man," the Judge said dismissively.

"How's your sex life, See-em?"

He slid the phone back onto the receiver. He didn't slam it—that would only give the caller pleasure.

Fifteen minutes later the Judge's Lincoln was cruising downtown through the pre-rush-hour traffic on the FDR Drive. Miles Davis' *Live at Carnegie Hall* was in the tape deck, filling his ears with the melody of "My Funny Valentine." He and Harriett used to go to jazz clubs all the time. It was their only extravagance back when he was a young criminal attorney and money was tight. He smiled slightly at the memory, but wasn't in the mood to revel in nostalgia.

Instead he turned down Miles and pulled out his mini tape recorder. His rhetorical muse was calling him. "The banality of evil," he said firmly, "is usually supported by the mediocrity of the masses." *Good one-liner,* he thought. *I'll save that for a speech. It's too good for a simple decision. Only a couple of attorneys would hear it then, and they'd never appreciate it.*

As he curved his car off the FDR onto the Brooklyn Bridge, the Judge glanced into his rearview mirror. Which one belongs to the PBA? There was a rumor they'd recruited a few Internal Affairs squad members to shadow him. He made a right onto the Cadman Plaza exit. The Judge was about to park his car when the muse hit him again.

"The dignity of the soul," he said softly, "each individual soul, is one of the most precious gifts God delivers upon us. But it is not invulnerable, inviolate, or constant. It can be taken and too often it is. Everyone has it usurped at one time or another, but when it's stripped clean and we lose our dignity to drugs or crime or homelessness or—" He paused. His eyes watered and a few tears trickled out. Then he pulled out his handkerchief and wiped his face. "Or viciousness"—the Judge continued—"then the depths to which we fall can be profound."

Inside the St. George Health Club the Judge worked out with passion: StairMaster, bike, free weights, and even a bit of 3 on 3 hoops, with the Judge shooting his one-hand push shot like Oscar Robertson. When he finished, the Judge sat in the steam room and took inventory. Despite his best efforts, the belly was softening. His legs, however, were hard and his arms sharply defined. *Damn good,* he thought.

Dinner was at Ken Wah Inn, a Chinese restaurant his wife liked on West 56th Street. Old friends in town for a surgeon's convention. Mrs. Johnson had gone to school with the Judge's wife at Fisk. Dr. Johnson was a Meharry graduate with a thriving practice in Charlotte. The Judge knew this was no idle meeting. As they sipped tea and cocktails, Harriett Peters was clearly trying to interest her husband in life back down South. She'd never say it directly. Harriett Peters, despite thirty years in New York, still retained a Southern reserve that kept her from confronting her husband on issues of discontent. But she was expert at communicating her desires to her husband via indirection, sly comments, and things she brought to his attention. So tonight Harriett, the doctor, and his wife ate sizzling pepper steak while comparing New York unfavorably with Charlotte. The Judge was uncharacteristically silent. He knew the drill. New York is dirty, mean, and impolite: Charlotte is clean, safe, and courteous.

But the Judge liked all that dirt and meanness. Gave him something to do. Gave his life purpose. Gave him a way to mess with white folks, and a great many black folks he didn't care for, too. Dr. Johnson was telling a dreary anti–New York joke when the Judge noticed that Dan Winfrey and his wife were four tables away, eating dumplings and reading through what the Judge assumed were printouts of polls. *Figures he'd be into computers and all that rahrah. Admirable. Smart. Too bad he's hollow. Like everybody else in his generation, Winfrey can talk it but can't walk it.*

The Judge excused himself and got up. He walked past the Winfreys' table without a glance and down the staircase toward the men's room. There was a phone next to the door. He got the urge to call Jacksina and was reaching into his pocket for a quarter when a voice said, "Judge Peters?"

"Yes."

"My name is Dan Winfrey."

The Judge said, "Oh, yes, I'm familiar with you," in a tone that let Winfrey know he'd be getting no respect tonight.

"And I with you, Judge," Winfrey said respectfully. "I wanted to meet you and to say that I admire your guts."

Using his best judicial voice, the Judge announced, "You have quite a few yourself, young man, seeing how you've decided to buck three generations of black advancement just to get on the idiot box regularly."

"Sorry you feel that way, Judge. But just as it's your duty to make the decisions you feel strongly about, I have to take stands on things I believe in."

The Judge was about to go on the offensive when a loud gagging sound came from the bathroom. He opened the door and saw that a stocky, light-skinned black man had thrown up his steamed dumplings on the floor. Poor T.J. was so sloppy drunk that he'd tried to do it in the sink but missed.

Despite his little accident, T.J. otherwise gave the impression of a neatly dressed, clean-cut young black businessman—a more middle-management, less-elegant version of Winfrey. The Judge, always a quick read, turned to Winfrey and said with wicked sarcasm, "Looks like a potential Winfrey supporter."

"Unfortunately you may be right."

The Judge walked past T.J., around his spreading pile of vomit, and stood in front of the urinal. "You joining me?" the Judge asked.

"I'll go tell the management," Winfrey replied politely.

T.J. looked at him and said, "Hey, Dan Winfrey! I *like* your stance, guy," and then extended a shaky hand in greeting. Winfrey said a hurried "Thank you," turned away, and retreated from the room.

"What's with him?" T.J. asked the Judge.

The Judge, having finished his business, zipped up his pants and surveyed T.J. "Son, his problem is he works in a world of theory and you quite clearly are a creature of reality. Excuse me." T.J. had no comeback to that observation. The Judge began to wash his hands at the sink next to T.J.'s mess.

"Don't I know you?" T.J. said finally, a glimmer of recognition rolling across his face.

"Not now, young man. But if you keep drinking it's inevitable we'll get real close." And with that he was gone. T.J., looking into the mirror at himself and his soiled and reeking suit, realized he'd just made a fool of himself in front of two very important men.

* * *

On the way uptown the Judge regaled his wife with the tale of his confrontation with Winfrey and how the young politician had been saved from a serious tongue-lashing by a drunk buppie in the bathroom. Of course, he made it a touch more dramatic than it actually was, but his wife knew that.

Up at 74th Street the car slowed down as it neared the Beacon Theater. Mobs of kids, mostly black and Hispanic, crowded off the sidewalk and into Broadway. Jeeps were double parked, and a police van sat on the corner. The marquee read, **GRANDMASTER FLASH AND THE FURIOUS FIVE, JOINT-SKI, DR. JEKYLL AND MR. HYDE.** The Judge didn't know what was going on, but he was glad it was happening in Manhattan and not in the Bronx.

Inside the Beacon, Joint-ski and Rahiem were rocking the house with "Break It Down," and a sixteen-year-old was being thrown from the upper deck into the mezzanine by a Dance Inferno regular named Sugar Dice. Joint-ski saw it from the stage, ignored it, and then started, "Throw your hands in the air and wave them like you just don't care!" Rahiem looked back down at the turntables and began scratching up "Break It Down" on his Technics turntables. At the same moment the Judge drove happily past the Beacon and turned left on 79th Street toward his home on Riverside Drive.

To Joint-ski, Rahiem, and the Judge, Sugar Dice was a face in the crowd, another stuck-up kid, another dark perpetrator who'd never mean a thing to them. At least not this day.

Jacksina hadn't seen much of Danielle since her roommate had moved back home. They'd talked on the phone quite a few times—including that one sad phone call—and exchanged very elaborate Christmas cards: Danielle sent her a Dial-a-Date card with pictures of obnoxious men you could meet if the spinning arrow landed on the wrong guy; Jacksina sent her a custom-made card with a color picture of herself in high heels and judge's robes (photographed by the Judge). It was inscribed, *Future Member of the High Court.*

So it was with great anticipation that Jacksina awaited

Danielle at Peretti's, an Italian restaurant on Columbus Avenue, one Saturday afternoon in April. When they'd lived together, Jacksina and Danielle had spent many mirth-filled hours looking out of Peretti's windows at the nouveaux riches, the trendy, and the semi-famous strolling along Columbus. Danielle walked into Peretti's with a big shopping bag from a local boutique. "What did you get?" Jacksina asked after they'd exchanged air kisses.

"Two cashmere sweaters. One for me and one for Dwayne."

"Still not a dresser, huh?"

"I'm doing the best I can, but he's not that interested, and since we're both busy, I don't really have time to polish him up."

"How do you feel?"

"Good. Better every day. What about you?"

"Oh, girl. I'm fine. I'm studying a lot harder—as you advised—and I've cut down on my extracurricular activities— as you advised. Aerobics only once a week."

"Getting serious. Finally."

"I tell you, Dee, one day I'm going to make a lot of money, have a nice condo, a few cars, and a truly fine husband. I'll pay back my family. I'll give to black charities. Don't worry about that. I'll be socially conscious."

"That's good, Jack."

"But I'm working harder for it now. You know, the Judge has really helped me understand my cases." Then she paused, knowing she was about to cause a fight, but she had to say it. "I think he wants to marry me."

Danielle, not wanting to start in, replied, "I'll say this, you two have been dating—if that's what you call it—longer than I ever would have thought."

"Over a year. Usually I'm bored by now. But Danielle, you know, it's still good."

"You're happy."

"Yes, I'm very happy."

"I'm really glad for you." In how Danielle said "for you" Jacksina could feel her friend's sadness.

"I knew you couldn't be over it yet."

No point in putting up a false front with Jack. "I'm really doing all right—but Dwayne." She paused. "Dwayne hasn't even begun to deal with it."

"If he loves you it'll be all right."

"I think—I know—he's still guilt-ridden over his selfishness."

"Selfish?" Jacksina looked at her friend as if she were crazy. "It would have been selfish to have a baby neither of you wanted."

Danielle screwed up her face and stared out onto Columbus Avenue. Then, with renewed conviction, she looked back at Jacksina. "It seems like I did the right thing for my career. But I know it would have been all right if I'd kept the baby."

Jacksina sat back and stared at Danielle. "What?" Danielle asked impatiently.

"You'll be all right, girl," Jacksina said slowly. "You've gotten over other men. You'll get over Dwayne one way or the other. The real problem is you. You're always the lover and not the lovee. You won't be happy until you cut that mess out."

"That's a selfish way to think."

In a singsong voice Jacksina said, "If you want to be happy for the rest of your life get a man who's a lover to marry you. I know I will."

Slightly pissed, Danielle barked, "Let's order."

"Better get a salad, Danny." Jacksina wasn't going to let up. She nodded at Danielle's stomach.

"Men still like me." Danielle was now very defensive.

"Men like most women. Particularly women as sexy as we are."

"I love Dwayne." Danielle sounded pitiful even to herself.

The waitress came over.

"Get this woman the healthiest salad you have."

"Jack . . ."

"Maybe two."

After their real orders had been brought to them, Jacksina and Danielle sat and people-watched, frequently giggling at the faces of the passersby. They agreed that many of them seemed to resemble the dogs that accompanied them. It was the most fun Danielle had had for months. Jacksina always meant laughs and always there was mental stimulation to accompany it. And it was she who eventually brought up the question of what to do about and with Mr. Dwayne Robinson.

Danielle was in Dwayne's bed, a place of pleasure before, a site of profound frustration tonight. "Why not?" she asked.

"I don't know. I just can't."

"Let me try something."

"No."

"No?"

"No." When Dwayne said that, Danielle turned away from him. Dwayne couldn't tell her why. He couldn't say he was afraid to get her pregnant again. He couldn't say that the idea of entering her again, of going back into the place he'd started a life before, was messing with his mind. He lay there, watching Danielle's back and thinking that if he said any of the things now in his mind he'd really be hurting her. He had to try, though he knew he'd sound damn feeble. He caressed her back but she didn't turn around.

"Are you listening?"

"I can hear you."

"Look at me, please." She rolled over to face him. She had been crying so softly that he didn't hear it. "I have a problem," he said. "I don't know why, but I have this fear of making love to you. I guess I don't wanna make another mistake. Does this make any sense to you?"

Danielle stared at him. Finally, in a monotone voice, she said, "When you're ready, let me know."

"It'll be soon," Dwayne whispered. "Trust me."

The next afternoon Danielle and Dwayne sat at his dining table. He was working on the proposal for his Delux book, *The Relentless Beat.* Danielle was writing sections of her Powell-Rangel project. Sitting there sharing tidbits of unearthed insight, they looked like two studiously matched bookends. He began looking over her handwritten outline. "There are a few sentences I'd like to tighten up for you, but otherwise this is superb. You really thought this through."

"You think so?"

"Oh, yeah. I love the section where you compare Powell and Rangel's responses to similar issues. A lot of people will debate you on your interpretations, but your arguments are strong."

"I'm really glad you like it. That means a lot to me." She studied the pencils on the table.

"Dwayne?"

"Yeah?"

"I've got to go."

"Go where?"

"Back home to type the paper."

"Do it here."

"No. I want to go home, clear my head, and do the final draft there."

"Okay, that makes sense."

Danielle gathered her papers and fled. On the familiar ride back to Arthur, she read over her report and scribbled notes in the margins. She studied Dwayne's suggestions for improving the writing. *He's really a good writer, but he can also be a mean, self-centered S.O.B. If he'd just extended himself a little bit, opened up a little more, I wouldn't be feeling so bad.*

The trees that Danielle saw out the train window were sprouting buds. It was warm, and she found herself unbuttoning the two top buttons on her blouse. She leaned back in her seat and sighed. *So what's next? I've been seeing him for a year—a great, rotten year. We should be able to put it back together. But the pieces aren't fitting. They're just not fitting.*

Two hours later, in the quiet of her family basement, Danielle dialed T.J.'s number. Her voice was warm, slow, and strangely otherworldly. It was as if her mind were a long way from her body.

"T.J., I want you to come over."

"What's up? Are you all right?"

"No, I'm not. Come over. I need your help."

"You sound strange."

"Just come on over."

"What's going on?"

"Come over." It was not a plead or request. It was an order.

"Be there as soon as I can."

T.J. ran three lights and almost slammed into a garbage truck on his way to the Embrys' house. He saw her in his mind's eye, and he was happy and he was tense.

The minute he entered the house Danielle took his hand and fixed him with a look he'd seen from her before but never aimed his way. It pleased him. It frightened him. So did her teary story of how Dwayne "Mr. Hot Pants," was cold and—maybe—impotent.

As Danielle related this tale of sexual woe, she pressed her head against T.J.'s shoulder and wrapped her arms around him as if he were a teddy bear. It was obvious how vulnerable she was. It was in her voice; in her body language.

"You don't feel too good right now, do you?"

"No. I feel—" She searched for a word. There were plenty in her vocabulary that might have described her frustration, but for one of those rare moments in her articulate life, she could not think of which to use.

"Danielle . . . you don't have to say anything else." T.J.'s voice was low and soothing. "You won't believe me, but I know how frustrated you must feel." Almost to his own surprise, he was being honest. Inside, in some dark place where jealousy had reigned for years, he wanted to take advantage of her. *Isn't that why you've been hanging around? Isn't that why you're here? You knew she'd be vulnerable.* Desire made his oatmeal complexion flush, but he was no longer the horny, opportunistic fool whom Dwayne, perhaps rightly, so disliked.

Danielle squeezed him hard but he refused to give in. Very gently he peeled Danielle off him, took her arms, and pushed her away.

"Danny, you need something. And I can't give it to you." It hurt him more than Danielle would ever know to make that simple statement. "And your parents can't and it's clear to you that Dwayne Robinson can't give it to you. What you need is unconditional love."

"No one gives that to you except your parents, T.J.," she protested, suspicious now, trying to figure out why he had rejected her and where he was headed.

"You're wrong. I know someone who will."

"Morris?"

T.J. nodded, and Danielle absently ran her hands through her hair, then adjusted her skirt to cover her knees.

"I mean Morris. Believe it or not, after all this time, and after the way you treated him, he's still silly for you."

"T.J., if you told Morris about . . . Dwayne, I'll kill you." Her tone of voice really frightened him.

"My God, no. What did you think? I didn't say anything about the abortion." He paused. "But I did tell him you were in pain and about how mean you've been treated."

"I couldn't go back to him. Not after the way it ended. He wouldn't have me."

T.J. smiled. "But that's precisely why you *can* go back. You ended it. You moved on. But he stayed in that same spot—and he's still waiting there."

"Danny, I'm pregnant."

"Oh, Jack. Is it by the Judge?"

"He's the only man I've been with for over a year."

"I'm more surprised by that fact than by you being pregnant."

"You really haven't been listening to me, have you?"

"I guess not."

"I'm having this baby."

Danielle looked at the phone as if it were the doorway to the Twilight Zone.

"The man is married!"

"I don't care. I love him and I want this baby."

"What about school? Your career? What about your dreams? That's why I didn't have mine."

"Danielle, don't lie."

"What?"

"Don't lie," Jacksina said coldly.

"Lie about what?"

"You had an abortion for the same reasons that I'm not—the prospective father wouldn't stand beside you. The Judge loves me. That's the difference. I'm sorry, Danielle. I'm sorry about what happened with you and Dwayne."

Jacksina waited for the explosion, but her friend merely asked, "So what are you going to do?"

"After I have the baby?"

"Yeah," Danielle said. "After the baby. About law school, work, paying the rent. All that."

"I think I can finish classes before the baby's born. Definitely I'll have to postpone taking the bar."

"The Judge should be lining up some kind of patronage job at the courthouse, so when the baby's born you can receive some civil service benefits."

"He said something about that, but I got the feeling some people at the court are trying to block it."

"Yeah. He's not very popular among pols. I assume he's going to pay the rent."

"Yes, yes. Money has already been set aside. He's happy. He wants the baby. We've talked about what if this happened."

"Jack, I'm jealous. I don't want to be, but I can't help it."

"Danny, you're my best friend. I love you and I know you love me. My doctor says, because of my previous abortions, that my uterus is weak. He says it could be a difficult pregnancy. So please don't envy me. And don't hate me."

"I don't hate you. I couldn't hate you. You must know that. I guess I'm jealous happy and happy jealous." They laughed.

"Have you been working out lately?" Danielle asked.

"No time. I've been under a lot of pressure."

"That's no excuse. What are you doing tonight?"

"Studying."

"Let's go to your health club."

"*You* want to go to a health club?" she asked suspiciously.

"Listen, girlie, I'm not letting you lose your beautiful figure behind this baby. Besides, I want a healthy goddaughter."

"Who made you godmamma?"

"I didn't hear that. I did *not* hear that. I'll be over in about ninety minutes."

"Okay, sounds good."

"Your being pregnant will be great for my wardrobe. I better bring my shopping bag with me."

"See you then. And when you get here, don't even walk by my closet."

Dwayne Robinson walked into Blackmon's Lounge, on State Street, in the heart of East St. Louis, Illinois. It was a down-home place where the city's over-forties and over-fifties gathered to talk business, politics, get a taste (or two or three), and listen to the grit sounds of Marty Abdullah, a Texas bluesman with a local following in that part of black America where blues still commanded respect. The jukebox was playing Z. Z. Hill's "Down Home Blues," and the air was thick with the smell of Kool cigarettes and bourbon. Dwayne surveyed this scene as he wiped early-summer sweat from his brow.

J. C. Rivers sat in a booth in the back with two older black men, swallowing shot glasses of Jack Daniel's.

"Hey, Dwayne!"

"Hey, J.C.!"

Dwayne slid into the booth next to Rivers.

"This is the young man I was telling you about—Dwayne Robinson."

Dwayne reached across the table and found that Ben Hemingway and James McDonald both possessed large, calloused hands with long firm fingers. Hemingway and McDonald were, according to Dwayne's *Village Voice* review of Chic's *Risque* album, "the only bassist-drummer combo to rival Stax's Duck Dunn and Al Jackson and Motown's James Jamerson and Benny Benjamin. They might even be better." Dwayne fought back the inclination to babble all this when he met them. Instead he sat listening to men twice his age and three times his experience talk about people and events that Dwayne had only read about. Legend was meeting reality. Mythology given human form. It was a process Dwayne found as intoxicating as alcohol.

Hemingway, McDonald, and Rivers recalled the time a now resurgent female rhythm-and-blues singer, noted for long legs and verbal husband-bashing, invited several young boys from the neighborhood by to watch her screw her teenaged guitar player on the kitchen table. And the way Jackie Wilson and Sam Cooke used to tease James Brown about his looks and steal away his women until Brown got revenge by putting together soul's most dynamic band. And how the Delux musicians struck for three weeks in 1970 to get their names on the album covers and how Delux's owner, Mulray, never forgave them. According to them, in 1972 Mulray purchased studios in Los Angeles and New York and tried to replace the original Delux players with rhythm sections on both coasts. In the process "the Delux sound" was lost and the spirit of the original team broken. Which is how the label went into a decline capped by Mulray's death by drowning in '73.

At 10:30 p.m. Hemingway split for a gig with a local jazz band, and at midnight McDonald left to pick up his wife at East St. Louis Hospital.

"That was great," Dwayne said to Rivers. "Thank you."

"Come on, Dwayne. It's a treat to be appreciated. Look at me now. We're old men who made records. Who knows us? Who gives a shit? Everybody just wants to meet the singers, as if they had a damn idea what was going on. You seem to know, though. Your pops must be proud of you."

"Unfortunately, I wouldn't know."

"Yeah? That's too bad. Your mother did a good job, huh?"

"Well, my father was around at first, but then he left home. You know how it is."

"Sometimes it takes a man a minute. I'm on my third family now. Got a kid five now." Rivers pulled out his wallet and showed him the picture of a little boy in a St. Louis Cardinals uniform. "I thought I was in love twice before. Then I figured out that love is more complicated and just as simple as any of those silly-ass Delux songs."

"How is that?"

"Well, it took me until I was about forty-eight before I could really say I loved somebody right, 'cause I finally knew *myself* from nostril to asshole to toenail, I finally knew who I was."

"Now that's knowing yourself," Dwayne said.

"That's knowing yourself," J.C. agreed.

"You got a lady?"

"Man, I really don't know. I used to have her, but I don't know if I need to. It seems like she wants all of me, but I'm just not ready to give it up."

"You love her?"

"Yes, but I love me more. Damn, that's fucked up. Let me put it like this: between a bad personal experience and trying to get this book off the ground, I feel I need to get my head together. It's sad to say you love yourself more than your lover, isn't it?"

"Shit, man, you just being real. The lyrics of all those hits can talk that lovey-dovey fantasy, I'll-be-yours-forever-and-thirteen-days shit. Life demands reality. And those that ain't real, they might as well make their heart a spit can."

"You are rough, J.C."

"R-E-A-L. Real. That's all, bro. That's all. Let me call you something else."

Dwayne said, "Go ahead." He was loving the attention and the old-school wisdom.

"When I was younger," J.C. started, "I used to walk fast, just like you. Cos I thought if I didn't, the world would get away from me and I'd always be behind. Now I walk slow. Know why?" Dwayne dutifully nodded "No." "Cos I know now it's always gonna be ahead of me and there's not a damn thing I can do about it. Now I enjoy the view. Now I realize most other people are walkin' at the same speed. Some a lot slower. You'll be all right soon as you find your own speed."

Back in his hotel room Dwayne showered out the stale aroma of alcohol and cigarettes from his skin, then stood in front of his bathroom mirror, gazed into his reflection, and started singing the Supremes' "Where Did Our Love Go?" imitating the moves of Diana Ross.

Danielle wasn't home that night when he called. Her mother said she was staying in the city with a friend. She called the next morning at 8 a.m.

"Hey, Danielle."

"Hello, Dwayne. How is life in East St. Louis?"

"East St. Louis is chilly and more than boring. How did your adviser react to your paper?"

"Professor Gaines was quite pleased. She forwarded it to a friend of hers at 'Like It Is.' There's a chance of a part-time job."

"That would be a good place for you. The only good black public affairs show in town."

"Yeah, I think so too."

"Danielle."

"Yes?"

"I gotta ask you something. Is it over between us?" It was a strange, awkward question. He knew that. Definitely could have said it better, sweeter, smarter. But he was impatient for whatever peace of mind this question might bring. He knew the question would offend her, but it seemed, at that moment, the best thing to do.

"Is it?" Danielle asked.

"I think so." He really wanted her to do it.

"Then it is. You started it, I guess you can end it."

"I don't regret anything that happened."

"It's too late for making nice, Dwayne Robinson. You bastard. I can't say I don't regret things, Dwayne. You've hurt me and then you call me long distance to ask if we're over. I thought more of you. But now I think T.J. was right about you from the first day we met to right now."

"What that jealous fool says or said doesn't matter. The truth is I didn't have what you wanted."

"No, that's not what happened. You just changed your mind about giving it to me. You just became a selfish motherfucker, or maybe you always were one and just teased me into thinking otherwise. No one has ever disrespected me the way you have." The phone line between East St. Louis, Illinois, and Arthur, Connecticut, was severed at the eastern end.

* * *

When Dwayne got back to New York he found a pile of letters addressed to him on the kitchen table. A *Village Voice* check. A letter from an agent interested in representing the Delux book. A bill from the phone company, on which Reggie had under-lined Dwayne's long-distance calls. A gas company bill. And one letter, with no return address, postmarked Arthur.

> You should be proud of yourself. You have taught me things about life my father and mother never did. You should feel good about yourself. You taught me about emotional de-ceit. And how could I forget your lesson on how to be de-tached and make it work for you.
>
> At first it was all hard for me to accept. But you told me and I've learned to believe you. Preachers, teachers, politi-cians tell us to strive for optimism, to look for a brighter day. Now, if I've truly learned your nasty lessons, optimism and love are just ways to disguise our inadequacies. Anything happy or good is bullshit, right? You have taught me that people mess you over and then act like nothing happened or, worse, that you ("you" being the person hurt) are overre-acting and that all this negativity is for your own good.
>
> What I don't understand is why learning your cruel lessons doesn't make everything as simple for me as it does for you? I'm in pain, Dwayne. But I bet you think that's all right. I don't think so. Why is that? Maybe you skipped a lesson, but I can't come back to school. Your classes are too damn expensive.

Danielle didn't even sign it. At the bottom, in big letters, she wrote GOODBYE.

Reaching into the envelope, Dwayne found Valerie Simp-son's earring. It was broken into six pieces. It looked like it had been hammered repeatedly. For a minute he tried to put the pieces together but the effort was futile. Right in his soul, he hurt. Right inside, where he hadn't hurt since his father left home. He'd been so wrong. No words. No more thoughts. Just dark, unbelievable pain.

Dwayne initially tried calling her parents' home, which resulted either in hangups or stony "I'll take a message" replies from her mother and father. His letters came back unopened and unanswered. In the months following the breakup there were other problems as well.

There were threats from the Mulray family about the book. He worried about his mother's nagging back ailment. His sexual desire returned, but he had trouble getting back into the game. There was a lot of talk around about this disease AIDS, but since it seemed to affect only Haitians and gays, it didn't worry him much. The real change was inside.

For her part, Danielle still followed his by-line—she even defended his critical credentials to Ernest when Dwayne had the nerve to write liner notes on a John Coltrane reissue. Still, she tried to move ahead, tried not to look back, but rarely succeeded. When a flyer at Columbia advertised a Hoboken sublet she jumped on it, and she vowed not to have a roommate, male or female, or even a boyfriend. Morris kept calling. T.J. continued to sing his praises. She crossed her fingers, hoping she could be happy by herself.

SIX

The smell of mildew, marijuana, and Harlem garbage steaming in the June heat filled Joint-ski's Apollo Theater dressing room. The aroma was rank enough to turn the stomach of even the most insensitive diner, so all Dwayne could down was some potato chips and ginger ale, avoiding the courtesy spread of cold cuts and mushy potato salad. Joint-ski, however, wasn't so wise and was now in the bathroom vomiting.

It had been a long day. Shooting a music video had been the idea of B.C.'s London office since "Break It Down" was a budding United Kingdom hit. B.C.'s U.S. staff couldn't care less. To B.C., rap was a novelty and nothing else, which is why no one at the label told the Brits that the Apollo had profoundly lost its glory since its historic days and that they'd spend much of the shoot dodging chunks of falling plaster. Adding to the day's difficulty was that the gap between Joint-ski's onstage charisma and off-stage insecurity had grown dangerously with each twelve-inch sold—they were up to 300,000 nationally. Vomiting was, in Dwayne's eyes, just one more manifestation of the strain.

Reggie didn't care. Well, Reggie cared but he cared more about his own peace of mind. Of all the rappers on the Dance Inferno scene, Reggie had picked Joint-ski to invest his money in. Reggie had given the kid a career, treated him like a son, and now both were reaping the rewards.

Reggie was in love as deep as his naturally cynical soul allowed. Time once spent scolding and tutoring Joint-ski after sessions was now spent riding the Metroliner to D.C. Reggie even missed the video shoot's start because his train was delayed in Wilmington.

Joint-ski came onstage in a red leather outfit, looking a bit pale but basically cool, and began rapping. The director tried to get him to wait, but he was feeding his ego, building himself up, banishing his demons, and he didn't care what anybody said.

"Mr. Robinson, could you please help us?" a Brit producer asked. "Your Joint-ski doesn't seem to want to stop talking, mate. He bloody well won't let us set up our shots." Dwayne peered at the Apollo stage, where Joint-ski, the microphone pressed to his lips, mumbled rhythmically about how "The sins of the father are visited on the son/and my black Daddy was a son-of-a-gun."

In the wake of "Break It Down" and a Dwayne Robinson piece in the *Village Voice*, The Dance Inferno was no longer an obscure ghetto club, but an "underground" spot, a designation that meant trend-pimpers of every variety—journalists, record executives, filmmakers, photographers, models, agents, visual artists—made pilgrimages to Inferno in search of thrills, spills, and greenbacks. Much of the art crowd was knee-deep into its flirtation with graffiti as art. Break dancing had already begun its long climb from urban battle style to music video irrelevancy. But rap was still too foreign, unproven, and unmusical for effective exploitation. In short, the Inferno still stank of angel dust and herb, but now a hint of designer perfume also hung in the air.

All this bothered the Inferno's back-room crew. Being a star in the ghetto, a house-rocking party starter, celebrated from the Bronx's Grand Concourse to Brooklyn's Belmont Avenue, was cool back when that was the best that rap could earn you. A rep for turning parties out meant quick cash—on a good night you could rock two or three jams, plenty of pliant dirty-sock girls, and earn respect usually granted ballplayers, pimps, and the dope man. Just as the Sugar Hill Gang's "Rapper's Delight" and Kurtis Blow's "The Breaks" had changed things for those kids, "Break It Down" revolutionized Joint-ski's life. To non-

Bronxites, Joint-ski "was" hip hop because he'd put out a record and none of the old-school crew had.

Soon that would change—all the back-room boys would eventually get their shot (and years later be nostalgic for life before records). But at this moment in time luck had conspired against them. They'd never respected him. Joint-ski. He was a joke the girlies liked. Now he was their worst nightmare—a sucka getting paid at their expense.

So the events that would transpire that July evening weren't a spontaneous explosion. It had been building since the Inferno regulars heard Joint-ski was doing a special appearance at the Inferno, along with two break-dance crews and a showing of work by the graffiti artist Samo. Television crews from Belgium, Germany, and the United Kingdom were to be in the house and everyone was encouraged to dress in their freshest sweat suits, gold chains, and Kangols.

Joint-ski, while by no means mature as a man, had grown tremendously as a performer. Despite the television crews and the hypsters and the old-school rappers in the house, he felt in control enough to sit in The Dance Inferno's minuscule dressing room with Rahiem, in a custom-made Gucci warm-up suit.

"Did you get the ass?" he queried Rahiem.

"What do you think, motherfucker?" said the usually taciturn deejay-valet-bodyguard.

"I didn't ask you to ask me a question. Either answer my question straight or we'll just squash the whole conversation."

"Yo, I got that ass, that mouth, the mole on her thigh, and both her big titties. Satisfied? I got it all."

"You ain't all that, nigger. Bring that girl back here after the gig and I'll get it from her direct."

"Why you gotta talk to her?"

"Yo, if your shit was correct no need to worry. Am I right? Nigger, you know I'm right."

"Maybe," Rahiem said reluctantly.

"Maybe what?" Joint-ski demanded.

"Maybe I'll bring her back."

"Maybe!" Joint-ski laughed. "Yo, man, I know you been

taxing that booty in the back ride. I know it. Least you can let me do is check out that pussy's aroma."

The way Joint-ski stretched out the word "aroma" made Rahiem laugh, though he really didn't want to. Joint-ski playfully hugged Rahiem around his neck. "Yo, you my nigger man. We been through a lot. Now we taking shit to the next level. We gonna bust out all the nonbelievers in here tonight."

An anxious Reggie entered the room, and Joint-ski's mood changed. "They're ready," Reggie said.

"No. The question is, Are you ready? Is the sound right? Are the few shitty-ass lights here coordinated? Since you got them D.C. skins, Reggie, your game has just gone left."

Joint-ski and Reggie's relationship had seriously deteriorated since Reggie had missed the British video shoot. He resented how Reggie's romance with Kelly Love Chase had changed him. Every free weekend was spent either in D.C. or in his Queens bedroom with her. No more club cruising at Leviticus or Othellos; no more pickup lines on the F train. Joint-ski understood it was Reggie's choice to live this way. But Reggie's obsession was hurting Joint-ski's career. Reggie was slow to respond to record-company phone calls. He was distracted in the studio because he was always thinking about calling Kelly or waiting for her to ring him.

At this key time in Joint-ski's life, when all his childhood dreams and adolescent insecurities were bubbling up through the prism of fame, he craved the fatherly authority that Reggie had provided and now didn't. So when Reggie reached over and grabbed Joint-ski by the collar, pulling him close to him, Joint-ski wasn't inclined to back down.

"Listen, boy." Reggie spoke with real menace. "Don't ever talk to me like that!"

"Fuck that, you fat bitch!"

Reggie slammed Joint-ski against the wall. Immediately he wanted to apologize, but he never got the chance. Rahiem pumped a right into his kidney and Reggie crashed to the floor.

"I'm sorry, Mr. Olds." Rahiem was genuinely contrite. "Real

sorry, but I couldn't let you do my man like that. Here—let me help you up."

Rahiem lifted Reggie up and sat him on a chair in front of the makeup table. Reggie, in considerable pain, moaned and squeezed his side. Joint-ski stood behind him, adjusting his gold chains, ignoring Reggie's groans. Randy, The Dance Inferno's owner, entered the room. "C'mon, guys, everybody's ready. What happened to Reggie?"

"Nerves," said Joint-ski. "Yo, we ready. Let's take it to the stage."

As they walked out, Rahiem told Randy, "You better get Mr. Olds a ginger ale."

Joint-ski followed Rahiem's back as he pushed toward the stage past Kurtis Blow and Afrika Bambaataa. Blue, the white woman promoter who wanted to bring hip hop downtown, was with the graffiti kid, Fab Five Freddie. Dwayne Robinson patted his back and Joint-ski smiled. Suddenly there was the stage. Time to blow up.

Dwayne wondered where Reggie was. He usually stood stage right, looking on like an anxious father-to-be. In his spot tonight were some crazy gangster homeboys with their arms folded and "show me" looks on their faces. As usual the girls were screaming, but this time the Inferno's stage was bathed in bright tv lights. Dwayne looked around at this strange mix of black and white, downtown and the Bronx, b-boys, Brits, and bohemians. *This is the joint! Something's going on here. Will it last? Hopefully long enough to get another* Voice *piece out of it. After that . . .* Dwayne never finished that thought.

"Yo, pussy! You nonrhyming, punk-ass pussy!" Joint-ski was about to introduce "Break It Down" when the hard-rock kid known as Sugar Dice, garbed in a green velour jogging suit, unlaced green Adidas, and a green Kangol, appeared stage left.

"Yo, homie, chill!" Joint-ski shouted. "You got beef wait till the gig's over."

"No, pussy!" Sugar Dice jumped onstage. "You ain't no real rapper. Just a punk white boys be gassin'."

Somewhere in the back of The Dance Inferno there was a commotion. Two black kids in green velour suits yoked an astonished and complaining German soundman. A chair flew by, launched by an unseen hand. A girl screamed, "Get the fuck off my man!" The crowd, as though impelled by an invisible hand, surged toward the stage. Sugar Dice leaped at Joint-ski and in a sign of total disrespect used his open hand to mush the rapper's face. Somebody shoved Dwayne from behind and he smashed facefirst onto the floor of the stage. More screaming. A few feet from him, Joint-ski struggled to free himself as Sugar Dice held his thick gold chain with one hand and smacked him one-two-three times. Dwayne saw Rahiem knock over a turntable, grab Sugar Dice, and begin to pistol-whip him about the head and neck with a .45 automatic.

Bam-bam-bam.

Rahiem let go of Sugar Dice and squinted out into the dim, smoky room, trying to spot who had fired the three shots. A boy lay on the stage, on his back, twisting in pain; his face covered with blood. Rahiem dove to the floor, expecting more gunfire. He looked up cautiously, then crawled over to Dwayne to see if he was okay. Joint-ski and Sugar Dice continued to wrestle.

Rahiem rose to his knees and raised the automatic. His eyes darted through the yelling, panic-stricken crowd. He turned and looked at Sugar Dice. "I should put a cap in that nigger."

"No, Rahiem!" Dwayne shouted.

"Over and out."

"No!"

Lavender. The sky over Manhattan's West Side was at that moment between dawn and day when an early riser could claim the sky was neither light nor dark blue, but lavender. The Judge reached out his hand to the New York Hilton window. Just then, lavender gave way to pale blue light.

"There are worlds in the mind other than the one we live in," he said. "There is the world we remember living in, though what we recall of it is only fragments of what that world is about."

The Judge turned from the window and the memory of lavender and, with arms folded, leaned against the sill and watched Jacksina roll her pantyhose up her long, brown, well-muscled legs. She looked up, smiled, said "I'm listening," and went back to her pantyhose.

"There is the world of accidental imagination. The world of innocent daydream. The world of exotic fantasy." Jacksina moved over to a corner of the room, where their clothes lay in a pile, pants atop silk dress, silk dress atop shoes. "There is the world of willed destiny or manifest dreams, which is sometimes called ambition. In that world you dream of where you're going and what you wish to finally achieve. This world can be most unsatisfying because what you will make happen never ever satisfies as profoundly as you think it will when you find you want it."

Jacksina, now fully dressed, walked into the bathroom to pull her hair back into a bun. "You had enough yet?" he asked as she twisted her hair.

"No, baby, go ahead."

"In some way that last world of ambition is the worst one because of the anticipation. You contemplate ambition for so long that ultimately it only really works as an idea, not as reality." He was dressed now, tying the knot in his tie, examining himself in the reflection of the window.

"I don't know for sure. I just know that 'willed destiny' is not nearly as potent or divine as it sounds."

Jacksina walked up behind him and put her arms around his waist. "But you still believe it."

"Do I?"

"Everything you do says you have a dream you care about." She reached around him and began stroking his groin.

"If I do, it's only because I no longer know the difference between ambition and routine."

He turned to face her and they kissed long and hard as the light outside grew brighter.

"I have classes today," she said as she slowly freed herself from his embrace. "And don't you have to go make some prose-cutors unhappy?"

"I love you."

"You don't have to say that."

"Why not? Haven't I been inflicting my philosophy on you? Now I say something from my heart—and you won't listen. I love you." Jacksina squeezed him harder.

Parked across the street, unknown to the two lovers of willed destiny, was a white man with a telephoto lens. He had been photographing their window since the sky had turned lavender.

Danielle left the offices of WABC on Columbus Avenue feeling as good as she had in months. She'd spent the last hour talking with Gil Noble, the host of New York's best (not best black, but best) local public-service program, "Like It Is." He'd read her paper, thought it well researched and, maybe, hopefully, per-haps, there might be an opening as a research assistant in three months. The pay would have been considered ridiculously low for a Columbia J School student. Furthermore, the show's con-tent was too overtly "black" for many. Noble had broadcast his-toric documentaries on Malcolm X and Paul Robeson. Most of the black students enrolled in Columbia's prestigious program sensibly looked for gigs more lucrative and mainstream.

But for Danielle "Like It Is" was perfect. She could live at home and do some freelance editing to supplement her salary. The job would be hard on her ego, but if she had been caught up in ego, she would never have left Doubleday.

She was walking past Lincoln Center when she felt a chill. She stopped. *What if I'd had the baby?* It was the first time that thought had occurred to her. *He or she would be crawling, drib-bling, laughing, crying right now. Ma would be picking up after him (her?), looking under the living room furniture for stolen curlers, and scooping up toys. Daddy Dan would have remod-eled the basement with wood paneling, linoleum, brighter lights. And me—what would I be doing? Yeah—what? Enough of that. It's done. What I wanted for Dwayne and myself, what we could have built together, all of it's over. I hate him some-*

*times. But what good does that do me? Besides, the good times
we had together were as sweet as any I've had with a man. I
shouldn't even bother with hating him. What's done is done.
Right?*

Danielle continued down Broadway and entered the enormous Coliseum Bookstore at Columbus Circle. It was Dwayne's
favorite bookstore, and frequent visits had endeared it to
Danielle as well. Dwayne always said that the Coliseum, an in-
dependent store, always had books before B. Dalton's, Walden,
and the other chains. *Let's see if he's right,* she thought. Instead
of walking to the familiar Political Science, Sociology, or Black
History sections, she ventured over to a part of the Coliseum
foreign to her, stopping in front of the New Age ghetto, where
tomes on holistic medicine, astrology, and self-help competed
for shelf space.

Danielle perused the section with great care, looking for a bit
of her past. On a lower shelf, far from the sightlines of its intended buyer, was *Stages of Romance*, by Dyana Williams,
Danielle's last editing assignment before leaving Doubleday.
Dyana was one black author who didn't use her blackness as
subject matter. Meditations on love were her specialty. "Color-
blind" is what Williams called her writing, and she'd built her
career avoiding the "black writer" label.

Danielle knew she could have gone in the same direction.
Relationships, astrology, cookbooks, travel, and health were all
areas an alert young editor could build a stable career around.
Luck-out and sign the right diet doctor, chef, exercise maven,
astrologist, or, above all, sex/romance shrink and regularly
scheduled bestsellerdom—and raises—awaited. But Danielle
had vowed that *Stages of Romance* would be her only contribu-
tion to the love life of supermarket America. She flipped the
book open to the table of contents. According to Williams, there
were five stages of romance:

1. *Rapture.* The newness of love inspires a euphoric state—
the most desirable state of all.

2. *Exploration.* Getting to know your romantic partner, sharing common interests and beliefs.

3. *Discovery.* As you become aware of your partner's basic components, you begin to identify differences, displeasing attributes, and problem areas.

4. *Conquest or Comfort.* Either one party attempts to change and control the other or there is an acceptance/respect for individuality.

5. *Expansion or Abandonment.* Positive development leads to a desire to solidify the relationship by living together, formalized marriage, children. Negative development leads to a feeling of being trapped and despondency. In both cases there is an ultimate desire to return to rapture, though only one road leads to that magical state.

It was, as pop books go, intelligent and well written. Williams meant what she wrote and she wrote with feeling. *Rapture.* Danielle knew what that was. It was Morris cooking dinner for her in his brownstone. It was Dwayne at a Hitchcock double feature. It was Dwayne in the Poconos and that night at the Funhouse. *Rapture . . . But maybe that's the problem with Dwayne. Chasing rapture. Rapture is a drug that fills you with longing for that original high. He keeps calling. Like a junkie he craves that original rush. Sometimes, I do too.* She put the book back on the shelf and left the store.

SEVEN

The yellow tape that read **CRIME SCENE—DO NOT
ENTER** was strung across The Dance Inferno doorway. A
large padlock decorated the doorknob. About three feet in front
of the tape stood a group of politicians and clergymen, and behind them were television crews, photographers, and journalists. Prominent among the community leaders present was Dan
Winfrey, looking sharp in a light-blue summer suit, custom-
made white shirt, and navy blue silk tie. He stood before the
collected media stern-faced, ready to deliver his message of
morality and order. Off to the side, away from the media folk,
with a small crew of rappers and Inferno regulars, was Dwayne
Robinson.

Dan Winfrey stepped up to the microphone and adjusted his
tie. The television lights came on, the camera clicked, and
everyone fell silent. "My name is Dan Winfrey, and on behalf of
all of us gathered here today, I thank you in the media for re-
sponding to this moral emergency."

Dwayne thought, *Come on, you fool. Get to the pitch.*

"Three days ago a young man was shot dead in this building.
Many others were beaten and robbed, including visitors to the
South Bronx from Europe. Right now the only people charged
are those who eyewitnesses say were seen carrying a gun."

Dwayne's mind flashed back three days to the huge .45 in
Rahiem's hand and to his relief when Rahiem didn't bust a cap
in that Sugar Dice kid. He recalled his disgust when, after it was
all over, Sugar Dice claimed that Rahiem had fired into the
crowd.

Winfrey went on. "We think the D.A. hasn't gone far enough in pursuing the root cause of this incident—the rap show itself. In every borough of this city so-called rap crews are growing. They give parties, such as the Zulu National does in this borough. The Dance Inferno has been a site for these activities for two years."

Now Winfrey's voice became more sonorous, more accusing. "They call themselves 'crews' and purport to be engaged in musical activities. We collected here today believe these crews are just a new name for an old concept—gangs. While the Jolly Stompers and Tomahawks have faded, these rap crews now use music to camouflage their antisocial actions. A message must be sent. We want Lawrence Davis, whose rap tag is Joint-ski, to be indicted for conspiracy to incite a riot, for being a public nuisance and endangering the lives of unsuspecting young people, lured by music into sites of organized thievery. What we are asking for is moral leadership from the Bronx D.A. against a new form of antisocial juvenilia. Let me end with this thought: The ability to communicate is a license to advocate, but these young men must learn this gift should not be an invitation to anarchy. Are there any questions?"

Dwayne shouted, "That's all bullshit, Winfrey."

Winfrey ignored him. "Questions from the press, please!"

Dwayne's shout *"I am with the press!"* was drowned by the voices of the other rappers and kids around him echoing his original charge of "bullshit" and adding a few of their own.

"Yo, you fuckin' Uncle Tom!"

"You don't know jack 'bout this shit!"

"Rappers ain't asking no one to rob nobody!"

The cameras swiveled to record the protesters. Winfrey positioned himself to confront them. He thought it would show his willingness to dialogue with urban youth. Dwayne saw it as a slick play for the evening news. Either way, the ensuing footage (Winfrey: "Young man, we've got to protect the innocent young people of our community—even if it means inconveniencing a few." Dwayne: "Rap is a new expression of black culture that deserves nurturing, not suppression") made di-

verting viewing at 6 and 11 o'clock. The *Post* gave it page one
(**POL RAPS RAP RIOT**). That caught the mayor's attention.
He liked Winfrey and savored any opportunity to stick it to the
city's blacks. Three phone calls later Joint-ski was up for indict-
ment and Rahiem was under arrest. The mayor commended
Winfrey for addressing the "underlying immorality that creates
black-on-black crime, something the black officeholders of
this city refuse to condemn," and reassessed his chances for another term.

By that time Dwayne's first-person account of the shooting
("**BAD RAP**") had received a box on the *Village Voice*'s front
page. In it he reported, "While Rahiem's gun was clearly
visible—he held it only three feet from my face—he pulled it
back from the side of Dice aka Glenn Murphy's head and stuck
it back inside his jacket. He then yanked Joint-ski and me to our
feet and, miraculously, guided us through the crowd toward the
dressing room. Rahiem kicked the door open and dragged us inside. Joint-ski's producer, Reggie Olds, who had stayed inside
to recover from a stomachache, was on the phone with 911.
'Hurry!' he screamed. 'Kids are being hurt!' Rahiem pulled in a
couple of girls, then he barricaded the door. Time passed—
maybe ten minutes—before we heard police sirens. The nightmare had ended; the nightmare had just begun."

Dwayne thought it was probably the best thing he'd ever
written for the *Voice*. His Delux book proposal, *The Relentless
Beat*, was receiving attention at St. Martin's Press as a result of
it. Still most of the news wasn't good. Rahiem was in Rikers
and, with his outstanding warrants, it didn't seem likely he'd
be leaving soon. Joint-ski was out on bail, holed up in the
Bat Cave. Reggie sat in the Parson's Penthouse, listening to
Coltrane as he wrestled with his anger at Rahiem and Joint-ski
for attacking him, anger at himself for allowing their trust in
him to deteriorate, and, finally, anger at the Bronx D.A., the
mayor, and Winfrey for railroading his boys.

Dwayne spent a lot of his time closeted in his bedroom,
trying to focus on the Delux Records book, when he really
wanted to be with Danielle, talking with her, holding her, loving

her. Now everything was deadlines and pressure. The trial was coming up. Word had it that the hearings were being directed to Judge Peters' court on purpose, and it was only a matter of time before the *Post* or the *News* cold-busted him with Jacksina. *Hope the fool doesn't go down until this case. The Judge is homies' only hope.*

Danielle left the 42nd Street Library and looked at her watch. 4:30 p.m. She frowned. The opening edge of rush hour on an overcast August afternoon. Instead of squeezing into the subway up to Jacksina's apartment, Danielle waited for the air-conditioned 104 bus, which would take her across 42nd Street, up Eighth Avenue, and then past Columbus Circle up Broadway. It wasn't the fastest way to reach 68th Street, but it was calm and leisurely, two elements sorely missing from her life.

The bus arrived almost immediately. Danielle paid her 75 cents, climbed aboard, and looked for a seat. There was only one available, a few inches between a fat white businessman and a white woman lost in the pages of *Barron's*. Danielle said "Excuse me," assuming they would make room for her. Neither passenger budged. She tried glaring. No reaction. Suddenly her unspoken rage seemed to flood from her body and envelope the two seated passengers and they simultaneously made room for her.

Thank God the project is completed . . . but my work isn't finished yet. Have to make photocopies of it that Dan's office asked for. I need more résumés. Dan was sweet, letting me sit in on those staff meetings. He even bounced a few ideas off me. Dan's got plans for me. Fair enough. I have plans for him too. He's going to be my political mentor.

As the bus inched past the tawdry marquees, fast-food joints, and soiled souls on the storied block between Seventh and Eighth avenues, Danielle thought about the men in her life. *Dan satisfies my political curiosity, T.J. is there when I need a shoulder, and Morris just wants me playing Trivial Pursuit in his fancy brownstone. Lots of attention being paid to me, no doubt about that.*

The 104 finally turned onto Eighth Avenue, across from the Port Authority Bus Terminal, and continued past the Show World porno emporium and three burlesque theaters, two that featured women and one that offered young men. The bus stopped in front of the latter and took on some passengers. Danielle was seeing all this, along with the restaurants, Korean tourist shops, and the dingy tenements that lined Eighth, but registering very little of it. *Different men for different needs,* she mused. *Still, do I need all of them to replace Dwayne? He never really cared much about politics, and he certainly never committed to me like Morris. Throw in T.J. and Dan, and I've more men doing more for me than ever in my life. Yet more isn't better and more isn't deeper. More is actually too much of not enough.* Erasing Dwayne from her heart was proving to be a difficult task.

She decided to think about Jacksina and the Judge. Not that their situation was any better—it just wasn't her drama, which made for an easier study. Disaster loomed. Jacksina was determined to have the baby, delaying and/or totally derailing her legal career. Danielle was certain the Judge would split to save his marriage and/or career, destroying Jacksina in the process. Some snoop would find out about Jacksina and the baby and ruin both their reputations. And there was no silver lining. *Maybe if Jacksina had an abortion and broke up with the Judge and no one ever found out about them. Sure. And if there was no traffic in Manhattan, I'd be at the apartment by now.*

She got off in front of the big post office at 68th Street and crossed Broadway, still lost in thought. *Jacksina and I are different,* she decided, *yet in some fundamental ways we're the same: we go for it, whether it's careers or love or these strange situations where the two connect. My mother would never have gotten into any of the weirdness we have, even if she was tempted. Too many consequences. She'd say we were immature.* But, as Danielle entered the grounds of the Lincoln Towers, she came to a different conclusion: *We're just not as afraid of the pain.*

When Danielle opened the door to her old apartment she saw

a red-eyed Jacksina sitting in a chair by the sofa, staring in horror at a bunch of photographs. The Judge, grim as—well, a judge—was looking over her shoulder. Playing softly in the background was Teena Marie's romantic, sensual "Portuguese Love," a song that did not at all match the mood of the persons in the room.

"What's the matter?" Danielle asked.

"Oh, Danny," Jacksina said, "*look* at this shit."

Danielle put her purse and shopping bag down and went over to the sofa. Jacksina grabbed a handful of glossies and thrust them at her.

At least they weren't X-rated. But they were sufficiently incriminating: shots of them kissing in the backseats of cabs, holding hands or hugging in some auditorium (Avery Fisher Hall?), and one especially tender shot of the Judge standing at what appeared to be a window in a large hotel. Jacksina's head was on his shoulder and his arm was around her waist. They were both apparently in bathrobes.

"Well . . . this is a nice shot," Danielle said and giggled nervously.

"Don't you joke about this!" Jacksina yelled. "It's not funny."

"Danielle's right." The Judge chuckled. "It is a nice photograph of a nice morning. I remember it well." There was a smile plastered on his face, but when he sat down on the sofa next to the photographs his body sagged, his expression became grim again, and for the first time since Danielle had met him Judge Peters looked his real age.

"Who sent these?" Danielle asked.

"His wife," Jacksina spat. "The bitch Harriett sent them." She began to cry.

"It wasn't my wife."

"Who else would have done it?" Danielle asked.

"My wife would never have sent these to Jacksina in the mail. She would have handed them to me after dinner, and she would have said, 'Shit or get off the pot.' That's what she would have done. No. It wasn't her. It was someone else.

Probably the PBA or some rogue cops or, who knows, maybe even the FBI. This is some kind of interpersonal terrorism designed to scare me."

"Are you going to call the police?" Danielle asked.

"No," he said. "I'll delay that treat as long as I can. I have a lot of enemies in the department, too many to trust anyone at One Police Plaza with this. I'll wait."

Jacksina had stopped crying. The Judge was still slumped over, but no longer looked afraid. Danielle scooped up the pictures and laid them, facedown, on the table. Jacksina reached over to hug Danielle and be hugged back.

"It's going to be all right. I'll be there for you, Jack."

The two friends embraced. The Judge seemed to be shrinking before Danielle's eyes, growing smaller with each moment. Would he be there for Jacksina? Danielle didn't think so.

Dwayne hadn't been back in the Greene Street studio since that wonderful fun night Joint-ski cut "Break It Down." Tonight the vibe was so different: somber, dark, melancholy. No girls. No laughter. No Rahiem. Reggie sat in the control room behind the console, talking to the engineer. At one point Kelly Love Chase called, but he got off the phone quickly. Joint-ski nodded when Dwayne said, "What's up?" but he was really deep inside his head. Standing with earphones on their heads in the studio were several old-school legends—Kurtis Blow, Busy Bee, Melle Mel—who were free-styling for each other while waiting for Joint-ski.

"Let the track ride, Reg," Joint-ski said.

"What do you mean?"

"Just let it ride all the way out. I'll do the rhymes, they'll do the chorus, and then we'll free-style it. I don't wanna do no punch-ins tonight."

"Okay," Reggie responded. "It's your statement."

Joint-ski went into the studio with the other rappers.

"Damn, he seems so focused," Dwayne observed.

Reggie just grunted. When Joint-ski put on his earphones, Reggie motioned for the engineer to start the track.

It was a beat Rahiem had laid down with a beat box and scratching. Unlike "Break It Down's" sunny r&b feel, this beat was mean and slow, more truly b-boy than any record he'd made to date. Reggie didn't love it—didn't think black radio would play it—but under the circumstances he didn't want to fight about it. That so many old-schoolers had agreed to participate was what sold Reggie. Their appearance was a statement of solidarity. Maybe Joint-ski was soft, but they were down with him tonight.

Joint-ski leaned into the mike:

> "You see it started for me back in the day
> with DJ's rocking beats in the park around
>   the way
> Mama said stay/DJs go away
> But I wanna rap/I wanna play
> You see to me rap is a music of affirmation
> for a man of my persuasion
> It is a power incantation for the downtrodden
>   of this nation."

The old-schoolers joined in on the chorus, shouting:

> "Rap is my religion and it's not a split
>   decision
> I pledge allegiance to the beat like a soldier
>   of this nation."

Joint-ski went solo on the verse, rapping so hard spit flew out of his mouth:

> "There will come a time to put your heart on
>   the line
> I don't fret that moment
> 'Cause I'm strong in mind
> My father disowned me

My girlie postponed me
The IRS decided to phone me, but—"

Then the old-schoolers, all fired up, joined in for the chorus:

"Rap is my religion, so I'm strong in mind!
Yes, rap is my religion so I'm strong in mind!
Rap is my religion! Rap! Rap! Break it down!"

Joint-ski came back, "I can't hear you!"
"Rap! Rap!" they shouted back.
Joint-ski then improvised a riff that went, "Rap is my religion! Rap is my religion! Rap! Rap! Break it down!"
Reggie surprised the engineer by pulling several levers on the console. Now except for the beat box, the rapper's voices were on their own and, encouraged by Joint-ski, the old-schoolers free-styled rhymes on the "Rap is my religion" theme.
Dwayne danced around the control room, laughing and yelling. "This shit is the joint! It is the crazy joint!" Reggie grinned wide from ear to ear, then picked up the phone to dial Kelly in D.C. This single would pay for their honeymoon. The other rappers were now dancing around with their earphones on.
Amid all this joy Joint-ski stood, swaying slightly but not smiling. As the beat boomed through his earphones, he spoke, "This is a shout out to my brother-in-arms Rahiem! Stay strong! We will rock again! Believe it!"
Dwayne stopped dancing and Joint-ski stared back at him through the glass separating them. Dwayne looked at him, not with compassion, but pleasure. This was the beginning of his next article—a tale of rap and violence and young black men. Dwayne felt slightly guilty about his mercenary attitude, but when he considered how much everyone in the room could make off the record his guilt abated considerably.

In front of Sikulu's Records Store on 125th Street the sidewalk speaker spewed "Rap Is My Religion" into the hazy late-summer air like it was the ghetto national anthem. A grainy blow-up 8×10 of Joint-ski and Rahiem hung in the window. Someone had written in on the white border under their names, *Live From Rikers Island!* Dwayne had to smile at that.

Then he turned and walked down 125th Street past incense sellers, t-shirt vendors, loose-joint dealers, booksellers, cops, church ladies of both the revivalist and Jehovah's Witness persuasion, and foreign-born salespersons with Asian and Islamic accents hawking cheap clothes and imitation gold chains. With a brown nylon travel bag hanging from his shoulder, Dwayne crossed Malcolm X Boulevard. He moved swiftly over to Lenox. There he made a left and went down two blocks to Sylvia's.

Standing in front of the restaurant was a nervous-looking Walter Gibbs. "Yo, Gibbs, what's happening?" Dwayne reached out his hand.

"I'm cool, Dwayne. You know how it be in this business."

"You know, I hear you." He handed Gibbs the brown nylon bag. "Is he inside?"

"Yeah, he's sitting in the new dining room. You got mine?"

Dwayne smiled. "Sure, man, right here in my pocket."

"Why don't *you* do it?"

"We both wanted a public place but not a public face, you know what I mean? Besides, don't you need this money?"

"And you know that, homie." Gibbs reached into his dungaree jacket pocket for a cassette. "Could you give this to Reggie? It's a track that could be nice for a rapper."

"Cool. He owes you one after this. I'll be at the counter."

Dwayne went in first and took a seat at the counter. He ordered fried chicken, greens, and potato salad. Gibbs came in a few minutes later and walked into the dining room. Dwayne ate slowly, flirted with one of Sylvia's big-boned waitresses, and leafed through a copy of *Starlite*, a giveaway pamphlet that promoted Harlem bars. He was contemplating photos of "wet bikini" night at Duke's Lounge on Edgecombe Avenue when Sugar Dice swaggered out of the dining room, wearing one of his trademark green velour sweat suits. Under his right arm was the Gucci suit worn by Joint-ski that fateful night at the Inferno.

He and two posse members disappeared out of Sylvia's front door. Dwayne paid for his meal. In the dining room Gibbs sat holding one of Sylvia's "world famous talked about" ribs in his chubby mitts.

"How'd it go?" Dwayne asked.

Gibbs nodded toward a legal letter that sat next to a grease stain on the table. Between nibbles he remarked, "He really wanted that suit."

"He didn't turn down those five Gs, did he?"

"But it was the suit, my man" Gibbs replied. "I'm telling you, that suit might have been why he went after Joint-ski in the first place. He told me, 'A sucka like Joint-ski don't deserve fresh gear like that.' "

"Whatever," Dwayne said disdainfully. "Long as he drops his civil suit and doesn't testify in the criminal case, he could have Joint-ski's entire wardrobe."

"This business is funny," Gibbs said as he wiped.

"Isn't it? But these b-boys aren't like r and b brothers who went to church and all that. They got some other thing going on. Their values—what they like, what they respect, what they hate—are black but it's a different thing."

"Yeah," Gibbs agreed. "That 'Rap Is My Religion' is a hit but it ain't music."

"Tell you what. You may have just helped Reggie make a lot more of them."

"Well, fuck good music then," Gibbs said and began chewing on another rib. Dwayne excused himself and went back into the room with the counter and the pay phones. Reggie was waiting at the lawyers' office. "It went smoothly," Dwayne reported.

"Bring that letter down here right now," Reggie said anxiously. "Grab a gypsy cab."

"You'll pay for that too?"

"Just come on. The record is the hottest thing in New York, Philly, and D.C. Two hundred fifty twelve-inches. Now B.C. finally wants to do an LP. The sooner we get this over with—"

"Let me go then. Oh. Gibbs gave me a tape for you."

"No more r and b," Reggie declared.

"He said you could use it for rap."

"Nigger's just trying to get paid."

"Look who's talking."

"Just come on down."

In New York in the eighties all roads led to court. Traffic violations, bankruptcy, divorce, break-ins, discrimination, and the three Ms (mugging, mayhem, murder) were as much a part of metropolitan life as the rumble of subways and the shouts of school kids. Dwayne had been lucky. With the exception of his parents' divorce proceedings (which he wasn't allowed to attend) and a ticket for using a high school transit pass while attending St. John's, Dwayne had happily led a life that avoided the courtroom.

Now he was a participant-observer in a worthless case. *It's all so silly,* he thought as he stood on 161st Street at the bottom of the long staircase leading to the Bronx County Court. Joint-ski was accused of inciting the Dance Inferno crowd to riot and was supposed to be culpable in the ensuing violence. Moreover, the Bronx D.A.'s office asserted that Joint-ski had been encouraged in these activities by Rahiem who, the police alleged, was in cahoots with the Velour Crew to rob the Inferno's patrons.

This legal lynching of Joint-ski was actually just a smoke-screen to trap larger prey. Dwayne didn't know that until he watched the crew gathered on the steps for Dan Winfrey's latest press conference: a Hispanic woman who claimed she'd been assaulted by a black teen but whom the Judge had accused of lying; the teacher who'd questioned the Judge's morality for sending a seventeen-year-old for psychiatric treatment, not to jail, after the boy had attacked the teacher for allegedly uttering a racial slur in class; and Mayo, progressive r&b musician, who'd recently railed in *Billboard* that "rap is the first sign of decay in black music's long and varied history." *These folks are a dark-skinned lynch mob of vested interest,* Dwayne thought, *who Winfrey—and the PBA and the mayor?—rounded up to make the black Republican larger by pissing on the Judge.* It was shrewd and it was ugly.

"Our minority children, who demographers tell us are the future majority of New York, deserve uplifting music and real moral leadership from all areas, especially the bench." Winfrey was rolling. "Just because a judge is black and supposedly sensitive to minority youngsters doesn't mean he's working in the best interest of our community. The certainty of justice reinforces the lessons of right and wrong we teach in our homes. When outside forces—be they drug dealers or musical purveyors of violence—violate those teachings, then it is up to us to make sure the fabric of our families is not worn down and, eventually, shredded. Calling for black pride is only a whitewash way it's used to condone self-genocide.

"Judge Peters is a black man. But he must understand that true commitment to his people, the kind of commitment I believe I have, leaves no room for liberal waffling or false black pride. Young people, black people, have been injured, and this music—wild, angry, rebellious—inspired this carnage. Judge Peters must now speak with a moral voice!"

Damn. Dwayne clicked off his tape recorder. *That speech was strong . . . if you go in for that kind of thing. My man is frightening—a black neo-con who can move the crowd. Winfrey ain't Thomas Sowell.*

"Hello, Dwayne."

Danielle stood next to him at the bottom of the courthouse steps, looking him dead in the eye. His knees felt weak and he gasped fitfully for words.

At first she wasn't going to say anything. She was just going to stand next to Phyllis Cole and watch from a distance. Maybe Dwayne would cause another scene and give T.J. and her mother something else to laugh about over dinner. She hoped not, though she had to admit there was something exciting about Dwayne challenging Dan Winfrey. And then, as if she were iron and he a magnet, she found herself moving toward him. It had been a while since they last saw each other. She inventoried him. His beard was neat, though too long. He wore a beige cotton shirt and the brown gabardine slacks she'd bought during a spring clearance sale at Barney's. His butt, she thought, still looked good.

"Preparing for another tv appearance?" she asked sarcastically. He ignored her comment and tried to pull himself together.

"Are we still speaking?"

"You look good on tv, Dwayne."

"So we are talking. How are you?"

"I'm fine. Sorry about Rahiem and Joint-ski."

"And I'm sorry you're hanging around Winfrey."

Slightly embarrassed, Danielle said, "He liked my paper. He's not a hundred percent right, but he's far from all wrong, you know."

"Same could be said of me."

"Please, Dwayne, don't try that one."

"Okay. I love you."

Just then Phyllis Cole, thirty-something, with thick glasses and an officious air, walked up to them. "Danielle, are you coming downtown with us?"

"Dwayne, this is Phyllis Cole, Dan Winfrey's press representative." They shook hands coldly.

As a peace offering Dwayne said, "Your candidate made a strong presentation."

"He always does," Phyllis said crisply. "Danielle—are you coming?"

"I thought," Dwayne interjected, "you were coming to the ball game with me."

"Really?"

"Like we planned."

"Like we planned? Oh . . . right." Danielle knew they had to complete this conversation. Cole minced off without even glancing at Dwayne.

"Thank you," he said.

"You may not be happy when we finish talking."

"At least we're talking." Dwayne risked a smile.

"Where to?"

"This way." They headed toward the stadium.

Dave Winfield's body reared back, waiting for the pitch from the Orioles' Mike Flanagan. A white blur flew from the left-hander's fingers and Winfield put his 6-foot 6-inch frame into a swing that sent a frozen rope of a line drive down the right-field line. It bounced into the right-field corner below Dwayne's and Danielle's seats and disappeared from sight until the Orioles' right-fielder threw it back toward the infield. Winfield coasted into second base with a double.

"I love to watch him play," Danielle said. "He's so long and graceful."

"Seems like you needed to do this," he said.

"Guess I did, though I didn't know that when you suggested it." The inning ended with a strike-out and the Yankees took the field. Long and lean Winfield ambled out to his position in right field, just below them.

"I told you I loved you," he said.

Now he was pushing his luck and she could stay cool no longer. "You think saying that will make everything all right? When I needed to hear it you didn't say it. Everything that happened—everything—was *your* choice. You tried to make it seem like I did it, but Dwayne it was always about what you wanted."

"Look, Danielle, I can say it now. I can express that feeling now. I couldn't before. Doesn't that make a difference?"

He tried to kiss her, but she resisted. "I'm going."

"No." He grabbed her arm.

"Yes." She pulled away.

"Don't leave."

"Please, Dwayne!"

There was the loud crack of the bat and the crowd went "AHHHH!" All around them people stood up. A ball was heading their way and Winfield was running right at them. He leaped so high you could see his glove over the edge of the fence. The ball landed just two rows in front of Dwayne. Hands reached. Bodies dove. Dwayne ducked, but it didn't prevent a fat, three-hundred-pound father of four from Yonkers from falling backwards onto him and knocking him to the ground. By the time Dwayne had crawled out from under the man and grabbed a breath of air, Danielle had escaped into the vastness of the house that Ruth built. Dwayne's clothes were drenched with beer. The colossus from Yonkers mumbled an apology as Dwayne stared down at Winfield, whose white-and-blue uniform was outlined against the stadium's grass as he moved back into position. *At least baseball makes sense,* Dwayne reflected gloomily. *Hit three home runs, you win. Give up three home runs, you lose. Life is something else. Saying you love someone isn't enough when you finally get around to it. People actually have to believe you mean it.*

Dwayne left the game early and walked over the bridge at 155th Street from the Bronx to Harlem. He'd wandered through the 150s and 140s before he realized where he was headed. On 135th Street and Adam Clayton Powell Boulevard, Dwayne went past the shuttered fronts of two legendary Harlem watering holes, Small's Paradise and the Red Rooster, where the low and high of Harlem once partied. The Renaissance Ballroom, long-ago home to big bands and a powerhouse basketball team, was up the boulevard a few blocks, but nothing was happening there either. The only still vital sign of old Harlem on this corner was the YMCA, once home to famous poets and artists and still an important social center. The boastful sign, **HARLEM PLAYS THE BEST BALL IN THE COUNTRY,** spread across the schoolyard wall on 135th Street near Lenox, a relic from the days when the public schools possessed, not just talent, but clean gyms and smart coaches. Nearing Lenox, Dwayne passed the old Schomburg Library, which had nurtured generations of scholars. On the corner the new Schomburg sat, a long, three-story building of brown brick in which Dwayne had spent many hours in search of history.

Dwayne walked slowly through the first-floor gallery, where the work of photographer Austin Hansen hung. Though the photos ranged from 1940 to 1980, he was drawn to the images from the early forties to the early sixties—the two postwar decades before heroin's conquest of Harlem; before the flight of the black working class to the other boroughs and the suburbs; before Charles Rangel's ascendence and Malcolm's assassination. Dwayne peered into the pictures, looking at a heritage he'd never fully reclaim. In black leotards, her left leg raised high as she spun, Eartha Kitt instructed a dance class at the Harlem Y in 1955. Talking to each other, confidently, casually, perhaps conspiratorially, were Malcolm X and Adam Clayton Powell, a picture Dwayne thought spoke volumes about Harlem leadership then and now. Hansen's street scenes captured a cluttered neighborhood of churches, social clubs, and neat homes that were now obscured beneath two generations of graffiti. In a crowd shot of Powell speaking to a huge gathering at the corner of 125th Street and Seventh Avenue, he saw men in wide-brimmed hats and baggy suits, and felt himself falling into the picture. Suddenly he was a little boy in the crowd and his father was wearing one of those funny-looking hats on a day back when Harlem was still vogue.

Dwayne was so young that when his dad said "Harlem," he heard "Holland," the legendary land of windmills. Yet he was already perceptive enough to recognize that it was Dinah Washington's voice he heard on the radio as his dad took him on his first trip "uptown." His dad, a Southern boy, fresh from Korea and backed by the positive push of the G.I. bill, had moved north with his young bride, gotten a comfortable government gig at the post office. Then, with remarkable alacrity, he was ground up by the real-life windmills of Harlem.

On the car radio, as they crossed 125th Street, Dwayne heard Washington and Brook Benton—one of his mother's favorite singers—dueting on "Baby (You Got What It Takes)." His father cruised over to a tenement on Lenox Avenue, where, briefly, they visited a woman and her two kids, neither of whom Dwayne liked. For some reason they called his dad "Pete," which was not his name, and they never addressed Dwayne by name.

But the centerpiece of the outing was a club on St. Nicholas Avenue which, years later, Dwayne saw on a real-life Dinah Washington video. The place was big and dark and cool and it was filled with that distinctive blend of relaxed, Southern-bred demeanor refined by the big-city sophistication known as cool. Around the bar, men sported straw hats, loose-fitting trousers, and broad suspenders, while young women with bright-red lips wore skin-tight sweaters and skirts, multilayered wigs, and powerful perfumes that pierced the haze of Lucky Strikes and Kools. Dwayne could still hear Washington singing "This Bitter Earth" on the jukebox, a song whose bluesy melancholy could drive an optimist to tears. The barmaid, a large, fleshy woman, placed a Coke spiced with a cherry in front of Dwayne as his father told him to wait and disappeared into a back room, and Washington's voice floated above the wigs and the clouds of acrid smoke. Dwayne sat at the bar, dutifully sucking on his cherry, wondering where Dad was. Couples ground their hips to the swaying tempo of the string bass as an endlessly repeated record that lasted only a few minutes seemed to malinger in the air for hours. Finally, just as the tears were beginning to rise, Dwayne's father emerged from the back room and they went home.

Back in the present, Dwayne recalled how disappointed he was when he learned at age seven that there were no windmills in Harlem. Now, outside the Schomburg, he opened his bag, grabbed his telephone book, and walked over to a pay phone. He looked up the number, fed in coins, and punched seven digits.

"Hello. This is your son. Would you like to get together sometime?"

His father said, "Hell, yes."

"All right, then."

Dwayne's dad elected that they meet the next morning at nine, at Perk's, on 123rd Street and Manhattan Avenue. It was a small soul-food restaurant built into the first floor of a brownstone. Dimly lit, homey, and quite country, Perk's was frequented by the sons and daughters of North and South Carolina and Virginia who'd come up the Eastern Seaboard during the fifties seeking gainful employment and a little urban romance.

Dwayne sat at a table near the door, nursed a cup of tea, and watched the nurses, garbagemen, McDonald's employees, mechanics, and cleaning women whose voices were a mix of Newport News and Gun Hill Road. The aroma of freshly fired bacon and pancakes filled Perk's while cuts from one of B. B. King and Bobby "Blue" Bland's live album filled the speakers. Dwayne put down his cup and looked at his watch. *He's late. Or am I just antsy? You call a meeting, you should have something to say. I don't. Not really. Just questions. Yet inside— really inside—I'm afraid. I want to get the hell out of here and get back to my real life and not deal with these fucking ghosts. I became a man without these answers. So why do I need them now?*

" 'Cuse me." The waitress, a short, round woman with silver hair sauntered over. "You wanna order?"

"No, I want the check."

"The check? Ain't you meetin' someone?"

"He's late."

"You ain't been here but fifteen minutes yourself, honey. Why don't you look friendly so when he do come your body's not ready to leave."

"Makes sense."

"Sally always makes sense," a male voice added. Then, as if by magic, Dwayne's father appeared next to her. He was wearing a red and black knit sweater, white slacks, and a black Kangol, which was very b-boy circa 1967.

"Robinson," Sally said. "Where you been, handsome?"

The elder Robinson gave her a soft kiss on the cheek that lingered two seconds beyond friendly.

"Been working, baby. See you met my son. Looks even better than me."

"Not much."

He kissed her cheek again. "I gotta watch that 'cause you might be habit-forming." He sat down across from Dwayne. "You order yet?"

"Waiting for you."

"I know your order," Sally said to Mr. Robinson. "What would you like, honey?"

Dwayne ordered a full breakfast, then focused his eyes on his father's face. Yeah, it was rounder, beardless, nicked by years of shaving, about two shades lighter than he remembered, and wrinkled around the eyes. Still, it was Dwayne's face. No doubt about that.

"I'm glad you called," Dwayne's face said to him. "Took you a long time to get back to me." Dwayne said nothing; he was mesmerized by his reflection in flesh.

"You gonna talk to me?" the face inquired. Dwayne didn't know where to start. His father filled the silence with the comment, "You sure look like me."

"You mean," Dwayne countered, "*you* look like *me*, except older."

His father smiled. "You'd get used to it if you'd called me back and come hung with me. You act like you don't have a father."

"I didn't. Not after I was fourteen."

His namesake just looked at him. Then he pulled a pack of Kools out of his pants pocket.

"Want one?"

"You know I don't smoke."

"Thought maybe you changed."

Sally came over with their food and her good cheer. Dwayne's father flirted with her a bit, while Dwayne looked on with a forced smile. When Sally was gone his father's face turned serious.

"You act like I owe you something."

"You don't think you do?"

"Son, you never missed a meal because I wasn't home. Unlike a lot of men out here I made sure you were taken care of. I never stopped loving you. You just got an attitude and been actin' like a baby ever since. That's the only problem."

"Did you love Ma?"

His father made a face and mashed out his cigarette. "Is that it? Is that what's been rolling around in your head all this time? Shit, we could have addressed this a long time ago."

"Well?"

"Yeah, boy, I loved your mother. Still do." He paused. He looked down at the table and then back at his son. "But we had disagreements from the very beginning." He paused again. Dwayne couldn't hear the jukebox or talk in the room—only his heartbeat. "Okay, let me say it straight: it got to the point either I would have killed her or she would've killed me. That's how rough it was between us before I left. I'm talkin' to you like a man now, son, and I'm talkin' about your mother like she's a woman."

"Fuck you," was Dwayne's measured response. His voice rose. "You were cheating on her. You say you loved her. Then you stepped out on her. That's what it's all about. Tell me I'm wrong."

Heads turned. A pair of old men at a nearby table gave him an openly disgusted look. Other customers stopped talking, wanting to hear some more dirt.

"Fuck me? Is that what you said? Well, I'll be damned. Try to treat you like a man but you ain't one yet. Shit. You still caught up in your mama's skirt. Don't want to hear the fuckin' truth."

Dwayne jumped up and shouted, "Don't curse her!"

Sally came over to the table. "Y'all gonna have to keep your domestic dispute quieter." They ignored her.

"Curse her?" Dwayne Senior stood up, hurt and mad. "I wasn't cursing Miriam, I was cursing you."

Father and son stood there, glaring at mirror images of themselves. Perhaps if Dwayne had been more open, better able to make small talk, perhaps if his father hadn't been so wounded by the "Fuck you!" they could have made something good happen. Perhaps if they'd merely sat their asses down . . .

"Sit down, boy," Mr. Robinson said.

Dwayne just scooped up his bag and walked away.

"Where you going?"

As his son disappeared out the door, Dwayne Robinson, Sr.,

pulled out another Kool and lit it with his silver lighter. "He left his food," Sally observed.

"That boy is a kid." He puffed on a freshly lit Kool. "Too long up under his mother. I thought I raised him right, but damn . . ."

"If that tall, bearded fella's a kid, then what are you?"

He looked at her with a long, lusty leer. "That makes me a young man full of fire."

For the first time since he entered, Sally's gaze was less than adoring. "Lordy, lordy, Dwayne Robinson," she said softly. "You're a mess. A pur-dee mess."

"I'm sorry for him personally." Dan Winfrey was driving his blue Toyota up the FDR Drive. Phyllis Cole sat beside him and Danielle was in the backseat. "And for the young lady as well."

"But it just confirms that our whole campaign was on target," Cole chimed in. "I hate to gloat, but it shows he's got no more morality than the average black Democratic politician. Judge Peters gained power by backing Rangel against Congressman Powell when Powell was in Bimini. And he kept it by ruling against the 'racist' judicial system. Now the public sees his true colors. I love it. It makes you look so good, Dan."

Throughout her gleeful diatribe Phyllis kept rubbing her hand over the front page of the *New York Post*, perhaps hoping the ink would enter her bloodstream. **JUDGMENT OF LOVE!** was the banner headline that ran down the tabloid's right side. Next to it was a large, grainy photo of Judge Peters standing at a hotel room window with Jacksina's arms around his waist and her head on his shoulder.

Danielle had seen the compromising photo before it showed up in the *Post*. Still, there was nothing like seeing it on the front page. Next week was Halloween, but the tricks had already started. And where was Jacksina? Her parents, sick with worry, had called Danielle in search of their daughter, but her best friend knew as little as they did.

Danielle didn't know that the *Post* had called the Judge at home for a comment. His reply to them was to curse *Post* owner

Murdoch's mother and her ancestry. He slammed the receiver down and called Jacksina. Too late—a reporter had somehow tracked her down and got through to her. And his wife, his too-long-suffering wife, overheard him tell Jacksina "I love you," and decided it was time to act—the judgment of love indeed!

All Danielle knew was that her friend had vanished and that Jacksina's love affair was spray-painted across the front page of a rag. And that she was sitting—at her own request—in a car with a politician and his sidekick, who were both crowing over these events.

"Who do you think planted the photo?" Danielle asked cautiously.

"Harriett," Cole said too quickly and too gleefully, as though she knew something.

"Harriett is a lovely woman," Winfrey said. "It is a family tragedy and I feel bad for her."

If that's the case, then why are you cultivating my young self? Danielle thought. *Forget holding your tongue.*

"It was the PBA," she announced. "Probably with the mayor's backing."

"What are you *talking* about?" Cole said almost hysterically. "That's a *very* irresponsible thing to say, Danielle."

Winfrey was much calmer. He peered into the rearview mirror and saw the scowl on Danielle's face. "If you have some information, Danielle, I suggest you share it with us." His voice was cold.

"I know Jacksina and I've met the Judge."

"Go on."

"She talked a lot about the harassment and the threats he received from the PBA. I think they finally decided to get him."

"You *knew* about this affair?" Cole was outraged.

"Jacksina was my roommate for two years."

Cole turned around to face her as the car navigated the traffic on the 155th Street Bridge. "You could have done this city a great service by exposing that old hypocrite. Did you ever think about that? You've been hanging around Dan for these last few months—you know his feelings about Peters—yet you said nothing about this. You hang out with *Village Voice* writers. What are you up to, Danielle?"

"Stop it!" Winfrey said. "Stop it right now!"

He pulled over to the curb on a street next to Babe Ruth Park, the athletic field across the street from Yankee Stadium.

"That was totally uncalled for, Ms. Cole. I won't tolerate that kind of talk around me. Understand?" Phyllis quieted, but her eyes still cut into Danielle. As far as she was concerned—suspicion confirmed.

"Danielle, you have said some very disturbing things," he said slowly. "You've shaken me, as you have Ms. Cole. But I can't worry about that right now. The media are collected in front of the courthouse, waiting for me to comment on the *Post* story. If you have some other information, kindly tell me now. Not later."

Danielle searched her mind as Cole and Winfrey glowered at her from the front seat. "Nothing concrete," she said hesitantly. "Nothing but what they said. . . . If there were letters or names of actual officers involved, I never saw them."

Winfrey thought she was lying. At that moment, however, a lie was fine with him. It gave him a clear conscience to do what he was about to do. "Okay." He looked at his watch, then softened the tone of his voice. "Danielle, I'm going to ask you to get out of the car. We are only a few blocks away from the court. We will leave a seat for you in the courtroom as we'd promised but, under the circumstances, I don't feel comfortable arriving with you."

Danielle got out. The car pulled off and she walked toward Yankee Stadium in search of a pay phone.

For Dwayne it was like watching an all-star game. Joint-ski strolled up to the courthouse with his mother and attorney. A few steps behind them came Reggie and his fiancée, Kelly Love Chase. Mayo, master musical conceptualist and budding neo-conservative, walked in with Seth Grassburg, a *Billboard* reporter. Mayo looked resplendent in a gray Nehru jacket adorned with three buttons: one said **BLACK POWER** in red letters on black, one was a small head shot of Jimi Hendrix, and the last bore an **MSS** aka "Marcus Silver Sings" logo. He was running his rhetorical game and Glassburg was going for it. Dance Inferno owner Randy Tarrentino and several old-schoolers— Kurtis Blow, June Bug Starski, Grandmaster Flash—emerged together from an enormous black Cadillac. Randy looked very unhappy. The small media group that stood in the entrance to the courthouse let these folks pass by—just some New York music types. Then they trotted down the steps to meet their designated champion: Dan Winfrey of the GOP. Cole read a prepared statement while the press encircled them.

Dwayne didn't care. No Danielle. He hoped she was with Jacksina in some safe place—if such a place existed in these parts—holding her hand and offering that love she'd tried so often to share with him. Looking at Winfrey preen himself, he concluded that he was the slimy son of a bitch who had leaked the photos.

"This is a profound public tragedy for this man, his wife and family, and for all New Yorkers," Winfrey began. "We've had our differences, as you all know, but I hate to see anyone's dirty laundry aired in the media. However I feel obligated to out—"

That's it. I can't listen to this, Dwayne thought. *Either I go after him and get busted for publicly denouncing him as a fraud in a Brooks Brothers suit, or I go inside, find my seat, and write the best damn story I can.* He turned around and walked in.

The Bronx courthouse hallway was crowded with white men in cheap, wrinkled, ill-fitting suits. Most carried brown briefcases in various stages of disrepair. Bespectacled legal-aid lawyers with serious, noncommital faces strolled about, speaking in subdued voices with black- or brown-skinned men and women—defendants, victims, and friends of both.

The air stank of defeat. Defiantly, Dwayne sucked it in. It was all so sad and desperate that he felt himself slipping into a detached, surreal dream to counteract the real darkness that was closing in on him. He closed his eyes for a moment and imagined himself back in his quiet room, reviewing a brand-new LP . . .

"Dwayne."

"Huh?"

"No time to daydream."

"Reggie. Yo man, did you see the *Post?*"

"Does a rat cut cheese?" Reggie asked.

"You know the Judge might just do Joint-ski to prove a point."

"That thought crossed my mind."

"But Reg, on second thought, he's too irascible to change his game. Damn, it's amazing isn't it? Look where this rap thing has taken us."

"You got a point. My life is so damn different. I got a woman. Hit records. A little cash in the bank. And soon as this is over, I'm through with Joint-ski."

"What?"

"I got an override on all his subsequent albums, so I'm selling my production contract with them outright to Mayo and B.C. I'm cashing out."

"I thought Mayo hated rap."

"You see the sales figures on 'Rap Is My Religion'? He's a businessman. That Marcus Silver project sank like a rock, so he's on to the next thing. Besides he's got some concept for smoothing out rap that he wants to try."

"Reg, this is not good news."

"Did that girl Danielle break your heart?"

"Right now it's just cracked."

"When it finally splits in two, you'll cry a little bit, maybe bug out. But, whenever you really fall in love, you'll understand why I did this."

"You're giving up music for your woman?"

"No, I'm just gonna get my money straight before I go on to my next project—making more babies."

"Damn, Reggie," Dwayne said.

Winfrey, the print reporters, and several highly interested spectators walked inside the courtroom. Dwayne and Reggie exchanged "Fuck him!" looks and followed.

Fifteen minutes later there was chaos in the hallway. The attorneys, the criminals, the victims and their friends who'd stood by the door as Judge Peters spoke, now fanned out throughout the building.

"Yo, the rappin' homie got off clean!" said a brother up for assaulting a bag lady on a D train platform. "The Judge had the gig, Holmes," said an Hispanic dude known for ripping off drug dealers. "You knew he'd let that kid step. I'm countin' on him to fix me. I'm gonna admit I take off dealers, but that I'm like Robin Hood and shit."

"You're over, blood."

"What you mean?"

"Judge Peters just quit."

"Ah, shit." The dude's eyes darted around the hallway. "Where's my fuckin' lawyer? Better take the motherfuckin' plea bargain."

Outside the courtroom a *Post* reporter stopped to get a comment from a shell-shocked Winfrey, while everyone else sprinted down the courthouse steps to where Judge Peters was to hold a press conference.

"What about Rahiem?" Joint-ski asked Reggie as they left the courtroom.

"It'll be okay," Reggie said. "Sugar Dice has recanted his story. The D.A. will drop those crazy charges. But I don't know about that gun possession charge. Rahiem's got a record and the D.A. will definitely want something to show for this mess." Joint-ski didn't say anything. He was happy about getting off, but the news about Rahiem made him uneasy. Again, on the plus side, he was relieved that he appeared to be back in full effect with Reggie. Then Mayo came over. Reggie said, "Joint-ski, this is Mayo, the best and smartest record producer in New York."

"Always been a fan of you and your music," Mayo said. "My man, you have so much potential."

Dwayne was one of the last to leave the courtroom. He had been too busy scribbling in his notebook. At the far end of the now almost deserted hallway he saw Danielle. Her face was tense and preoccupied. He hurried toward her. She didn't appear to see him and quickly disappeared through the entranceway.

"Danielle!"

Dwayne rushed out of the building and promptly bumped into the D train mugger and the Hispanic Robin Hood, almost knocking them down. "Get the fuck off of me!" the mugger screamed.

"Sorry, my man," Dwayne said.

"Brother better watch himself," Robin Hood mumbled.

Dwayne looked down the steps, toward 161st Street, where he could see the Judge, holding hands with Jacksina while addressing a battery of photographers, reporters, and tv cameras.

"The banality of evil is usually supported by the mediocrity of the masses. That's why the mayor, the head of the PBA, the Bronx D.A., and my sepia-toned Republican friend all have jobs. I can't prove the direct involvement of each in the smear campaign against me, but I do have enough circumstantial evidence for some of you more aggressive reporters to have a nice couple of weeks of headlines. Always remember: the ability to communicate is a license to advocate."

"What about your wife?" a black woman from the *Amsterdam News* shouted. The reporter was talking to the Judge, but her eyes were glued to Jacksina's growing stomach.

"My wife has stood by my side for over twenty years. I owe her the respect of not further embarrassing her by trying to speak for or about her at this time. Jacksina, since the media people know who you are already, please hand out that information to the press."

There was shouting from behind the Judge. He and everyone else turned toward the courthouse where, at the top of the steps, several men were engaged in a furious fistfight. "I'll miss New York," he said and then laughed loudly.

"That's Danielle!" Jacksina screamed.

At the same moment the Judge began addressing the media, a melee had started at the doorway, instigated by Dwayne Robinson. First his eyes had been drawn to the press conference on 161st Street. But then, looking to his left, he saw an image that taunted him like a heckler. Danielle and T.J. stood on the steps talking. T.J. held both her hands in his. Standing nearby, whispering anxiously, were Winfrey and his faithful Ms. Cole. Dwayne collected himself and moved toward them. When he got there he acted as if T.J. were invisible. "Danielle," he said. "I need to talk to you."

"Well," T.J. cut in, "she doesn't need to talk to you."

"T.J., no!" Danielle said sharply. He let go of her hands.

"I love you, Ersatz," Dwayne said.

"What mess are you saying now, Dwayne?" T.J. demanded. Dwayne turned toward him. A nasty smile appeared on his face. "I know *you* ain't talking to me, you oreo motherfucker."

T.J. reared back to throw a punch. Jealousy was clearly on his side. But years of alcohol and no exercise made him slower than a young man should be. Dwayne, however, had a lot on his side—class resentment dating back to high school, the fact that he was still pissed about what went down with Evette in St. John's, and his own jealousy. Dwayne's accumulated grievances made him quick enough to deftly duck T.J.'s awkward, head-hunting right. As T.J.'s fist flew by, Dwayne sent a straight right into his ample stomach. T.J. doubled over in pain. Winfrey, after a moment's calculation, decided it was in his best interest to play peacemaker. He pinned Dwayne's arms from behind to stop him from harming T.J. any further.

That could have been the end of it, but when Joint-ski, who had been parlaying with two old-school rappers, saw two suit-and-tie Negroes trying to yoke Dwayne, he charged Winfrey from behind. At the same moment T.J., not fully revived but still game for a fight, rose to his feet. The four of them slammed together in one clump and fell to the steps. Dwayne was trying to pump a right hand into T.J.'s unwilling face, while T.J. struggled to get a grip on Dwayne's neck. Joint-ski was working on pushing Winfrey's telegenic face into the steps, while the taller Winfrey was furiously pumping elbows into the rapper's ribs. A battery of officers emerged from the courthouse to subdue the battling brothers.

By now the reporters had climbed the stairs and were snapping and videoing and feeling good about themselves. Visuals always told a story better. Danielle stood among the media, as fascinated as they were by this spectacle, but not nearly as happy. If she didn't know and, in fact, love some of the men involved, the whole thing might have been funny. But her only thought was a sad one: *Maybe, from the beginning, I've been giving men way too much credit.*

It was early on moving day at the Parson's Penthouse. Boxes were everywhere. Crates of records were stacked on top of each other in the living room. The sofa was gone—in its place were three years' worth of ground-in dirt, lint balls, small change, and two used condoms. Dwayne sat on the steps to the living room, drinking orange juice from a glass and looking out the window at the hazy summer light. Occasionally he would flex his left hand, which was wrapped in an Ace bandage.

Back to Brooklyn in style. That's how I'm living. Duplex. Brownstone. Fireplace. High ceilings. Backyard. All that. It's good. My mother loves it. Women will love it. Yup. If that's what I want. Lots of women. But that isn't what I want. It would make everything a lot easier if I really did.

Wearing pajama pants and a Joint-ski shirt, Reggie came out of the hallway, surveyed the room, then sat down next to him. "So how you feel today, Sugar Ray?" Dwayne chuckled. Reggie continued. "I hear the Golden Glove people are anxious for your next bout."

"So I'm Sugar Ray now, huh? Should I take that as a compliment or are you just being your usual sarcastic self?"

Reggie was a bit surprised by Dwayne's sour tone. "Have I done something wrong? You've been really nasty towards me lately. I don't need you mad at me now. I've got enough stress as it is."

"Stress? Reggie, please. You got a real woman. You got paid by selling Joint-ski to Mayo. You're moving to the suburbs. *I'm* the man with stress."

"Okay," Reggie admitted as Dwayne sipped his juice. "My

stress is different from yours. All I have to do is live the way people are supposed to. Have kids. Mow the lawn. Make love only to my wife." Reggie sighed theatrically. "Your stress is that you got to live with messing up your love life."

"That's right."

"But do yourself a favor."

"What's that?"

"Blame your motherfucking self."

"What?"

"Don't blame your father. Don't blame your mother. Don't blame your ex-woman. And don't blame me." Dwayne didn't speak. He just took his empty glass and flung it against the wall, spewing fragments of glass around the living room. Then he stood up.

"Don't worry! I know I fucked up! I-KNOW-I-FUCKED UP!" He stomped across the living room to the windows and began pacing in front of them. Reggie remained calm. "Dwayne," he said. "Dwayne. Dwayne, listen!" Dwayne stopped pacing. "I may have influenced you. A lot of other people may have influenced you. But in life you are alone. You can have lovers and family and friends. But the decisions you make are yours. I didn't know how much I needed Kelly until I met her. I had to make the decision to open myself to her and I did and it's fine. Scary but fine."

Dwayne turned around. He was still upset but the embers of anger inside him had cooled. "And I didn't for Danielle?"

"You know it yourself. It wasn't your time, Dwayne. That's all. You're not evil, my man. You have a hell of a time paying your bills and you can't cook at all, but you're not evil. You just gotta be patient."

"Thanks."

Reggie got up and walked across the now empty living room. He embraced Dwayne as an older brother would have. When they let go, Reggie reached into his back pocket and pulled out a copy of *Essence*. "You know, I really came in here to compliment you. This essay is one of the best things you've ever written. I'm telling you, Dwayne, one more heartbreaking romance and you'll be ready for prime time."

Dwayne took the magazine out of Reggie's hand and looked at his narrow, hairy, nicely retouched face peering back at him. He had finally written his "Say Brother" piece. It was called "My Dream Girl." With a forced smile Dwayne said, "Joint-ski called and said I went out like a sucka."

"Well, Dwayne." Reggie paused and put his hand, now more fatherly than brotherly, on Dwayne's shoulder. "You love rap and all that. But you are no b-boy. You are an r and b man. One thing about r and b men—they ain't afraid to whine for a woman and, brother, you do some world-class whining in here." With a smile Reggie added, "My wife-to-be loved it." Reggie moved back up the steps toward the hallway. "When are your movers coming?" he asked.

"In about two hours."

"Kelly and her brothers will be here this afternoon. Wish the phone was still on."

"Don't you talk to her enough?"

"Not yet," Reggie said and then disappeared down the hallway. Dwayne looked down at the "Say Brother" and began reading himself to himself. He liked the second paragraph:

> "The reality of my desires, though, is that my kind of dream girl has very definite dreams of her own. Quite often (too often for my peace of mind) her dreams conflict with mine and can turn this self-confessed romantic into a mean, tear-inducing nightmare. Adjusting to her dream (or accepting the fact that I can't) has been one of the major learning experiences of my young adulthood."

In her Hoboken studio apartment Danielle finished that paragraph and frowned. She was sitting curled up barefoot on her black futon. She'd been flipping through three months of unread magazines when Dwayne's name in the table of contents caught her eye. Nothing unusual except that he'd written a "Say Brother" and not a music piece. There was his picture: boyish, cute, arrogant, insensitive. The pull quote ("My Dream Girl is beautiful, smart, ambitious, but can I deal with her in real life?") had made her groan. She didn't want to read it but she had to.

Farther down it read, "Love is a dream on the tip of my tongue. Love is a memory of things not done. Love is moments lost in the search for feelings unspoken." The phone rang. The answering machine clicked on. Her voice announced, "This is Danielle Embry. Life is fascinating, so tell me about it."

There was a beep and then Morris's voice said, "Danny, T.J. and I played racquetball this morning." Danielle frowned. "We were thinking we'll go to the Winfrey fund-raiser at Tavern on the Green together. I tell you he's beginning to make sense to me. Me, you, Ernest and Von—and T.J. will bring a date. I think it's a great idea. I'm sure I could sell some real estate there. Besides, we all should be hanging out together again. That's the way it should be, you know. I'm going to look at some buildings, so call me later. I love you."

Danielle could have picked up the phone, could have spoken with the man who loved her unreservedly, the man who wanted her in his house, in his space, in his blood. But Dwayne Robinson had written something she wanted to read and, at that moment, it was more important.

She picked up the "Say Brother" where he'd written:

You don't want to have any regrets, because regretting is remembering bad things, remembering mistakes, remembering the taste of her mouth and the way the tip of her tongue felt against the tip of mine. It's remembering her breath on my pillow. It's remembering how much she loved me and how I toyed with that love like a child with a video game and then discarded it for something newer and easier. Regretting is knowing how stupid you acted and the pain that makes you cry way behind your eyeballs.

I do that a lot these days. In a meeting or in the street I'll feel a spasm of regret cut through me and the tears behind my eyeballs begin to flow. What's really scary though is that I even cry that way when I'm alone. I can't cry like I should.

No water. No sobbing. I just can't seem to give in to regret. Too unmanly, I guess. But one layer below the surface I'm blubbering like a baby. I just don't trust myself to let it out because once unleashed I don't know what'll happen.

I'm lonely and regret tells me I didn't have to be. It was my choice to be. It was my choice to be this way. My whim. My silly whim. Sometimes I just want to curl up and forget everything—even my name. Just be a dark, clean blank slate. But it's too late for childish escape. I am this person— tortured as all hell, empty as a dockside after a ship has sailed. I want to cry but all I can do is feel as a dockside after a ship has sailed. I want to cry but all I can do is feel the water behind my eyeballs and the backup has me thinking I'm about to drown.

That was all she read. That was enough. She cried now. Tears, thick tears, she wished the writer could share. Tears about love, tears about death, tears about the very need for tears. Then Danielle dried her eyes, put *Essence* down, and remembered a number she vowed to forget. Dialing it seemed so easy and so dangerous. Her hands were as moist as her eyes. *I don't know what to say,* she thought. The phone rang once, then twice. *What do I say?*

And then it didn't matter. "This number is no longer in service," the pre-recorded voice announced. Danielle hung up, as relieved as she was disappointed.

She picked the phone back up again and, with a quickness, was dialing again. When Morris answered she felt as if a fever had suddenly broken. He was about to go out but said, "I always have time for my baby." As Morris talked of plans for the Winfrey fund-raiser and, he hoped, a summer vacation, Danielle ripped Dwayne's "Say Brother" into smaller and smaller pieces, as if her memories of urban romance could be scattered like paper.

Now that you've enjoyed a little
Urban Romance, it's time you got

SEDUCED
by
Nelson George

**"As compelling and soulful as a
great r&b love song."**

—Bebe Moore Campbell
bestselling author of *Brothers and Sisters*

In *Seduced*, Nelson George serves up a twenty-year
slice from the life of Derek Harper—an r&b purist
artist and struggling songwriter trying to sell soul
without selling *his* soul. From the shark tank of the
1980s music biz—where hip-hop is making killer
waves and wannabe stars and predatory execs cruise
relentlessly for hits—George reveals a generation's
tragicomic affair with sex, success, and stardom.

"[A] smart, funny, and resonant novel."
—L.A. Times Book Review

A One World/Ballantine trade paperback
$12.00
ISBN 0-345-41266-4
For credit card orders dial
1-800-793-BOOK (2665)

Nelson George
is the author of nine books, most recently *Hip Hop America*. His other works include *Elevating the Game*, *The Death of Rhythm and Blues*, which was nominated for a National Book Critics Circle Award, *Where Did Our Love Go?*, *Seduced*, and, *Buppies, B-Boys, Baps & Bohos*. A graduate of St. John's University, he was *Billboard*'s black music editor for seven years before becoming a regular columnist for *The Village Voice* in 1989. He is a coauthor of the screenplays for the films *Strictly Business* and *CB4* and a Grammy Award winner for James Brown's album *Startime*. George was born and grew up in Brooklyn, New York.

Printed in the United States
by Baker & Taylor Publisher Services